PRAISE FOR

The Collectors

A Schneider Family Book Award Honor Book

A Minnesota Book Award Finalist

"Original, brave, and addictive. West has created creatures cuddly and terrifying and hilarious, and a protagonist you will love. This is a world you're gong to want to return to long after the book is done."
—Adam Gidwitz, bestselling author of the Newbery Honor book *The Inquisitor's Tale*

"Magic and mystery lurk behind every shadow in this inventive, engrossing, and wonderfully strange adventure. In *The Collectors*, Jacqueline West gives readers a book to adore."
—Anne Ursu, author of *The Real Boy*

"*The Collectors* is made out of dangerous and delightful magic."
—William Alexander, award-winning author of *A Properly Unhaunted Place*

"*The Collectors* has the whole package—a brilliant premise, a compelling hero, and a crackling sense of humor. It's everything a young reader could wish for!"
—Jonathan Auxier, *New York Times*–bestselling author of *The Night Gardener*

"A brilliant fantasy adventure exploring the consequences of getting what you wish for."—*Booklist*

"A gentle, triumphant reminder that being different doesn't correspond to weakness. . . . West's magical adventure offers humor and warmhearted adventure."—*Publishers Weekly*

"West has constructed a fast-paced and engrossing tale of a boy wrestling with the consequences of power and responsibility. . . . Readers may not wish to leave this magical world."
—*Kirkus Reviews*

JACQUELINE WEST

GREENWILLOW BOOKS
An Imprint of HarperCollins*Publishers*

This book is a work of fiction. References to real people, events, establishments, organizations, or locales are intended only to provide a sense of authenticity, and are used to advance the fictional narrative. All other characters, and all incidents and dialogue, are drawn from the author's imagination and are not to be construed as real.

Published in hardcover by Greenwillow Books in 2018;
first paperback publication, 2019.

 Printed in the United States of America. For information address HarperCollins Children's Books, a division of HarperCollins Publishers, 195 Broadway, New York, NY 10007.
www.harpercollinschildrens.com

The text of this book is set in 10-point ITC Stone Serif.
Book design by Paul Zakris

Library of Congress Cataloging-in-Publication Data

Names: West, Jacqueline, author.
Title: The Collectors / by Jacqueline West.
Description: First edition. |
New York, NY : Greenwillow Books, an imprint of HarperCollins Publishers, 2018. |
Summary: Overlooked in class, a hearing-impaired boy who collects lost or discarded trinkets discovers a dangerous underground world full of stolen wishes and the people who collect them.
Identifiers: LCCN 2018027798 |
ISBN 9780062691699 (hardback) | ISBN 9780062691705 (pbk. ed.)
Subjects: | CYAC: Wishes—Fiction. | Magic—Fiction. |
Collectors and collecting—Fiction. | Hearing impaired—Fiction. |
People with disabilities—Fiction. | BISAC: JUVENILE FICTION / Fantasy & Magic. |
JUVENILE FICTION / Action & Adventure / General. |
JUVENILE FICTION / Social Issues / Friendship.
Classification: LCC PZ7.W51776 Co 2018 |
DDC [Fic]—dc23 LC record available at https://lccn.loc.gov/2018027798
20 21 22 23 PC/BRR 10 9 8 7 6 5 4 3
First paperback edition

Greenwillow Books

For Beren, who'll read it someday

Contents

1
Small Things

THE spider dangled above the table.

It was a large table in a busy restaurant, but it was wedged into the dimmest corner, and the spider's web was strung between the curls of an old wrought-iron chandelier that no one ever remembered to dust.

A family sat at the table below: three grandparents, an aunt and uncle, a mother and father, and a child who was exactly four years old.

The spider positioned herself above the child's chair. She waited there, watching, her eyes glittering like the bumps on a wet blackberry.

When several waiters trooped into the corner, carrying a special little cake with four burning candles on top, the spider inched a bit farther down her thread.

The waiters and the family all sang and cheered.

"Make a wish!" said one of the grandmothers.

The child huffed out the candles.

Everybody cheered again.

And in that moment, while everybody was smiling and clapping and getting ready to slice the cake, something rose up into the air on a spinning wisp of candle smoke.

The spider caught it. It was what she had been waiting for.

She bundled it up into a ball of strong, gluey thread. Then she scuttled across the ceiling to the nearest window and wedged herself through the gap above the sill, dragging the bundle behind her.

Outside, a gust of cool evening air swept over her, making her clutch the restaurant's brick wall with six legs. But she didn't lose her grip on the bundle. Once the gust had passed, she lowered it slowly, carefully, toward the sidewalk.

A gray pigeon hopped down from its perch on a street sign. It glided below the restaurant window, snipped the spider's thread with its beak, and flapped away up the twilit street, the bundle dangling under it like a tiny broken pendulum.

The pigeon landed on the shoulder of a woman in a long black coat. The woman held up one hand. The pigeon dropped the bundle into it. The woman tucked the bundle safely into one of the coat's many pockets.

Then the woman turned and strode off into the shadows with the pigeon still perching on her shoulder, and the spider squeezed back through the window gap, and nobody noticed the small, strange, terribly important thing that had just happened.

That's the thing about small things.

They're very easy to miss.

This makes small things dangerous.

Germs. Thumbtacks. Spiders—both the black widows that lurk under rotting woodpiles, and the patient, watchful ones that live in the chandeliers of old Italian restaurants.

Most of us don't spot them until it's too late.

So it's a good thing for us that *someone else*—someone quiet and sharp-eyed, and also very easy to miss—is always keeping watch.

2
A Damp Squirrel

ONE summer afternoon, in the middle of a very large city, at the edge of a very large park, sat one very small boy named Van.

His full name was Giovanni Carlos Gaugez-Garcia Markson, but nobody called him that. His mother, who'd given him all those names in the first place, called him Giovanni. Most people just called him Van, which he liked much better. And the kids at school called him Minivan, which he didn't.

Van was always the smallest kid in class. Because his mother was an opera singer whose work took them all around the world, Van was always the newest kid too. And he was generally the only kid with a tiny blue hearing aid behind each ear. He tended to like different games, and watch different shows, and read different books than everyone else. He was used to being on his own.

In fact, he'd gotten very good at it.

So, on this particular afternoon, Van was sitting on his own on a wide stone bench. His mother was trying on shoes in a shop across the street, and every now and then, she'd look up and check on him through the plate-glass window. She'd warned him not to leave the bench. Van didn't mind. He was more interested in looking around than in getting up, anyway.

There was plenty to watch. People were picnicking in the shade, jogging on the pathways, playing fetch with their dogs on the soft green grass. Pigeons waddled everywhere. A man with a pink guitar sang a song whose words Van couldn't quite catch. And just a few feet away, a huge stone fountain splashed and shimmered, droplets of water falling from one bowl to the next like curtains of glass beads.

A boy on a bicycle zoomed past the fountain, his tires flattening a strip of grass.

And that was where Van saw it.

A small red plastic arm stuck up from the crushed grass of the tire track. Its hand was open, and its palm was turned out, so it looked like it had an important question and was just waiting for someone to call on it.

Van glanced over his shoulder. His mother was sitting in a shoe-shop chair, her head bowed over a pair of high heels.

The arm was still waiting. Van scooted his behind toward the edge of the bench.

Then, with a last quick look at the shoe shop, he slid off the bench and dashed across the grass.

He crouched beside the red plastic arm. The rest of its body—if there *was* a rest—was buried in the dirt. Van took hold of the arm and gave a tug, and a small red man popped out of the ground.

The man had a red plastic space suit, and bendable red plastic arms and legs, and a helmet that looked like a bubble of fossilized chewing gum. Van crumbled a bit of dirt off the man's shoulder. Then he put him in his jacket pocket and took a careful look at the grass all around. Perhaps a red plastic spaceship had crash-landed somewhere nearby.

Something glimmering in the mulch turned out to be a blue glass marble with a glittery gold swirl inside. Van rolled the marble back and forth on his palm, watching it sparkle in the spring sun. He dropped it into his pocket. To the spaceman, the marble could be a distant planet, or a meteorite full of some powerful and unearthly element. Van was trying to decide what sort of element it should be when he spotted something else gleaming on the pavement just ahead.

A bristly man in a Windbreaker noticed the gleaming thing at the same time. The man bent to pick it up. Then he turned toward the fountain and gave the gleaming thing a flip off the tip of his thumb.

Van watched the coin arc through the air. It spun toward the largest bowl of the fountain, where it hit the water with a soft, splooshing *plop.* To Van's ears, there wasn't really any sound at all, but his mind filled in what he would have heard if he had been several feet closer.

The man turned around again. He noticed Van watching him and gave a bristly half smile. "No army is she, right?" Van thought he heard the man say, over the noise of the park. *No harm in wishing, right?* The man tucked his hands into his pockets and shuffled away.

The next instant, there was a wild shiver in the bushes to Van's left.

Van turned.

A squirrel—a pale, almost silver, very bushy-tailed squirrel—shot out of the leaves as if it had been fired from a grenade launcher. It bounded onto the edge of the fountain, swishing its tail and chittering excitedly.

An instant later, something else burst out of the bushes.

This something was a person—a youngish, girlish person, with brown hair tied back in a ponytail and a long, dark green coat that had clearly been made for someone much bigger. The girl bolted to the spot where the squirrel stood. Without even stopping to push up her floppy coat sleeves, she plunged face-first over the lip of the fountain.

Van generally liked talking to adults more than he liked talking to other kids. Adults didn't call him Minivan. Adults didn't think that tweed vests or cashmere cardigans were hilarious things to wear. As far as Van could remember, no adults had ever flicked anything that had come out of their noses at him. But there was something about this girl, with her weird coat and sloppy ponytail, that drew him closer.

He inched forward.

The girl sprawled on her stomach over the fountain's side, with the squirrel crouched beside her. Van stopped just out of range of the girl's kicking legs. From there, he could see that she was pawing at the scummy bottom of the fountain, scooping together a mound of even scummier pennies.

Van's voice, like the rest of him, was small. "Um . . . ," he said politely. "You probably shouldn't do that."

The girl shot up as though Van had screamed, *"Look out! Rabid badgers!"* straight into her ear. She whirled around, her ponytail spattering Van and the squirrel with a gush of fountain water. She gasped so loudly that Van gasped too.

The squirrel shook its wet fur.

"I'm sorry." Van threw up his hands. "I didn't mean to startle you. But—"

"What?" shouted the girl.

"I said, 'I didn't mean to startle you,'" Van repeated, slowly and clearly.

Now that the girl was staring straight at him, he noticed that the rest of her features were small and round, but her ears and her eyes were large. He wasn't sure about the expression in those eyes, but if he'd had to guess, he might have called it *fear.*

The girl reached out one cold, wet finger and touched the center of Van's forehead. She gave a little shove. Van wobbled.

"You're *real,*" the girl breathed.

Van's hearing aids made voices louder—but they made everything else louder too. In big cities, even in peaceful spots like parks, they filled his head with several sounds at once: motors, echoes, horns, tires, chirping birds, splooshing fountains. Still, Van was close enough to the girl, and her voice was clear enough, that he was pretty sure he'd heard right. Even if what he'd heard didn't make sense.

Maybe this girl was one of the crazy people his mother said lived in the park. Van took a cautious step backward.

"Yes. I'm real," he said. "But you—"

"Who are you with?" the girl cut him off, in a quick, sharp voice. "Why are you talking to me? You can't stop me, you know. If you're working for *them*, you're too late. It's mine."

The squirrel hopped toward Van on its hind legs, raising both little squirrelly fists and making itself look as large as possible.

Now Van was almost sure that the girl was one of the crazy people. Maybe the squirrel was one of them too.

"I'm not working for anyone," he said, glancing down at the squirrel, who he could have sworn was making little punching motions. "I thought . . . maybe I could help you."

"Help me?" The girl frowned.

"Like—if you need money for something." Van nodded at the water. "Maybe to buy food, or to get a ride somewhere. My mother could—"

"Money?" the girl repeated.

She stepped closer to Van. The squirrel crept toward him too, its little nose quivering and its ears flicking. Van got the sense that they were both smelling him. Or maybe not *smelling* him, but trying to sense something about him, something that Van himself couldn't quite smell or hear or see.

The girl stared into Van's eyes. She had to tilt her head down to do it. Her eyes, Van noticed, were a pretty shade of greenish brown—like a mossy penny at the bottom of a fountain.

"Who are you?" the girl asked.

"My name is Van Markson," said Van politely. "What's yours?"

The squirrel chittered loudly. Its high-pitched little sounds sounded almost like words. *"Quickquickquick!"* it seemed to squeak.

"I *know,*" said the girl, and this time, she was definitely not talking to Van.

Her gaze flicked down to the mound of submerged

pennies. Then, keeping one eye on Van, she reached down into the fountain.

Van couldn't help himself. "That water is full of germs," he said.

The girl pulled a dripping handful of coins out of the water and stuffed them into one of her coat's huge pockets.

"And you probably shouldn't take those coins," Van soldiered on. "They're people's wishes."

One of the girl's fine brown eyebrows went up. "I *know,*" she said again.

"Then why are you taking them?"

"Because," said the girl impatiently, "you made me lose track of the one I was *trying* to get."

"Why were you trying to get just—"

"QuickquickQUICK!" the squirrel chittered again.

Van had never been interrupted by a squirrel before. But he'd been interrupted by other people often enough to know when it was happening.

"I've never seen a tame squirrel in person," he said, hoping to move the conversation in a more pleasant direction. "I mean, I've seen Alvin and the Chipmunks, but they're a cartoon. And they're chipmunks."

The squirrel blinked at him.

"Does it like popcorn?" Van asked. "Because I could get some money from my mother and—"

"So, you're just a normal little boy," the girl interrupted again, stuffing one last fistful of coins into her pocket. "You're a little boy sitting here in the park. And you saw me take some pennies. That's it." She waited, watching Van closely. "Right?"

Van didn't really like this description of himself. He didn't like the "little" part. And he especially didn't like the "just" part. But there wasn't much else to say. There was no easy way to explain to this weird big-coated girl that he hadn't *just* been sitting in the park. He'd rescued a spaceman, and discovered a meteorite, and noticed other things that everyone else seemed to ignore. This wasn't the sort of thing you said to a stranger. At least, it wasn't the sort of thing *Van* said.

So, instead, he said, "Right."

The squirrel leaped onto the girl's shoulder and chittered into her ear.

"No. There isn't *time* for popcorn," the girl muttered. She looked back at Van. Her feet made an anxious shuffling motion. She tugged her bulky coat tighter around herself, even though the day was warm. "I don't mean to be mean," she said. The words seemed to fall out of her unintentionally, like objects slipping out of a pocket. "I just . . . people don't usually . . ." She broke off, tugging at the coat again. "They don't usually talk to me." The girl turned. "I've got to go."

"Wait!" said Van, before she could dart away. He groped in his pockets. He wanted to give this girl something better than slimy pennies. Something a little bit special. His fingers closed around the smooth, curved surface of the mysterious meteorite.

"Here." He held the marble out toward the girl. It sparkled in the sunlight between his fingers.

The girl frowned slightly. "What is it?"

"I found it. I just thought . . . you might like it."

The girl took it from Van's fingertips.

"I notice things sometimes," Van blurted. "Interesting things."

The girl met Van's eyes again. She gave him a long, hard look. "What do you mean?" she asked. "What kind of things?"

Before Van could answer, a ringing voice said, *"Giovanni Markson!"*

Van whirled around.

His mother towered over him.

If Van's mother had been a building instead of an

opera singer, she would have been a cathedral. She was a big, sturdy, elegant structure, with a dome of upswept coppery hair on top. Any sounds that came out of her rang as though they'd traveled through a huge stone hall. Van knew why opera singers don't use microphones: they don't need them.

"I told you to stay on that bench, didn't I?" said Ingrid Markson, in that ringing voice.

"Yes," said Van. "And I *was* staying. But then—"

"And I come out of the shop to find you all the way over *here,* completely out of sight. Haven't we talked about this?"

"Yes, Mom," said Van. "But there was—" He glanced at the spot where the girl had stood just a moment before. But she and the silvery squirrel had vanished. "There was this—"

"If I can't trust you to stay where you've promised, you'll be stuck with me in a lot more shoe shops." His mother lifted her shopping bag demonstratively. "Now, let's go home."

Side by side, they strode through the park gates.

"I almost forgot," said his mother, who was already starting to look less like her angry self and more like her usual glowing self again. "We have to make one more stop. It's an *extremely* important errand. Shall we go to the ice-cream parlor on the corner, or the gelato place across from the train station on Twenty-Third?"

"Gelato," said Van, although he wasn't really thinking about sweets at all.

As they turned down the street, he glanced all around, hoping to spot some trace of a baggy-coated girl with a squirrel on her shoulder. But the crowds quickly grew thicker, and the streets got louder, and the city crashed around him like a tide, washing everything else away.

3
SuperVan

VAN couldn't quite remember his father.

So he imagined him instead.

"Your father was a magic worker," his mother would say, whenever Van asked about him. For years, Van had pictured his father wearing a long silk cape and shiny top hat, flourishing decks of cards, and making rabbits disappear in little puffs of smoke. Eventually he realized that this wasn't what his mother meant.

In fact, his father was a stage designer. His name was Antonio Phillippe Gaugez-Garcia, and he created the kind of special effects with light and fabric and shadows and dry ice that made audiences gasp. As far as Van knew, he was still out there somewhere, probably in some busy European city, sketching scenery and hanging strange contraptions from fly rods.

If Van had ever missed his father, he couldn't remember that, either.

But he had inherited something from him—something besides his dark eyes and hair, and parts of his too-long name.

A model stage.

His mother had been about to get rid of it. According to her, there was no point in saving a bunch of bulky things when you were going to move again in six months, so she was always throwing things out, and Van was always rescuing things from the about-to-be-thrown-out pile.

And the model stage was especially worth saving. It had a black wooden floor about one foot deep and two feet wide, and black velvet walls around the back and sides, and a fancy gold proscenium with red curtains that opened and closed when you pulled a cord.

It was the perfect size for Van's collection.

That evening, as soon as he and his mother got back to their current apartment, Van scurried through the kitchen, down the narrow hallway, and into his bedroom. He closed the door behind him. He took off his hearing aids and set them down in their spot on the bedside table. Van usually took the hearing aids off as soon as he was home for the day. Removing them felt like having a big broom whisk through his head, sweeping all the dirt and clutter away. Now he could focus on the important things.

Van hurried across the room and knelt down in front of the miniature stage.

He tugged a heavy plastic box out from under the bed. Inside the box were hundreds of small things—things that other people had lost, dropped, thrown away, or forgotten, and that Van had found, picked up, cleaned off, and saved.

There were tiny plastic swords and paper umbrellas from sidewalk cafes. There were miniature animals and cups and cars, and broken jewelry, and tokens from board games. There was a tin soldier he'd found on the London Underground, and a tiny stone frog he'd sat on in a German train, and a three-legged lion from a public bathroom somewhere in Austria.

Van had been to a lot of places. Most of them were a blur—London was a big grayish blur, Paris was a big ivory blur, Rome was a big sunny blur—except for the objects that he collected. These stood out in his mind like rubber ducks floating in a big, blurry sea.

Now Van took the red plastic spaceman out of his pocket and added him to the box. He dug around until he'd found a miniature mirror and an old egg cup. He balanced the mirror on the cup and placed it in the center of the miniature stage, where it looked a little bit like a fountain. There were a few plastic trees in the box, and Van set these up around the stage's edge. He didn't have any squirrels in his collection, but there were two cats, and one of them was white, with a plumy tail. It was close enough. Van examined a few dolls, but they were all too poofy and princessy to be the girl in the big coat. He thought about using one of the plastic army men, or the little statue of a saint he'd found on a sidewalk in Buenos Aires, but in the end, he settled on a wooden pawn from a chess set. It wasn't right for the strange girl, but it was the only thing that didn't feel *wrong*.

The role of Van would be played, as always, by a little plastic superhero in a black cape.

SuperVan.

Van set the cat-squirrel next to the fountain. He scattered a few of his foreign coins over the top of the miniature mirror. Then he posed the pawn beside it. The pawn leaned in to grab a coin. SuperVan strode onto the scene.

"You know, you really shouldn't take those," SuperVan said boldly. "They're people's wishes."

Instead of whirling around, splashing the squirrel, and shoving Van backward with a wet pointer finger, the pawn bowed its knobby head.

"Oh," Pawn Girl said. "I'm sorry. I didn't know. I just need the money so much."

"What do you need money for?" asked SuperVan. "Are you hungry? Do you need help?"

"Yes," said Pawn Girl. "Yes, please. I'm so hungry. . . ."

"Wait right here," commanded SuperVan.

With SuperVan in his fist, Van dug through his treasure box. He found a set of beautiful plastic fruits he'd almost stepped on in a park in Tokyo, and a little silver goblet that had probably once belonged to a little silver king, and a pizza and a hamburger and several other miniature snacks that were actually erasers.

"Look out below!" shouted SuperVan. He soared over the stage, dropping food items like edible bombs. Pawn Girl and the squirrel cheered.

"You saved me!" cried Pawn Girl, as SuperVan landed gracefully on top of the fountain. "I'll never forget you! What's your name, so that I can find you again?"

"You can call me SuperVan. And what's your name?"

"I'm—"

Van paused, twirling the little wooden piece around in his fingers. What was the right sort of name for a girl who wandered city parks with a too-long coat and a noisy squirrel on her shoulder? He thought about the names of the girls at his school, and at his last school, and at the school before that. None of them seemed quite right. In fact, there was no ordinary name that he could think of that would suit this strange, squirrel-wearing girl.

He was still twirling the little pawn back and forth when his bedroom door swung open. Van smelled his mother's lily perfume just before she touched his shoulder.

"Playing with your maquette?" she asked.

Van's mother liked to call things by their fanciest names. The little stage was a maquette. A movie theatre was a cinema. Coffee with milk was café au lait. Van's mother was never "in the bathroom." She was *indisposed.*

"Kind of," said Van.

"I just realized that I forgot one of our errands today," said his mother, swishing away and sitting down on the edge of Van's bed. Van followed her with his eyes. "We should have picked up a birthday present for Peter Grey."

Van gave a little jerk. His elbow bumped the stage. SuperVan toppled into the fountain. "Why do we need to get a birthday present for Peter Grey?"

"Because you're going to his party on Saturday. I told you about this." Ingrid Markson looked into Van's wide eyes. "I *thought* I told you about this. He invited you weeks ago."

"He invited me?"

"Well . . . Charles invited you on Peter's behalf."

"Who's Charles?"

"Mr. Grey." His mother smiled brightly. "He has a first name, you know."

Mr. Grey was the artistic director of the opera company that had hired Van's mother for the season. Van knew he was important. Mr. Grey obviously knew it too. He always wore a suit, and he always spoke with a British accent that Van thought might have been fake, and he always seemed a bit bored with everything happening around him. His son, Peter, was just the same—minus the suit and the accent.

"Do I have to go?" Van asked.

His mother leaned back on the bed and patted her upswept hair. "Do you really need to ask that question?"

Van set the pawn on the stage. "No."

"I'll pick up a gift for Peter tomorrow," his mother said. Van looked up at her face again. She rose from the bed, stretching languidly. "There are plenty of leftovers from Leo's in the refrigerator, when you're hungry."

His mother signed the last word as she spoke it, cupping one hand and moving it downward over her chest. His mother always spoke aloud while she signed—which wasn't very often. Van had been almost five years old when his mother had noticed the trouble with his hearing. Since then—besides getting the little blue hearing aids—he'd become an expert face watcher and sound follower. While Van thought it might have been cool to use a secret, silent language with his hands, there was really only his mother to use it *with*. And she didn't do *anything* silently.

"Okay," said Van.

His mother swept out the door.

A minute later, Van caught the faint trickling hum that meant his mother was at the living-room piano. The higher, clearer hum of her singing followed it. Her voice glided up the scale like a paintbrush moving across a canvas, its colors fading out at the edges, where the notes grew too high for Van's ears to catch.

Van pushed his door shut.

Then he knelt back down in front of the little stage and picked up SuperVan and Pawn Girl. But now, for some reason, he couldn't think of anything to make them say. He set them down again and picked up the cat-squirrel instead.

"Quickquickquick!" it said.

Van set it back down too. He let out a heavy sigh.

At the moment, Van would rather have been headed to the bottom of a scummy park fountain than to Peter Grey's birthday party. But he didn't have a choice.

4
Something Dark

LATE that night, something pushed Van over the edge of *asleep* and into *awake*.

After he opened his eyes, Van couldn't remember what had done the pushing. He lay in his bed, trying to think backward. Had it been a dream? Or something tickling his arm? Or a flash of lights in his window? He wasn't sure. But as he lay there, and the minutes ticked by, he became more and more sure of something else.

He was thirsty.

Van threw his legs out of bed and padded to the door.

The hall was dim. Van and his mother had stayed in so many different places, every time Van woke up he had to stop and look around to remind himself where he was. Now he glanced carefully to the left and right.

His mother's bedroom door, to the left, was closed. The kitchen waited to his right. His striped pajamas whisked softly around his legs as he hurried out the door and down the hall.

The lights of the nighttime city dusted the kitchen with silver. Van yanked open the heavy refrigerator door, pushing aside stacks of cardboard takeout containers until he'd uncovered the jug of orange juice. He had to climb up onto the counter to reach a drinking glass. Then, with his full glass of juice, he tiptoed out of the kitchen and across the living room, past the piano, to the big dormer window.

Van knelt on the padded bench and leaned his forehead against the cool windowpane. If he leaned steeply enough, he could imagine he was flying, just like SuperVan. He was soaring over the sleepy streets, taller than the trees, taller than the buildings, taller than the tallest kids at school. Van wriggled his toes and sipped his orange juice.

It had rained lightly during the night. The streets were black and glittery. A gust of wind blew, and a few wet petals shivered down from a tree across the street, glinting in the lamplight. A taxi streaked by. If he had been looking at one of the puddles in the gutter, Van might have seen the tiny reflected wink of a falling star.

But Van didn't see that falling star. What he saw came immediately after.

What he saw was something dark.

It seeped out of the shadows. It scuttled out of sewer grates. It crept around corners. It ducked behind tree trunks. It moved so smoothly, at first Van thought it must be one large, singular thing, like a flood of black water. But then the flood began to break apart, and Van saw that it wasn't a flood of water at all, but a flood of thousands of small, dark animals: rats and raccoons and mice and bats and birds and creatures he couldn't identify. Some of them scurried up the stoops of the apartment buildings. Others clambered up fire escapes and drainpipes. The ones with wings soared up to the rooftops and windowsills.

Van watched, keeping perfectly still.

The winged creatures wriggled between closed curtains, slid through blinds, slipped under sills. Seconds later, they reappeared. Meanwhile, the scurrying shapes that had squeezed up the drainpipes and through cracks in doorways squeezed out again. And now, several of those creatures carried with them tiny, glimmering lights.

Van squinted. He pressed his forehead against the glass as hard as he could.

The creatures hurried into the street, little golden lights glinting in their beaks and mouths and claws. Soon dozens of steady golden sparks seemed to mix with that sea of shadows, like a swarm of fireflies on a black river.

The shadows and sparks swept back up the wet street. Before Van could blink, they had poured back through the sewer grates, glided around corners, and disappeared as quietly as they had come.

A droplet of orange juice slid over Van's fingers. His entire body had been so focused on the shadows that his hand had forgotten what it was supposed to be doing. Van straightened the glass. Then he pressed his forehead back to the windowpane.

The street below him looked perfectly normal.

A car shushed past, its roof sheening under the street-lamps.

For several minutes more, Van watched the street, his eyes catching every glimmer of motion. Each glint turned out to be nothing but a wet leaf or a blowing candy wrapper. Still, Van went on staring until his eyes itched and his feet fell asleep.

Finally he inched back off the bench and tiptoed down the hall to his bed, where the rest of him quickly fell asleep too. By the time he woke up the next morning, the small, scurrying shadows seemed as unlikely as a dream. And Van told himself that was all they were.

But he didn't quite believe it.

5
Petty Theft

INGRID Markson turned to Van, who sat beside her in the back of the cab. "I'll be back for you in three hours," she said, in a voice that made the whole taxi ring. "You've got the gift?"

Van held up the package containing a Lego spaceship.

"Good," said his mother. "Be sure to thank everyone. Especially Peter. And have fun!"

Van wriggled out onto the curb. He stared up at the Greys' house, an imposing four-story stone house in a row of imposing four-story stone houses. He was still staring up at it when the cab whizzed away behind him.

There was no escape now.

Van hadn't been to many other kids' birthday

parties. In general, he and his mother didn't stay in any one place long enough for him to get to know any kids who were having one. His own birthday parties were usually made up of a bunch of singers and musicians from his mother's current show, or sometimes they were just Van and his mother. The two of them would visit a zoo or amusement park, and then go out for big dishes of gelato, and those turned out to be the best birthdays of all.

But now he was on his own.

Van climbed the broad stairs, stepping twice on each one. The Greys' front door looked so solid and shiny and unfriendly, knocking on it would have been like punching an armored giant. Van pressed the doorbell instead.

The door flew open. A young woman with glossy brown hair smiled down at him.

"Hello," said Van as politely and clearly as he could. "I'm Van Markson. I'm here for the birthday party. You must be Mrs. Grey."

The woman giggled. "Oh, no, I'm the nanny. But you're at the right place. Come on inside."

Van stepped through the unfriendly door and flinched as it boomed shut behind him. The nanny spoke at the same time. Because she was behind him, and because the noise of the door soaked through her words, Van couldn't quite decipher them. At first he thought she'd said, "The poison's on the eater's spoon," but that didn't seem likely.

The nanny pointed toward the staircase. "Go on up and join them."

Oh, thought Van. *The boys are up in Peter's room.* A little better than poison. Maybe.

The nanny had already bustled away. With one last deep breath, Van ventured toward the staircase.

The stairs curved around the high-ceilinged foyer. The wall that curved with them was lined with opera photographs. Van glanced at the singers' wide-open mouths as he trudged past, imagining that they were trying to swallow him, like greedy fish lunging up from a pond.

He reached the upper hall. The first door on his left led into a bathroom. For just a second, Van pictured himself hiding in that bathroom for the rest of the party. Then he pictured one of Peter's friends running in to use the toilet and finding Van crouched inside the bathtub.

Probably not a good idea.

The next door was shut. Van tugged it open

cautiously, and found himself staring up at shelves full of towels.

The door beyond the towel closet stood open. Flashes of colored light and rumbles of noise poured through it into the hallway. Van let the flashes drag him the rest of the way into what was obviously Peter's room.

There were eight other boys inside. Their heads swiveled around as Van tiptoed in. They all stared at him for a second, their faces as identically blank as eggs in a carton, before swiveling back to the game on the TV screen.

"Hello," said Van, because nobody else said anything.

Nobody said anything to that, either.

"Happy birthday, Peter," said Van.

A boy with light brown hair and a controller in his hands said, "Thanks." His eyes didn't leave the screen. "On a hiccup at camel back."

Van altered the sounds in his head, rearranging them like figurines on a little stage. *Connor, pick up that camo bag.* Or maybe, *Colin, pick up that ammo pack.* It didn't matter. Either way, Peter wasn't talking to him.

Van inched farther into the room. Peter and three other boys were holding controllers. Four more boys were sprawled on the carpet beside them. Avoiding the logjam of legs, Van backed into the corner and sat down on the edge of Peter's bed. He looked around.

The walls were painted pale gray and hung with framed movie posters. The huge TV took up most of the opposite wall. Video games and consoles and wires spilled out of the cabinet beneath it. On the built-in shelves above the bed, just to Van's right, an army of action figures and models and finished Lego spaceships stood in silent rows. One of the spaceships, Van noticed, was the very same ship that was currently waiting downstairs, wrapped in sparkly blue paper, with a tag that read *To Peter, From Van.*

Van swallowed.

The screen gave off a bright red flash, snagging his attention. The four boys who had been playing handed over their controllers to the four boys who had been watching. Nobody mentioned giving Van a turn. He waited for a few minutes, watching futuristic soldiers charge across a nighttime desert, trying to decipher the muddle of sounds that came from the game and from the boys playing it.

When there was a lull in the shooting, Van asked politely, "What's the name of this game?"

The other boys kept their backs to him, but one of them nudged Peter in the arm.

Peter whipped around, scowling. "I was *talking*," he snapped.

"Oh," said Van. "I couldn't tell. Sorry."

Peter turned back to the screen without answering the question.

Van edged backward across Peter's gray bedspread, pulling himself toward the distracting shelter of the shelves. He examined a row of tiny metal soldiers. Their uniforms had tiny wrinkles, and they carried teeny guns, and their faces wore teeny-tiny expressions of stoicism. Van's eyes wandered down to the next shelf. This one was filled with miniature animal figurines. There was a bear, and a stag, and an otter, and a raccoon—and beside them, its tail quirked like a sideways question mark, was one tiny, pale gray squirrel.

"Sniper behind the watchtower!" one of the boys shouted. "Use your flamethrower!"

"No, use the grenade launcher!" shouted someone else.

Van's fingers perched on the edge of the shelf. They sat there casually, pretending not to be interested. There was a *BOOM* from the video game, followed by a cheer from the eight boys. Van's fingers closed around the squirrel. In one quick, smooth motion, they wedged the squirrel into his pocket and darted out again to sit innocently in Van's lap.

Van's heart thundered.

He couldn't believe he had just done that. Or that his fingers had. The things in his collection had been lost, or forgotten, or thrown away by someone else. Van had rescued them. He'd never *stolen* a single one.

But he needed this squirrel, Van reasoned. There were so many things in Peter's room—not just on the shelves, but in every corner and on every surface—that he would never notice one missing figurine. That squirrel had probably sat on the shelf, neglected and ignored, for years. In a way, Van *was* rescuing it.

Van swallowed again.

The thunder in his chest began to fade.

"Guys!" The nanny's voice was muddled by distance and electronic bombs. "Come down for agonized screams!"

Before Van had figured out that she'd probably said *Come down for cake and ice cream,* the other boys had jumped up and stampeded toward the door.

"I call a corner piece!" someone shouted.

"It's my party," said Peter. "*I* get to decide who gets the corner pieces."

"So, can I have one?"

"Maybe." Peter's voice dwindled into the hall.

When the last of the boys had shoved his way through the door, Van stood up. He touched his pocket, making sure the bump of squirrel was still there. Then he followed the crowd down the staircase.

The table was set in the dining room.

Van hung back as the other boys grabbed their seats. They were all talking at once, and the noise made his head ache, and Van didn't know whose face to look at. He looked around the dining room instead.

This room was too neat and stylish to have many interesting things in it. But he noticed that the light switches were the funny old push-button kind, and the beveled crystal knobs on the doors were shaped like giant engagement rings, and tall, narrow windows gazed out over the walled backyard. One of the windows was standing open. The branches of a birch tree leaned close to it, its pale green leaves fluttering into the room like a bunch of impatiently waving hands.

"That was *amazing*." Someone's voice cut through the din. "I can't believe you hit him from that distance!"

"It's like the game knew it was your birthday," said a boy with freckles.

"Yeah! Happy birthday, here's a dead alien!"

"Oh man," sighed a boy with tight black curls. "That's what *I* got you."

The other boys laughed.

Van remembered the duplicate Lego spaceship waiting in the pile of presents. His stomach began to tighten. He stared at the open window. The birch tree's delicate branches swayed.

"Here we are!" sang the nanny, bustling into the room with a big sheet cake.

She set it in the center of the table. The boys craned forward, kneeling on their chairs for a better look. From a few steps away, Van looked too. The cake was frosted with a swirling blue-purple galaxy. Spaceships zoomed between the planets, shooting flares of white laser icing. Twelve candles stuck up from frosting stars.

"I call a spaceship!" shouted the freckled boy.

"I said *I* get to choose who gets what," said Peter.

"All right, everybody lean back." The nanny picked up a box of matches. "I don't want to set anyone on fire."

"Shouldn't we—" said Van, before he could stop himself.

Everyone turned to stare.

"Just . . . shouldn't we wait for your dad?" he finished.

Peter frowned. *"No,"* he said, as if Van had just suggested that they squirt the cake with ketchup. "He's at *work*. That's why *the nanny* is here."

One of the other boys snorted.

"Oh," said Van. "I guess that makes sense."

"Come and take a seat, Dan," said the nanny distractedly.

Van stayed where he was.

The nanny struck a match, and everyone started shouting again. Van took a small step backward. He gazed past the table, toward the waving birch leaves. And as he watched, a pale, almost silver, squirrel jumped out of the birch tree and through the open window.

It perched on the windowsill for a second, its eyes bright, its tail twitching. Then it leaped toward the chandelier hanging above the table.

The nanny had finished lighting the candles. The other boys bumped one another, craning closer to the flickering cake. None of them paid any attention to the squirrel dangling from the chandelier just above their heads.

"Everybody ready?" the nanny prompted. "Happy birthday to you . . ."

The other boys joined in. Van's lips moved along to the words, but his eyes stayed on the silvery squirrel.

"Happy birthday, dear Peter . . ."

The squirrel's bright black eyes landed on Van.

The squirrel froze. So did Van.

The squirrel's eyes flicked toward the backyard. So did Van's.

His gaze landed on a familiar face—the face of a girl with a brown ponytail and a much-too-large coat. She was standing just behind the trunk of the birch tree, her eyes fixed on the squirrel. But now her eyes darted from the squirrel to Van. They widened.

"Happy birthday to you!"

"Make a wish!" crowed the nanny.

There was a cheer as Peter blew out the candles.

The squirrel twitched back to life. It coiled to the bottom of the chandelier, holding on tight with its back feet. Its tiny front paws reached out. Van watched as they snatched at the rising candle smoke. But as Van watched, he realized that what the squirrel had caught wasn't smoke at all. It was something that looked like a wisp of curling, sparkling, silvery silk. With the wisp clamped in its teeth, the squirrel sailed back toward the open window.

Van had already surprised himself twice today. He had gone to a party with a bunch of boys he didn't know, for a boy he didn't even like. He had stolen a china squirrel from the birthday boy's bedroom. Now he was about to surprise himself again. He could feel it.

Before the nanny could cut the first slice of cake or Peter could decide who got to eat it, Van bolted to the open window. He shoved the frame outward. If anyone behind him called out, Van didn't hear. He wasn't really listening, anyway. Keeping his eyes on the face behind the birch tree, he swung one leg over the sill, braced his arms against the walls, and dove out into the backyard below.

6
Spy vs. Spy

FORTUNATELY, the ground wasn't very far away.

Van tumbled onto the damp grass. His knees hit the ground, which hurt for a second and would definitely leave a stain on his nicest pants. But he decided not to think about this. He decided not to think about the boys who were probably gaping out the window behind him either. He sharpened his vision into a straight, bright beam, just like he did when he was searching the sidewalks for lost treasures, and he focused that beam on the brown ponytail that was already flying over the brick wall at the very back of the yard.

"Hey!" Van yelled. "Girl from the park!"

The girl didn't look back.

Van climbed onto a sturdy cement planter and

hoisted himself over the brick wall. He landed on both feet in the alley just beyond. He gave the lump in his pocket another pat, making sure the china squirrel was still there.

Meanwhile, the real squirrel was bounding down the alleyway ahead of him, its tail brushing the hem of the girl's long coat.

"I'm the one who gave you the marble, remember?" Van called, breaking into a run. "I just want to talk to you!"

The girl didn't slow down.

At the end of the alley, she and the squirrel veered left. Van raced after them.

"Why won't you tell me your name?" Van yelled. "Is it Anna? Is it Ella? Is it Bob?" Maybe if he guessed right, she would finally turn around. "Is it Rumpelstiltskin?"

The girl ran on.

They tore through blocks of quiet houses and rustling trees. With each block, the buildings got taller. Shops and restaurants grew thicker. The sidewalk got busier, and the world got louder. The girl and the squirrel slipped through the crowds like a pair of scissors through tissue paper. Van wasn't as smooth, but he was small enough that no one seemed to notice him either.

"Why do I keep—seeing you?" Van was beginning to lose his breath. "Are you—following me?"

At that, the girl finally glanced back. "Am *I* following *you*?" Van heard her shout.

"Well—not right now," he puffed as he chased her over a crosswalk. "But—it can't be a coincidence—that in this whole huge city—I keep seeing you."

The girl glanced back again. Her voice was clear enough that Van caught a few words, even though he was panting and traffic was grumbling and the wind was whipping the air between them. ". . . *Can't* see me!" she shouted.

"Yes I can!" Van shouted back. "You're wearing the same dark green coat as before. And there's a squished French fry on the bottom of your right shoe. And—"

And, so suddenly that Van couldn't even finish the sentence, the girl disappeared.

There was no puff of smoke, no trapdoor. She just wasn't *there* anymore. The squirrel wasn't there either. The patch of sidewalk they'd occupied was empty.

Van raced to the spot where the two of them had vanished. He looked carefully in all directions.

Just behind him was a store with a bright neon sign. EXOTIC PETS, it flashed, as waves of shifting neon light sloshed around it. Tanks of chameleons and anoles and snakes with skin like fancy bathroom tiles filled the huge plate-glass window. Farther inside, Van could see rows of bubbling aquariums, and gorgeously plumed parrots preening on high perches, and a giant cage of what looked like spiny hamsters. He didn't see the girl or the squirrel anywhere.

Two doors down was a bakery. In its window, cakes drizzled with chocolate and topped with berries sat on sheets of paper lace. Delicate French cookies formed pastel pyramids, and cupcakes topped with icing roses glistened in the background. The dizzying smell of warm sugar floated through the bakery's open door. The scent was so distracting, Van almost forgot what he'd been looking for.

The girl. That was it.

Had she gone into the bakery or the pet store?

Van took a small step backward, trying to choose. Bakery or pet store? He bit his lip. Pet store or bakery? And then, for the first time, he looked at the building wedged between them.

It was an office. A small, grayish, closed-looking office. Its single window was covered by plastic blinds. A colorless sign reading CITY COLLECTION AGENCY hung beside the door. It was the kind of place most people wouldn't even notice. *Van* almost hadn't noticed.

As if an invisible hand was pushing him closer, Van stumbled toward the office's dingy front door. It swung open when he turned the knob.

Inside, the office was dark. Only a whisper of daylight slid through the blinds. As Van's eyes adjusted, he saw that the office was not only dark, but empty. There were no desks, no file cabinets . . . no furniture at all. He patted the walls, but there didn't seem to be any light switches either. A funny smell, like old paper and spices and candle smoke, wafted through the air.

He ventured across the carpet.

At the very back of the room, half hidden by a dividing wall, was another closed gray door. Van reached for the knob, expecting to find a musty little bathroom, or maybe an empty storage closet.

What he found instead made him gasp.

On the other side of the door was a steep stone staircase—a staircase so long that Van couldn't see the bottom. It led straight downward, growing so dark in the middle that it seemed to disappear entirely. But farther down, from somewhere deep beneath the dingy office, far below the city streets, there glowed a green-gold light. A gust of spice and smoke fluttered the tips of Van's hair.

Van inched onto the steps. The heavy door thumped shut behind him. Slowly, silently, he crept through the darkness, down toward that green-gold light.

7
Underground

THE scent of old paper and smoke grew stronger. The green-gold light grew brighter. Holding his breath, Van tiptoed to the bottom of the long staircase, pressed his back against the chilly stone wall, and peered out.

He stood at the edge of a massive underground chamber. Pale green stones tiled its floor, its walls, its high, arching ceiling. It almost reminded Van of a subway platform, except that there were no trains or tracks, and the space was ten times larger than any subway station he'd ever seen. Rows of tulip-shaped lamps with petals of green and gold glass dangled from the ceiling. Flocks of pigeons waddled over the stone floor, along with several rats and streams of scurrying mice. There was no girl and no squirrel to be seen, but Van had the feeling—the absolutely positive, skin-tingling feeling—that they had been there moments before, almost as if he could feel himself stepping in their footprints. Straight ahead, just beyond a green stone banister, Van spotted the head of another staircase.

He hurried to the banister and craned out.

Below him was a hole: a huge, hollow, whispering chasm. It was dizzyingly deep and impossibly dark. Flights of stairs hugged the walls around it, forming an angular downward spiral. At each landing, where the stairs made a sharp turn before plunging down again, entrances to other underground chambers branched away into the dimness. When he looked straight down, he couldn't see any bottom at all.

The girl with the squirrel had to be somewhere down *there.*

A shiver rattled through Van's body. The thought of heading even deeper underground, farther from light and daytime and everything familiar, filled his mind with a low, terrible hum.

He clutched the banister.

What was he doing here?

What was he thinking, wandering down into some giant sewer or station or bomb shelter or whatever it was, chasing a girl who didn't want to talk to him anyway? He should turn around, climb back up the steps, and run back out into the daylight before anyone spotted him. He should find his way back to Peter's house, and—

And what? an imaginary voice from his pocket spoke up. *Go back to that awful party like nothing happened? Forget you ever saw that girl and that squirrel? Never learn what this place actually is?*

Van slipped a hand into his pocket. His fist closed around the miniature china squirrel. He'd come this far. He could go a little bit farther.

Before he could change his mind, Van started down the staircase. He clutched the banister with one hand, trying not to think about the bottomless dark on the other side, and held on tight to the little china squirrel with the other. The shuffle-pat of his feet hung in the chilly air.

Van slowed as he reached the first landing. An archway more than twice his height loomed ahead of him. Above the arch, tiled into the green stones with tall black letters, were the words THE ATLAS.

Van slipped through the archway.

He found himself in a chamber almost as large as the one above. It had the same pale green floor and ceiling, lit by rows of the same petaled glass lamps. Its walls seemed to be coated in layers of tattered, patchy wallpaper. When Van looked closer, he saw that it wasn't wallpaper at all, but maps: maps of all kinds, some full of illustrated trees and houses, some grids of lines, some just mysterious swirls.

Several people in long dark coats were gathered at tables in the center of the room. Their heads were bowed. They pointed at things on huge sheets of paper. None of them were girls with squirrels on their shoulders, but as Van watched, one of them turned and strode straight toward him.

Van threw himself backward into the shadows. He pressed his shoulders to the wall, holding his breath. The man in a long black coat swished straight by. He came so close that Van could see the glittering black eyes of the owl on his shoulder. But the man strode through the arch and down the staircase.

Once he was sure that the man with the owl was out of sight, Van crept back out onto the landing. He looked down the next flight of stairs. At the bottom, disappearing through another archway, he spotted something that looked like a bulky green coat, topped by the puff of a pale gray tail.

Van pelted down the staircase after it.

The air grew colder. The smoky, spicy scent grew stronger. The darkness coming from below seemed to rise up around him, swirling over his skin as lightly as mist.

The next archway gaped ahead of him like a waiting mouth. In the stones above the arch were the words THE CALENDAR. Van darted inside.

The room he entered was busier than the one above. It was as large as the Atlas, with the same arched ceiling and stone walls, but it was filled with bookshelves: rows and rows and rows of them. Dark-coated people bustled between the shelves, taking books down, putting them back. To Van, it looked a lot more like a library than a calendar—but as he crept between two shelves, he noticed that all the books were the same. Every single one of them was a large, plain volume bound in black leather. They would have been completely identical, except for the delicate markings on their spines. Van skimmed the nearest row. *May 11—Da. May 11—Dal. May 11—De.*

Van was just about to grab one of the books when a pale, puffy flash snagged his eye. He peered through the shelves.

The girl with the squirrel was hurrying up the next aisle.

Van scurried sideways, keeping her in view. Yes, it was definitely her, with the mossy eyes and sloppy ponytail. The girl strode toward the far end of the room, where a man sat behind a huge wooden desk. Van scuttled after her, peeping out around the edge of a shelf.

The man at the huge desk had long, iron-gray hair and delicate features. He spoke. The girl answered. The man bent to scribble something in one of the big black books, and Van caught sight of a tiny, sleeping bat dangling upside down from the man's right earlobe. The girl said something else—Van thought he heard the words *ray* or *wait* and *birthday* or *worthy*—and the man said something like *very good,* and the girl whirled around and darted away.

Van turned to follow her, but a line of people in long black coats had begun to fill the room. He ducked and dodged to stay out of sight. By the time he reached the archway, the girl had raced down to the next flight of stairs.

Van paused on the landing.

It was cold and dark already. Deeper down, it could

only be worse. Van clenched his hands. What would SuperVan do?

SuperVan would go on. He would streak straight down those steps and never stop until he'd learned all there was to learn, and given all the help there was to give.

Van went on too.

The air grew colder and colder. The darkness thickened, pasting itself to his face like mud.

Van didn't like the dark. Because he couldn't hear everything there was to hear, he liked seeing all there was to see. And he often saw things that other people didn't. Usually this balanced things out. But in darkness, he felt unsafe and small, like SuperVan stripped of all his powers.

And there were *things* here, in the dark. He could feel them. Small black shapes—birds or bats or something else—flitted and skittered around him. Once, he was sure he felt a wing brush the side of his neck, and a moment later, something with long, thin legs seemed to be crawling over his hair. But when he swatted at it with one hand, there was nothing there.

At first, when the sound began, Van thought his imagination was playing another trick on him. But the sound grew louder and louder until it couldn't possibly be only inside his mind.

It was a huge, rumbling, horrible sound. It was a roar. A howl. It made the walls shiver. Van could feel the sound thrumming into the soles of his feet. He couldn't tell what was making it, but whatever it was seemed to be far, far below.

His entire body—toes, knees, spine, stomach—all wanted to turn around and bolt back up the staircase, away from that sound and the cold and the dark. But Van held on to the banister. He took deep breaths. He had nearly steadied himself enough to take another step when, from ahead of him, there came a blast of silvery light.

Van squinted. Another archway stood before him. It was twice as wide and twice as tall as the openings above. And over the arch were two words that made Van's skin prickle from head to toe.

THE COLLECTION.

Van flew down the rest of the steps and through the archway. The blast of silvery light was already dimming—because, as Van saw, it came through a pair of massive wooden doors, which were quickly swinging shut. And disappearing between those doors was a silhouette.

The silhouette of a girl with a squirrel on her shoulder.

Without giving his brain the chance to think twice, Van raced after her, straight through the closing double doors.

8
The Collection

BEYOND the doors was the largest chamber yet.

It was so large that it made the other chambers look tiny. It was larger than any cathedral or concert hall Van had ever seen. Its stone floor dwindled away into the distance like a narrowing carpet. Its walls were so high that they seemed to lean inward. Its ceiling, instead of being arched stone like the others, was a mosaic of glass shards, which let in a wash of silvery light. Its size and its light, shot through with the smells of metal and spice and smoke, were dizzying.

Van forced his eyes to focus. The towering walls were filled with shelves: rows and rows and rows of shelves, rising all the way up to the ceiling. Ladders and scaffolds and spiraling iron staircases chased the shelves upward, metal rungs twisting and crisscrossing like spiders' threads. People in dark coats bustled up and down the ladders. More people filled the floor below, scribbling in ledgers, making notes on string-tied paper tags, knotting or pasting labels onto glass bottles of all sizes, shapes, and colors.

Because that was what filled the shelves.

Bottles.

Green and turquoise and indigo bottles. Bottles that sparkled. Bottles that were thick with dust. Bottles as large as milk jugs; bottles small enough to fit inside a closed mouth. Their glitter was dazzling. But Van couldn't make out what was sealed inside.

And there wasn't time to get closer. The girl with the squirrel was rushing toward the center of the room.

Van hurried after her, ducking for cover behind stairs and ladders. None of the dark-coated people seemed to notice him. As Van watched from behind a spiral staircase, the girl made her way toward a high podium, where a spectacled man the size and shape of an emperor penguin was scribbling in a massive book.

The girl stopped at the podium. The little man nodded. The girl passed something small and soft and silvery to a dark-coated woman at a table to the right. The woman slipped the silvery thing into a blue glass bottle. A man beside her tied a tag to the bottle's neck. A third person, a woman with what looked like an opossum draped around her collar, grabbed the bottle and hurried toward the back of the massive room.

Van scurried sideways, keeping the bottle in sight. He skirted a mound of tarnished pennies that covered a patch of the stone floor, and a pile of what looked like small, shattered bones, and watched as the woman set the bottle on a low shelf. Van waited until she had hurried away again. Then he lunged.

The bottles on the shelf before him were small, about the size of his hand. Some were tinted with color, some were icily clear; some were spotless, and some were muffled with blankets of dust. The emerald-green bottles were shaped like mason jars, and each of them held something that glowed like a small golden coal. The tag dangling from one green bottle read, in faded black ink, *Elizabeth O'Connell. August 12, 1900. Perseid meteor shower.* Even through the thick layer of dust, Van could see the golden coal glowing inside.

But Van was looking for a different bottle.

And there it was. On the edge of the shelf just in

front of him stood a small, sparkling, indigo-blue bottle. A silver wisp spun gently inside.

Van read its paper tag. Then he read it again, making sure the words and numbers were still there.

Peter Grey. June 8. Twelfth birthday.

Van's memory replayed the last moments of the party. The spaceship cake. Peter blowing out the candles. The squirrel with the silvery wisp in its teeth.

Van stretched his fingers toward the bottle, and the silvery wisp spun faster.

It was like the raised arm of the spaceman buried in the park. It was like every other forgotten, ignored little object that Van had found and saved. It was waiting for him.

With such small motions that only someone watching closely would notice them at all, Van grabbed the bottle and slipped it into his pocket, along with the miniature china squirrel.

The weight of a hand landed on Van's shoulder.

"What are you doing?" said a voice in his ear.

Van whirled to the right.

No one was there.

No one but a silvery, tufty-tailed squirrel, who was

perched on Van's shoulder, watching him with bright eyes.

"What?" Van whispered.

The squirrel blinked. "What?"

"Did you just say, 'What are you doing'?"

"Maybe. Probably." The squirrel's eyes coasted past Van's face and landed on a sparkling bottle. "Ooh, blue! Blue's my favorite color. And green. And brown. And pink. And blue. Ooh, look! Blue!"

Van held his breath. His whole body trembled. He wasn't sure which thing was more impossible—that the squirrel had just talked to him, or that he had heard it speak so clearly that its voice seemed to come from inside his own head.

"Am I imagining this?" Van kept his voice to a whisper. "Like I imagined hearing the squirrel in my pocket?"

The squirrel on his shoulder looked surprised. "You have a squirrel in your pocket?"

"I—"

"Which one? Cornelius? He's small. Or Elizabetta? Or Barnavelt? Wait. No. *I'm* Barnavelt. Is it Cornelius?"

"Are you . . . ," breathed Van. "Are you actually *talking*?"

"I'm not talking. You're *listening.*" The squirrel cocked his head. His tiny nose quivered. "Do you smell popcorn?"

"What?"

"Maybe somebody wished for popcorn. I love popcorn." The squirrel's eyes focused on Van again. "Hey! What are you doing with that bottle?"

Van put a telltale hand over his pocket. "What bottle?"

"The one in your pocket. With Cornelius."

"Oh. I . . ." Van stammered. "It belongs to a friend of mine. Kind of. I'm just keeping it safe for him."

"But Pebble said—" The squirrel's body stiffened. *"Hawk!"* he screamed, lunging inside Van's collar.

Van glanced up. A broad-winged bird coasted over them, its shadow dimming the rows of bright glass.

The squirrel waited until the hawk was out of sight. "I don't like hawks," he whispered, inching back out onto Van's shoulder. Then his body stiffened again. "Hey! *Pebble!*"

Van spun around, ready to duck from any little rocks that were flying in their direction.

Behind him stood the girl with the ponytail.

Her mouth hung open. Her mossy penny eyes were wide.

"Pebble!" the squirrel gushed. "It's so good to see you! It's been ages!"

Pebble didn't answer. She just stared at Van. Van stared back. They stared at each other for so long that Barnavelt grew distracted and started loudly grooming his paws.

"What are *you* doing here?" Pebble finally asked.

"What are you *doing* here?" Van blurted, at the very same second. "What are *all* of you doing here? Why are you collecting old pennies and smoke from birthday candles?"

Pebble's eyes grew even wider. Over her shoulder, Van spotted a man at the podium pulling a handful of coins out of his pocket. As he raised the coins one by one, a round, glimmering light emerged between the man's fingertips, as though it had come from within the coin itself. There was a greenish flicker as the man passed the tiny lights to another man, who slipped each one into a pale blue bottle and sealed the top with a cork. Then the first man tossed the coins onto the pile and strode away.

"I'm pretty sure I smell popcorn," said a small voice in Van's ear. "Does anyone else smell popcorn?"

"No, Barnavelt," said Pebble and Van at the same time.

Pebble's eyebrows shot up. Van sucked in a breath. Before he could move or speak or even think of what to ask next, Pebble's hand lashed out and grabbed his arm.

"You need to get out of here *right now,*" she growled. Then, still holding tight to Van's arm, she shot toward the double doors.

"Why?" Van asked as Pebble dragged him toward the doorway, Barnavelt still clinging to his shoulder. "Why can't I be here?"

"Because someone could *see* you," Pebble hissed. "I can't believe they haven't *already.*"

"What would happen if they saw me?"

"I don't know." Pebble yanked him through the doors, into the dark of the staircase. "But it would be bad."

Van stumbled up the steps behind her. "Would they hurt me?"

Pebble paused in a way that made Van's stomach twist. Then she climbed faster, mumbling something he couldn't hear.

"Yeah! Come on!" cheered the squirrel on Van's shoulder. "Giddyup!"

"I didn't *do* anything," said Van, which was almost

not a lie. The thought of the bottle in his pocket made his stomach twist again. "I just looked."

"That's bad enough!" said Pebble, her voice echoing in the dimness. ". . . Supposed to see *any* of this!"

"Why not? What are you . . ."

But the rest of Van's words were lost in a rising roar.

The same terrible sound he'd heard before came crashing up from below, filling the darkness and the inside of Van's head until everything rang. The steps beneath his feet began to shake. Van ripped his arm out of Pebble's grasp and grabbed the stone banister. It was trembling too. Van squeezed his eyes shut and held on tight.

Finally, with smaller and smaller tremors, the sound died away. The chilly air went still.

Van pried his hands off the banister. He looked up at Pebble, standing just beside him. "What *was* that?"

Pebble blinked. "What was what?"

"That sound."

"What sound?"

"You have to have heard it. That *sound*. That huge, roaring, howling sound!"

Van looked from Pebble to Barnavelt. The squirrel

stared back at him. Then it took a flying leap toward Pebble's shoulder.

"I think it's coming from below us." Van craned over the banister. Darkness fell away beneath him, endless and empty. "Are we above a train tunnel or something? Or is there some giant animal down there?"

Pebble's voice sounded funnily strained. "I don't know what you're talking about."

"That *sound,*" said Van, exasperated now. "I *felt* it. I—"

He whirled back toward Pebble.

But it wasn't just Pebble anymore.

A knot of people in long, dark coats surrounded them.

Someone grabbed his arm. Van glanced up, straight into the eyes of a large black bird.

The bird was perched on the shoulder of a big man with dark eyes and long black hair. The man wore a coat covered with straps and hooks and small leather bags. Just below his collarbone, a vicious-looking knife gleamed in a sheath.

He lifted Van by two handfuls of his shirt.

"Little boy." The man's voice was deep and hard. "You have made a serious mistake."

9
A Serious Mistake

VAN had never climbed stairs so quickly.

Of course, he wasn't really climbing them now. Several hands were locked around his arms, and several other hands grasped his collar, and all the hands hauled him up the steps, across the next landing, and into the Calendar, with its big black books. Van caught a last flash of Pebble and Barnavelt before the crowd closed around him. He tried to think of something to say, something that would fix everything, but words scrambled out of his reach like the pigeons scuttling out of their way.

The crowd dragged him to the center of the big stone chamber. Everyone was speaking at once. Van heard something like *ordinary boy* and someone shouting *couldn't find his way* and the big man with the raven on his shoulder snarling something about *including* or *intruding, danger* or *dagger.* The crowd grew even thicker, and the noise of the arguing voices grew louder, and Van felt himself sinking down into a tarry, sticky blackness where there was nothing to hold on to anymore.

He closed his eyes. The voices faded.

Van started to hum to himself. It was a little tune without words that he had made up years ago. He thought of it as SuperVan's theme. Now he hummed it just loudly enough that it filled the inside of his own head.

Dun da-dun DUNNN . . . dun da-dunnn . . .

The plugged-out voices shouted at one other. Van felt something with paws and whiskers sniffing at his cheek, and something smooth and furry rubbing at his shins, and then a sudden bump on his shoulder as two grown-ups started shoving at each other.

"Enough!" boomed a voice.

Someone grabbed him by the shirt once more.

Van opened his eyes. The big man's face loomed in front of him. The raven on his shoulder twitched its wings.

"No more discussion!" the man shouted over the crowd. "I'm taking him down to the Hold!"

"Loosen your grip, Jack," said a deep, clear voice.

The crowd hushed. Van, dangling from the big man's fists, couldn't see where the voice was coming from, but in the silence, he could hear every one of its words.

"He must weigh all of fifty pounds," the deep, calm voice went on.

"Fifty-seven," squeaked Van.

"Fifty-seven pounds," the deep voice repeated. "Do you really think he's going to break free?"

"Freee!" the raven squalled. *"Seeee!"*

"He *sees* us," said the man called Jack. "He got down here without any of us noticing him. What is he?"

"I don't know," said the deep, clear voice. "Why don't we let him tell us? Now, *loosen your grip, Jack."*

Very, very slowly, Van felt himself being lowered back to the floor. Jack's fists released his shirt. Van staggered backward, disoriented by the swirl of voices and bodies, and took his first good look around.

Dozens of people surrounded him. They wore long, dark coats with many pockets, or with hooks and buttons and attached pouches hanging on crosswise leather straps. Some were men and some were women; they had hair and skin of all shades, and eyes that glimmered like puddles. A gray pigeon nestled against the neck of one sleek-haired woman. A live raccoon was draped around the collar of a man with a pony-tail. A few people wore giant spiders on their lapels like brooches. One very tall, thin man with tousled gray hair and rigid cheekbones carried two big black rats on either shoulder.

There was so much to see that, for just a second, Van forgot to be terrified.

"So, boy," said the very tall man with the rats and the rigid cheekbones, and Van realized that this was where the deep, clear voice had come from. When he spoke, everyone else went silent. "Tell us who you are."

"I'm . . . I'm Van," Van gulped. "Van Markson." He stuck out one trembly hand. "Nice to meet you."

The man stared at Van's hand for a moment. When he finally reached out to grasp it, Van's hand disappeared completely in his. "I am Nail," said the tall man.

Without letting go, Nail took a slow, appraising look at Van, cocking his head to either side. Suddenly he stiffened. His hard cheekbones and long, narrow nose flashed closer, bringing both gigantic rats along.

"What is *this*?" he asked, straight into Van's ear.

One of the rats put out its front feet and balanced

itself on Van's shoulder. Its whiskery nose sniffed at Van's earlobe.

"Oh. That." Van raised his free hand, brushing the whiskers away. "That's my hearing aid."

Nail's eyes narrowed. "Are you recording this? Or transmitting it to someone?" There was a murmur. The encircling crowd tightened. "Who are you working for?"

"I . . . I'm eleven," said Van shakily. "I don't work for anybody."

"Then why do you wear a hidden microphone?"

"It's not just a microphone," said Van. "It helps me hear. It's an amplifier and . . ."

But the crowd around him wasn't listening. Their mutters and whispers surged over Van, swamping him in a dark wash of noise. Van's heart pounded. He started to hum again, just loudly enough that his own voice pushed back against the wave of angry sound.

Dun da-dun DUNNN . . .

The rat continued to sniff at his earlobe. Her whiskers, as fine as frayed velvet, whispered against his skin. At last Van turned to face her—he felt strangely sure that it was a her—and found her beady eyes staring straight back into his.

Van was so used to *not* being noticed, even by other people—even by people who matched him in age and grade and number of legs—that being looked at so deeply was disconcerting.

Hello, he thought.

The rat stared at him for another moment. Then she turned and scampered back to her perch on Nail's shoulder. She pressed her nose to Nail's ear.

"Thank you," Van thought he saw Nail's lips murmur. His eyes flicked back to Van. "Other than the device in your ear," said Nail, in a voice that made everyone else go quiet again, "you are *ordinary*?"

Van didn't like the sound of this. The other-than part or the ordinary part. He didn't like it any better than when Pebble had called him "just a little boy." But the circle of dark-coated strangers still loomed around him, and the flight of stairs leading out of here was very long and very far away.

"Yes," said Van. "I'm just a person."

"A person," Nail repeated. "But who are you with? Who do you belong to?"

"Well . . . I live with my mother," Van began. "She's a singer. She's kind of famous. If you like opera, anyway. But right before I came here, I was at a birthday party, so I was *with* a bunch of people, if that's what you—"

The big man named Jack pushed closer to Nail. ". . . found his way inside *on his own*," Van heard him snarl.

"Yes." Nail put up a hand, waiting for the crowd to still. "How *did* you manage to get inside, Van Markson?"

"I—I just . . . ," stammered Van, "I followed the girl. Pebble. The one with the squirrel."

"The girl?" Nail echoed. "*This* girl?" He nodded toward Pebble, who stood nearby, anxiously clenching and unclenching both hands. The squirrel on her head rose onto his hind legs and chittered defensively.

"I didn't do anything wrong!" Pebble shouted. "I didn't bring him here. I was just making a collection. I don't know how he saw me!"

Nail turned back to Van. "How *did* you see her?"

"Well . . . the first time, she was right there, taking coins out of the fountain in the park. And the second time, at the birthday party—"

But the crowd had broken out in furious murmurs once again.

"Twice?" Nail's voice barely carried through the rumble.

"We talked," said Van. "She splashed me. I gave her a marble."

But nobody was listening to him. Words overlapped, hisses and vowels smashing into each other, tangling into knots that squeezed around his body.

". . . *spoke* with him?" boomed a voice from somewhere over Van's shoulder.

"Little boy!" shouted another voice. ". . . standing . . . seen!"

Jack's raven screeched.

A lanky black cat peeled out of the shadows, winding itself around Van's ankles. Its bright eyes glittered up at him, slit pupiled. Predatory.

Once more, Nail's deep, clear voice sliced through the din. "And just what *has* he seen?" Nail waited for quiet before continuing. He turned to Van, opening his hands. "Why don't you tell us, Van Markson, *exactly what you have seen.*"

Van swallowed. "Well . . . ," he began. He glanced at Pebble, hoping for some subtle signal that would tell him just how much to say. But she and the squirrel just stared back at him, petrified. Van pulled his eyes away. "I . . . I noticed that the floors are pretty clean, even though there are a *lot* of pigeons down here."

Nail's lips twitched. "And?"

"And . . . I noticed the room full of maps and charts.

The one named the Atlas." Van glanced nervously from Nail to Jack, who had once again taken the spot just over his right shoulder. "And I noticed that all the books in this room match, so I suppose they're more for writing things down than for reading things. I think maybe they have something to do with birthdays. And I noticed there are a whole bunch of things sealed in bottles down there in that huge room, like little glowing coins, and something that looks like candle smoke. I noticed Pebble *really* doesn't want me here. And I noticed that—I *think*—there's something really, really big down there in the dark, and that Pebble won't talk about it. But that's . . ." Van stopped, his mouth going dry. "That's all."

The crowd around him had fallen silent. No one moved, not even the spiders or the birds. An echoing absence hung in the air.

"That's all," said Nail at last, very softly.

"He's dangerous. I told you." Jack's voice was like a blade on the back of Van's neck. "He needs to be contained."

"We can't keep him," said the sleek-haired woman with a pigeon on her shoulder. Van turned to watch her face. "People will search. Is that what we need, Jack? A city full of people *trying* to find us?"

"What do you suggest, Sesame?" Jack growled. His dark eyes snapped to Van. "If you don't want to keep him, shall we get rid of him entirely?"

Van's heart shot into the back of his mouth. His body tensed to run.

"No," said Nail.

Jack's raven gave a little *caw* deep in its throat. No one else spoke.

Nail bent close to Van's face. His eyes were gray and cool and steady. "By coming here," he said, "by speaking to us—just by *seeing* us—you have put yourself in serious danger. You must never let *anyone* know about us. Do you understand?"

Van nodded, because there was nothing else to do.

"Do not come back here. Do not mention anything about us, or about this place, to anyone. We will be watching you. If you *do* tell anyone, *we will know.*"

Van swallowed.

Nail leaned even closer. "And if we find out that you *have* spoken of us, you and anyone you've told will have to be . . . *removed.* Understood?"

Van nodded again.

Nail put out one long-fingered hand.

Van stuck out his smaller one. They shook.

"We have your word." Nail straightened up to his full height. "Now," he said, "Pebble will escort you out."

The chamber exploded into action. Birds soared off in all directions. Rodents skittered for the staircases. Dark-coated people strode back to the shelves and tables or disappeared through the chamber's entrance. Even Jack, after one more look at Van, stalked off into the darkness.

"Really?" Pebble whispered to Nail, just loudly enough that Van could hear.

"Take him back where he belongs." Nail didn't whisper. "If he's not a total fool, he'll realize how lucky he's been." He nodded at Van. "Good-bye, Van Markson."

Pebble hesitated for an instant. Then she turned and hurried toward the staircase. Van ran after her. When he glanced back one last time, he saw that Nail and his rats were still watching him, all of them standing utterly still in the lamplight.

Fear usually made Van even quieter than usual. But now the quiet just made him feel alone. And the only person who made him feel less alone was the weird girl with the mossy penny eyes.

"So . . . ," he began, as he followed her up the flight of stairs. "Your name is Pebble?"

Pebble didn't answer.

"That's a funny name."

Pebble's head whipped around. "*Van* is a funny name," she said. "Especially for someone your size. They should have named you Minivan."

"Ha!" cried Barnavelt. "Minivan! I get it! *Minivan!*"

Van sighed.

The squirrel went on chuckling all the way up the flight.

"Why did you name him Barnavelt?" Van asked when the squirrel finally stopped laughing.

Pebble glanced back. Her eyes were sharp. "Who told you his name was Barnavelt?"

Van pretended he hadn't heard this. He looked over his shoulder, toward the archway of the Atlas, where a few dark-coated grown-ups hurried about their work. "Are there any other kids down here?"

Pebble didn't turn around this time, but Van saw her spine stiffen. "Not right now," she said.

For a moment, Van kept quiet, watching the bottom of Pebble's coat whisk ahead of him across the floor of the huge entry chamber. He waited until they were halfway up the flight of stairs that led to the City Collection Agency before asking, in the most casual voice he could manage, "What *was* that huge sound?"

Pebble hesitated. "What sound?"

"That *sound*. That huge earthquake sound."

"Nothing. Just—something in the Hold."

"What's the Hold for?" asked Van.

"Holding things," said Pebble.

"What things?"

"Lots of things."

"Lots of things," echoed Barnavelt. "I know lots of things. My name. Your name. How to open a walnut. When a twig is too thin. Lots of numbers. Like three. That's a number. Twenty-one-hundredy. That's another number. . . ."

"And the big room full of bottles," Van plunged on. "What's the glowing stuff inside all of them? What does it have to do with coins and smoke and little bones? Is it chemicals, or atoms, or—"

Pebble turned around so suddenly that Van almost crashed into her. The squirrel on her shoulder gave a start. "Well, hello there!" Barnavelt squeaked, as though he was seeing Van for the first time in days. "How have you been?"

"You ask too many questions," said Pebble, in a voice

like the edge of a steak knife. "You can't know because you *can't know*."

But Van had just put the pieces together. His thoughts weren't going to be sliced apart now, not even by a steak knife. The chamber full of bottles. Piles of coins. Smoke from birthday candles. Tiny broken bones.

Wishbones.

"Are you collecting people's *wishes*?" he breathed.

Pebble grabbed Van so hard that he let out a squeak. Without a word, she shoved him through the hidden doorway, across the dingy office of the City Collection Agency, and straight out the front door.

Van stumbled onto the sidewalk. The daylight was blinding. In the street, cars vroomed and honked. The sudden noise of the city pounded against the pulse in his head. By the brightness of the sky, he could tell that it was still afternoon, but that was all. He could have run away from Peter's party an hour ago. Maybe two hours. Maybe more.

Pebble, hurrying through the door behind him, said something Van couldn't hear. Then she broke into a run.

Van jogged after her. His legs ached from climbing hundreds of stairs. His chest hurt. The world was much too loud and cluttered. But even worse than all that noise was the thought of what his mother would do when she learned that he'd run away. He could picture her terrified face, smell her perfume as she reached out to grab him . . . and there his imagination switched off. He couldn't begin to guess what his mother would do next. Because Van had never done anything even *half* this bad in his entire life.

He staggered down the next sidewalk, and the one after that, and the one after that, chasing the ends of Pebble's flying ponytail.

Are you . . . , he thought he heard Pebble yell.

Are you what? Maybe she'd just said *hurry up*. Van was running as fast as he could. But after all those staircases, and all those long city blocks, his legs were turning to rubber.

Abruptly Pebble stopped. Van saw her stare at something just across the street. Her body went rigid. She reeled backward.

"Go!" she yelled, shoving Van in front of her. "You're almost there!"

Van stumbled over the curb and into the street.

In his last glimpse of her, Pebble was whirling around, her face tight with panic, tearing back in the direction from which they'd come.

A sound like the roar from the Hold hammered in his ears. The air turned foggy, as if a dense cloud had burst just above him. And then, as Van took another staggering step—

The world tilted.

There were a few long, frozen moments when Van realized that he was flying. But not like SuperVan would fly. More like a plant would fly if you knocked it out of a window.

Then his right side seemed to catch fire. His head thumped cement, and he felt one hearing aid slip out of his ear and tumble away. The roar thickened. His head clanged. Above him, the sky spun with rooftops and the leafy tips of trees.

Between Van and the spinning sky stood a giant yellow insect. The insect seemed to be saying something. A second later, a pair of hands hoisted Van gently off the pavement and onto his behind.

Van sat up, blinking.

The insect turned into a man in yellow spandex, a bike helmet, and sunglasses.

Somebody put the lost hearing aid in Van's hand. Van worked it back into position.

"—ook both ways," the insect-bike man was yelling. "Rang my bell . . . shouted . . ."

"He may not have heard you," said a smooth voice from just over Van's shoulder. "He's deaf."

"Hard of hearing," Van corrected. The pounding in his head made him close his eyes.

An arm braced Van's shoulder. "Are . . . right? . . . Hurt?"

"I . . ." Van touched his sore hip. He had landed on his side. The side with the glass bottle in the pocket. He wriggled his stinging hand through the cloth.

The bottle was there. Safe and sound.

But his pants had a dirty, rubbed splotch on the hip, and when he pulled his hand back out of his pocket, he saw that his palm was scraped raw.

". . . hit your head?" said the close voice.

"That landed second," said Van. "I just bumped it. I think."

More words and noises dribbled around him, but Van wasn't really paying attention anymore. Confusion coursed from his pounding heart out through the rest of his aching body, and by the time his eyes focused again, the insect-bike man was whirring away.

Van turned to the right.

Seated beside him on the curb was an older man in a white suit. He had neatly wavy gray hair and blue eyes surrounded by crinkly smile lines. The smile that went with them was encouraging and warm, like a doctor might give you after a booster shot.

"I'm sure you don't remember me," said the man. "I am Ivor Falborg."

"I'm—"

"You are Giovanni Markson," said the man. "Or Van, for short."

Van blinked. "How do you know?"

"Oh, I'm quite the opera aficionado," the man explained. "I met you and your glorious mother at an Opera Guild party a few months ago." He rose to his feet, pulling Van with him. "Are you sure you're all right? I'd be happy to hail a taxi."

"No," said Van. "I can walk. I think."

"Then I hope you'll let me walk you home, at the very least. I live in your neighborhood."

"Oh . . . I'm not going home," said Van, with a fresh sinking feeling in his stomach. "I have to go back to the Greys' house."

"Charles and Peter Grey?" Mr. Falborg's smile crinkled again. "They are dear friends of mine! Now you *must* let me escort you. We're only a few minutes away."

Mr. Falborg was right. As soon as they turned the next corner, Van recognized the row of snooty stone houses and wide front steps.

And there, at the foot of one set of steps, was a police car.

A few of the boys from the birthday party were gathered on the sidewalk, throwing acorns at one another. Peter sat on the curb with his arms folded over his chest. Peter's nanny was sobbing something to a police officer, who was jotting on a tiny notepad. Standing on the sidewalk, one hand clenching the silk scarf around her throat, her eyes flicking up and down the street, was Van's mother.

Van's stomach suddenly felt like a bowl of cold oatmeal. He slunk up the sidewalk toward the crowd, squeezing as much of himself into Mr. Falborg's shadow as he could.

The nanny spotted them first. Van saw her mouth open wide as she shouted something, her finger pointing in his direction.

Ingrid Markson whirled around. *"Giovanni!"* In spite of her high heels, she was next to him in two seconds. She wrapped him up in both arms. Van sagged against her for a moment, feeling safe and grateful and very glad it was her hands clutching him instead of Jack's—although he wished it wasn't right in front of a knot of staring boys.

"What were you *thinking*?" his mother demanded, pulling back so that Van could see her face—although she was speaking loudly enough for Van (and the entire street) to hear. "Why would you jump out of a window and run away? In a city like this? What on *earth* were you *thinking*?" She grabbed his scraped hand. "And what happened to you? Are you all right?"

Van's mouth opened. Nothing came out.

"A minor collision with a bicyclist," said Mr. Falborg. "I saw it happen. I was too late to do anything else, I'm afraid."

"You were *hit by a bicycle*?" His mother squeezed Van's face between her lily-scented palms. "Are you hurt? Did you hit your head?"

The police officer and the crying nanny were heading toward them. The other boys, except for Peter, had edged closer. They were still throwing acorns at one another, but they were clearly eavesdropping at the same time.

Van still couldn't quite shove his thoughts into order. And his mouth was too tightly squished between his mother's hands for any words to get out anyway. "Uh," he began.

"I believe he landed on his side," Mr. Falborg put in helpfully. "I hope you won't mind me intruding, Signorina Markson—I'm Ivor Falborg. I'm a member of the Opera Guild. We first met at the gala last March."

"Oh, yes. Mr. *Falborg,*" said Van's mother. "How lucky that you were there." Her eyes flashed back to Van. "You *still* haven't explained what you thought you were doing."

Van swallowed. His mind hopped from the open window to Barnavelt the squirrel to the white cat he had used as a squirrel stand-in on his miniature stage, and from there to—

"I saw a stray cat," he blurted.

"A stray cat?" his mother repeated.

"It was in the yard. I thought it might be lost. So I tried to catch it."

Van's mother looked as though he'd just tried to force-feed her a dog biscuit. She leaned back, lips pursed. "You jumped out of a window and ran away from a birthday party because you saw a *cat* that *might* have been lost?"

The police officer and the weeping nanny joined them. The other boys sidled even closer.

"Yes," said Van. "That was why."

Ingrid Markson rose gracefully to her full height. "Apparently he was chasing a stray cat," she told the crowd. "I'm so sorry for the trouble, officer. And Mr. Falborg, it was very kind of you to give us your time."

"Ms. Markson," said the nanny, looking very wobbly, "I am so—so—I just didn't—"

"It wasn't your fault." Van's mother patted the nanny's arm. "It wasn't anyone's fault but Van's."

"And the cat's," said Van, but everyone ignored him.

". . . like everyone is where they should be," said the police officer. He nodded at Van's mother and the nanny before turning toward the police car. "I'll let you finish your party."

"The party's over," said a loud voice.

Everyone looked around.

Peter hadn't moved from his seat on the curb. "David already had to leave," he said. "Everyone else is getting picked up in ten minutes. And we spent the whole time out here, staring into people's yards. I didn't even get to open my presents."

"Peter!" said the nanny reprovingly. "Van is safe. That's what matters."

Peter's eyes met Van's. Peter's eyes were that cool shade of blue that made Van think of outdoor swimming pools. They narrowed, and the water darkened, and Van could practically feel Peter's chilly hatred flooding up and over him.

"I'm sure Giovanni is very sorry for disrupting the party." Ingrid Markson's voice was loud enough to push Van forward. Her fingers finished the job. *"Aren't* you, Giovanni?"

Van took a step toward Peter. "Yes. I'm sorry."

Peter turned his face to the side. His voice was only a mutter, and Van couldn't quite follow his lips, but he was pretty sure Peter had said, "You should be."

Van slid a hand into his pocket and pressed the little china squirrel between his fingertips. "Thank you for inviting me to your party," he said, giving Peter his brightest smile. "I had a wonderful time."

When they reached the apartment, Van's mother washed his scraped hand, tutted over his scuffed pants, and then sent him straight to his room.

Van had been about to go there anyway.

After making sure the door was firmly shut, Van took out his hearing aids and pulled his collection out from under the bed. He rummaged through the box until he uncovered the velvet drawstring bag he'd found on the floor of a French department store.

Van tugged the blue glass bottle out of his pocket. Holding it up to the light, he turned the bottle from side to side. *Peter Grey. April 8. Twelfth birthday.* Inside, the silvery wisp glimmered softly. Peter's wish.

What had Peter wished for? Van wondered. He squinted into the bottle, searching for a clue in the spinning silver smoke, but there was nothing. Nothing that Van could see, anyway. How many other stolen wishes were sealed up in that underground chamber? Millions? Billions? And why were the dark-coated people stealing them in the first place?

Slowly Van slipped the bottle into the drawstring bag. He placed the bag at the very bottom of the box, under a heap of other treasures.

Van turned to the miniature stage. He cleared away the plastic dinosaurs he'd arranged there yesterday, and placed SuperVan and Pawn Girl in the center. He set the stolen china squirrel between them. He rummaged through the treasure box until he found the rusty model garbage truck.

Vrrooommm. SCREEEECH. The garbage truck hurtled around a busy city corner. The tiny gray squirrel had no time to flee. Pawn Girl watched in horror as the truck's heavy tires barreled closer—

And then, from above, there came a streak of red and black.

SuperVan swept in front of the garbage truck, diving so close that his cape whooshed across its front bumper like a big dustcloth. He scooped the squirrel into his arms and soared back into the air, while the truck rumbled away into the distance.

"You saved Barnavelt!" shouted Pawn Girl as SuperVan landed gracefully on the sidewalk.

"Yeah! You saved me! You're a lifesaver! I love Lifesavers!" cheered the squirrel. "And I love Skittles, and Starbursts, and—"

"It was nothing," said SuperVan modestly.

"No. You're a hero." Pawn Girl moved closer. "You've proved that we can trust you. So now . . . we're going to tell you all of our secrets."

Van looked at Pawn Girl. He looked at the miniature squirrel. But for some reason, here, in his own ordinary bedroom, he couldn't imagine what might come next.

He was still gazing at the silent stage when a raven landed on his windowsill.

Its clever, pointed face flicked from side to side. It took in the scene behind the glass: the preoccupied boy, the miniature stage, the tiny china squirrel. Its beady eyes winked. Then it spread its wings and soared down to the shoulder of a man in a long black coat who was waiting on the twilit sidewalk.

The raven croaked softly into the man's ear. Then the man turned and strode away, with the raven still perched on his shoulder, and no one on the sidewalk, or in the street, or in the high, busy buildings to either side noticed that they had been there at all.

10
Hair Wreaths and Even Stranger Things

"WHY can't I just stay at home?" Van asked the next morning, as he scurried along the sidewalk in his mother's lily-scented shadow. "I don't want to spend a whole Saturday at your rehearsal."

"You *know* why," said his mother. "You've shown me that I can't trust you to stay where you're supposed to. This is a big, dangerous city, and you're very small and very special." She placed a hand on Van's head in a way that made Van squirm away. "Besides, I happen to know that Peter will be there."

The memory of Peter's ice-water eyes—and the thought of the stolen squirrel and the little blue glass bottle, both of which were currently hidden in his treasure box—pulled Van's stomach into a knot.

"Peter hates me," he said.

"I'm sure he doesn't hate you," said his mother. "But maybe you could be especially nice to him to make up for disrupting his party."

"Maybe," said Van doubtfully.

"Charles and I would love it if you two spent a little more time together," his mother went on. "You'd be good for each other."

"*Good for* each other?" said Van. "Like . . . broccoli?"

"Like broccoli and broccolini!" sang his mother.

For a second, Van thought about making a break for it. He pictured himself taking off like SuperVan, his body a caped streak bulleting through the city. . . . But even his imaginary self couldn't outrun his real mother. She'd have nabbed him by the next corner.

Van slumped over and stared at the sidewalk.

Wads of old gum. Bottle caps. A few crumpled flower petals. And there, under a shrub, something with glittering black eyes.

Van crouched so suddenly that his mother nearly knocked into him.

"Giovanni, what on earth—" she began.

But Van wasn't listening. He edged closer to the thing in the leafy shadows. Maybe it was Jack's raven, with its beak like a sharpened pencil. Maybe it was one of Nail's rats. Whatever it was, it was something *alive*. Something that stared back at him. Heart thumping, he reached out and swept back the branches.

Beneath the shrub was a tiny, trembling ball of gray fuzz.

"It's a baby bird!" cried Van. The bird blinked at him with ink-drop eyes. One crooked wing gave a twitch. "I think it's hurt!"

"Oh," said his mother. "It must have fallen out of its nest. Poor thing."

"What should we do?"

"Giovanni . . ." His mother sighed. "These things happen. And we have to go, or I'll be late."

Van pulled his arm out of his mother's grasp. "We can't just leave it!"

His mother sighed again. "It's outdoors, where it belongs. Don't touch it. I'm sure it has mites or rabies."

"Birds don't get rabies," said Van, who actually wasn't sure about this. "We have to help it!"

"Giovanni, it's a wild creature. You can't just bring home a crow or a sparrow or a—a—"

"A baby robin," said a polite voice.

So quietly that Van hadn't noticed it, a man in a

white suit had stopped beside them. Van looked up and found himself washed in the warmth of Mr. Falborg's crinkly smile.

"You have sharp eyes, Master Markson." Mr. Falborg beamed. "And Signorina Markson, what a pleasure to run into the world's greatest lyric soprano two days in a row! My lucky stars must be aligned."

"That's very sweet of you, Mr. Falborg." Van's mother glowed back at him. "Van and I were just on our way to the opera, as a matter of fact."

"*I* wasn't," said Van. "I'm not leaving the bird here."

"Giovanni," said his mother, in a voice that began to take on that cathedral ring.

"May I make a suggestion?" Mr. Falborg asked. "I could take the robin to an excellent animal hospital nearby. It's where I bring my Renata for her annual checkup. Renata is my Persian cat. Like Renata Tebaldi, she's quite the diva." His smile shifted back to Van. "And if it's all right with you, Signorina Markson, I'd be happy to take Van with me."

Van whirled around. "Can I, Mom? Please?"

"I'll bring him directly to the opera house afterward," Mr. Falborg offered. "If you say yes, that is."

He paused, waiting for an answer. Mr. Falborg's face

looked so warm and crinkly, Van didn't know how any-one could have said no.

Van's mother didn't say it either. "All right." She bent down to give Van a kiss on the forehead. "But you behave yourself. Do you hear me, Giovanni?"

"I hear you," mumbled Van.

"It's a good thing you spotted that little creature," said Mr. Falborg as Ingrid Markson hurried away. He tugged a blue silk handkerchief out of his vest pocket. "Without you, he probably wouldn't have survived. There." He bent down and swaddled the bird in the handkerchief. "It can think it's safe in the sky."

The animal hospital was just two blocks away. On the walk there, Van found a quarter and a Lego knight, which made the morning seem even sunnier. They left the baby robin in the care of a friendly veterinary tech-nician, who promised that the bird would be cared for and released into the wild, and Mr. Falborg asked her to send the bill to his home address, and he and Van strolled back out into the street.

They gave each other job-well-done smiles. Then Van thought of Peter Grey, and of the rehearsal room at the opera where everything was loud and blurry and boring, and of all the other things he could be doing on a sunny summer Saturday. He let out a sigh.

"Something wrong?" asked Mr. Falborg.

"Just . . . I don't really want to go to the opera. And rehearsal doesn't get done until three, so I'll have to sit there for hours."

"Hmm." Mr. Falborg looked thoughtful. "What if you were at the opera house long before the end of rehearsal, but you spent the rest of the time at my home instead?"

Van felt his face crinkle into a Mr. Falborg kind of smile. "That would be good."

Mr. Falborg's house, like Mr. Falborg himself, was tall and tidy. Its five stories of white brick were wreathed by a yard of sculpted bushes and trees, and its door was painted the same shade of sky blue as Mr. Falborg's handkerchief.

"Please come in," said Mr. Falborg, as they stepped over the threshold into a high-ceilinged foyer.

Van, who had expected to see numbered apartment doors on either side, let out a little gasp. "You have the *whole* building?"

"It's been in my family for quite some time. Ah! Gerda!" Mr. Falborg exclaimed, as a middle-aged lady in a neat gray suit appeared at the other end of the hall. "Let me introduce Giovanni Markson, son of renowned soprano Ingrid Markson."

"People just call me Van," said Van timidly.

"Ni-yis to meet you." Gerda spoke with a swoopy accent that Van couldn't quite identify. She gave him a warm smile. "Mr. Falborg . . . tree calls from the Venetian dealer dis afternoon."

"Thank you, Gerda." Mr. Falborg turned toward Van. "Would you excuse me for just a moment? Please make yourself comfortable in the front room." He ushered Van toward an arched doorway. "Perhaps Gerda can find us some refreshments."

Gerda strode down the hall toward the back of the house, Mr. Falborg turned to the right, and Van was left to tiptoe through the arched doorway.

He found himself inside a large front room. The walls were white, and chandeliers hung from the white ceiling, and white armchairs were arranged around a large fireplace whose bricks and mantelpiece had all been painted white. But that was where the whiteness ended. Jungly ferns poured from hanging baskets. Built-in bookcases shone with worn, warm-hued hard-covers. The walls were covered with frames of all shapes and sizes, and each frame held something different: a cut-paper silhouette, an antique postcard, a bunch of butterflies pinned in place.

More curios covered every flat surface. Glossy seashells. Wooden ships in bottles. Old metal toys. Lifelike flowers carved out of stone. Very carefully, Van touched the trunk of a cast-iron elephant. The trunk bent down and snapped back up into place. Van jumped.

"Lemonade and ginger cookies," said Gerda's voice, making Van jump again. "Please help yerself." She set a tray on a table and whisked back out the door.

Van sidled around the low white couch and took a nibble of one of the cookies. It was so brittle and spicy that it seemed to be trying to bite him back.

". . . see . . . fresh mints every . . . ," said Mr. Falborg's voice over his shoulder. *I see the refreshments have arrived.*

Van turned. "Mrs. Gerda . . . um, Mrs. . . . your wife brought them."

"I hope my wife wouldn't call me 'Mr. Falborg.'" Mr. Falborg smiled. "Gerda and her husband, Hans, help run my home. They also help to manage my business matters—sales and purchases and so forth. And they make this big place less lonely. Otherwise, it would be just me and my collections." He gestured around the room. "They take up plenty of space, but they aren't much company. Mechanical banks, stamps, marbles, hair wreaths—"

Van was pretty sure he'd heard this wrong. "Hair wreaths?"

"Victorian arrangements made from human hair," Mr. Falborg explained. "I've only been collecting them for the last decade or so. But some of my collections are the work of a lifetime. My opera albums, my paperweights . . ." His blue eyes grew even brighter. "You can see for yourself, if you'll come with me."

Mr. Falborg led the way through another arch, around a corner, to a pair of closed doors. He threw the doors open and flicked on the lights. The entire room twinkled to life.

"Ohhh," Van breathed.

The room was packed with lighted glass cabinets of the kind that Van had seen only in fancy jewelry stores. Each shelf of every cabinet was filled with glass bubbles, all different colors, all glinting softly. Van's mind flashed to the chamber full of shimmering bottles . . . but Mr. Falborg was opening a cabinet and lifting something out, and Van quickly dragged his mind back.

"This is one of the oldest in my collection,"

Mr. Falborg said, holding out an orb of green glass clustered with gold spirals. "I found it in an antique shop in New Orleans when I wasn't much older than you are. With that, I was hooked."

Van gazed around at the galaxy of paperweights. Some were filled with frozen cyclones of bubbles, some with layers of colored glass that looked like jellyfish legs, some with flowers that must have been picked a hundred years ago. "Wow," he murmured.

"Collecting is a slippery thing," said Mr. Falborg, bending down beside him. "The whole world becomes a curiosity shop. Your next discovery could be anywhere. And you know that looking at the world this way is making you distracted and strange, but you can't help it, because the minute you stop looking, you might miss a genuine *treasure*."

Van turned away from the cabinets and stared up into Mr. Falborg's face. There was a funny prickly feeling in his spine—very much like the feeling he got when he noticed something special waiting for him on the ground.

"And once you *do* spot that treasure," Mr. Falborg went on, "you simply have to have it. You need to add it to your collection, because—"

"Because it belongs there," said Van.

Mr. Falborg's eyes sparkled. "Exactly." He put a hand on Van's shoulder. "I *knew* I'd spotted a fellow collector. And what is *your* passion? What do you collect?"

"Just . . . little things that I find," said Van. "Stuff other people drop or throw away."

"Intriguing," said Mr. Falborg. "Would you care for another cookie? Or would you like to see the hair wreaths?"

"Hair wreaths," said Van quickly.

Mr. Falborg guided Van back through the doorway, around several corners, past many more closed doors, and up a long staircase.

Mr. Falborg's house was much twistier on the inside than Van would have guessed. Every hall seemed to split in several directions, and every nook and shelf was cluttered with strange treasures. One stretch of wall was hung with hundreds of masks. Another stretch was coated with old circus posters. An entire hallway was filled with the glimmering bodies of stuffed and mounted snakes. By the time Mr. Falborg threw open a door, Van had nearly forgotten where they were going.

This room was narrow and long, with dark paneling and red velvet curtains that shut out most of the light. Brass contraptions sat on polished wooden tables. Van saw something that looked like a typewriter, and something that looked like a very old cash register, and something that might have been a sewing machine or a dentist's drill. Mr. Falborg turned on the chandelier, and Van could suddenly see that the walls were covered with hanging glass boxes, each one holding something that looked like fancy embroidery without any fabric behind it.

Van moved closer.

Instead of colored threads, the embroidered things were made of thousands and thousands of human hairs. The hairs had been knotted and coiled into tiny buds and trees and leaves and stems—things that should have been green, or pink, or white, but that were all a sort of dusty brown instead.

"These *are* weird," Van said at last.

Mr. Falborg nodded. "They are indeed. And just imagine the Victorian craftspeople picking strands out of their hairbrushes night after night."

"*Really* weird," said Van.

"If we had more time, I would show you my music boxes—but they're down in the cellars. Perhaps on another visit."

Van smiled up at Mr. Falborg. "That would be great."

Mr. Falborg smiled back.

And then, just over Mr. Falborg's shoulder, something caught Van's eye. In the farthest, darkest corner of the room, inlaid with panels of painted silk and nearly hidden by the red velvet curtains, stood a pair of gleaming black doors.

"What's in there?" Van asked. "Another collection?"

"Ah." Mr. Falborg glided between Van and the gleaming black doors. "That is a collection I don't show to guests, I'm afraid." He gave Van an apologetic smile. "It is the most valuable of all my collections. Its safety is paramount."

Curiosity—and Mr. Falborg's kindly face—made Van bolder than usual. "I'd be really careful," he promised, with another look at the doors. "You can trust me."

But he'd barely finished speaking before several secrets loomed up in the back of Van's mind.

Peter's stolen squirrel. The way he'd sneaked inside the dingy collection agency, through the endless underground halls, into the chamber full of bottled wishes. The blue glass bottle with its spinning silver wisp wedged into the treasure box under his bed. Of course he would never steal from Mr. Falborg . . . but he hadn't meant to steal anything from Peter Grey or the underground collection either. Maybe he *couldn't* be trusted.

"Oh, I'm certain I can trust you," Mr. Falborg said, in a voice that made Van feel steadier. "But there are others who . . ."

Mr. Falborg stopped. His eyes locked on a tiny spot on the wall, not far from the half-hidden black doors. Van followed Mr. Falborg's eyes. When he squinted, he could tell that the spot was a small brown spider, holding perfectly still.

Mr. Falborg whipped the blue handkerchief out of his pocket. With a vicious *thwack,* he smashed the spider against the wall. Van winced. The sound of Mr. Falborg's hand against the wall was surprisingly loud, even to Van. Louder than it needed to be to smash a tiny spider.

Mr. Falborg turned away from the wall. His gaze landed on Van, and the look of cold distaste on his features melted quickly back into a smile. He dropped the handkerchief onto the nearest table. "Not *all* creatures are our friends," he said. He glanced at his wristwatch. "Oh, my. The time has gotten away from me. We'd better make our way to the opera house." He gestured to the door. "After you, Master Markson."

The walk to the opera was short and lit by streaks of afternoon sun. Mr. Falborg kept up a stream of stories about unusual marbles and extremely rare stamps that Van could only half hear, and Van found an old-fashioned key in the gutter, and by the time Mr. Falborg opened the opera house's lobby door for Van and bowed good-bye, Van couldn't quite remember why the tiny seed of a strange, unsettled feeling had rooted deep in the pit of his stomach.

11
We Will Come for You

THREE minutes after midnight, Van's window inched open.

Van, who was fast asleep with his hearing aids in their usual spot on the bedside table, didn't hear the window creak. He didn't hear the click of talons on his bedpost. He didn't hear the *thunk* of a heavy metal hook catching over the windowsill. A gust of cool air washed through the open window, fluttering the ends of Van's hair. Van stirred slightly. But he didn't wake up.

Two pairs of booted feet climbed up the brick wall beneath his window. Two long, dark coats rustled over the windowsill. Van didn't hear this, either.

It wasn't until a shadow fell over him, blocking his nightlight's misty glow, that Van's eyelids finally slid open.

Two dark-coated men loomed over his bed. One had a live raccoon draped around his collar. The other had a hard face, glittering eyes, and a huge black raven on his shoulder.

Before Van could scream, Jack's big hand clamped over his mouth.

Jack's lips moved. The other man nodded, whipping back the covers. Van didn't even have time to wish that these two hadn't seen him in his model train pajamas before he was thrown over Jack's shoulder. Someone tugged a black cotton bag over Van's head.

Van felt the jostle of being lifted over the window-sill, the rush of damp night air through his pajamas, the jut of Jack's shoulder in the middle of his stomach. He tried to scream, but the bag seemed to trap the sound inside his own head, where he could barely hear himself anyway. For an instant, he thought he was falling, and then another pair of hands caught him, and Van felt himself being hefted onto a narrow, springy seat. Someone sat down beside him.

A moment later, a jerk made Van sway back. A breeze told him he was moving forward. Fast.

They must know about the bottle, Van realized. They knew he had stolen it. His body went cold.

"Please," he gasped through the black bag. "I'll give it back. I'll do whatever you—"

The big hand clamped over his mouth again. If anyone answered, Van couldn't hear.

With Van's breath and sweat and that big heavy hand sealing the air inside, it didn't take long for the bag to grow stuffy. Soon it was stifling. Very slowly, trying not to panic, Van let his head droop sideways. The hand stayed where it was. At last, the bag had twisted just enough that Van could peek past its bottom edge.

He was seated in a small open carriage. It had black leather seats and large, spidery wheels. Two men on bicycles pulled it along, their dark coats flaring behind them.

The carriage turned into an alley, and then into another alley, and then another. Soon Van had lost track of their path. He supposed it didn't matter. He already knew where they were going.

At last the carriage rolled to a stop. Van was hoisted over Jack's shoulder again, and the bag slid back down over his eyes. He felt the dim enclosure of the empty office, and the chilling of the air as they all climbed down the steep stone staircase.

"Please," he begged. "I'll do whatever you want. Please."

The body carrying his didn't even pause.

More turns. More stairs. Down. Left. Right.

Then, with dizzying speed, he was set on his feet. Hands shoved him backward. Van staggered onto a cold metal surface that vibrated and swayed beneath his bare toes. Someone wrenched off the bag.

Van blinked, woozy and light-headed, and found himself staring down into bottomless, waiting dark. He let out a shriek. Without his hearing aids, the sound was muffled and dim, even inside of his own head. Could anyone else hear it at all?

He stood in some kind of swaying elevator—or really, Van realized, in some kind of hanging cage. Its walls were grates of wide-spaced metal bars. Just inches beyond his toes, one side of the cage hung open, revealing the plummeting depths below.

Standing on a solid stone platform a few feet away were Jack and two other hard-faced men. Jack's hands were clamped around a handle that spoked from a large metal wheel. The wheel led to a pulley and a set of cogs and cords.

Van saw it all in a flash: They were going to lower

him into the darkness. Into that deep, blinding black, along with whatever monstrous thing had made that stone-shaking roar. Into the Hold.

"NO!" he screamed. "Don't! Please! I'll give it back!"

Jack's mouth moved. He stopped, waiting.

"I can't hear you!" Van shouted.

Jack's lips moved again. Van couldn't make out a single word.

One of the other men said something into Jack's ear. Jack's eyes narrowed. The raven on his shoulder lifted into the air.

"Lies!" Van heard the bird cry. *"LIES!"*

Jack cranked the handle.

The cage plunged. It halted a few feet down, swaying wildly. Van skidded on the metal floor, grabbing the edge of the open wall so hard that he thought his bones might snap.

"PLEASE!" he shouted toward the men on the platform above. "I don't know what you want!"

The man with the ponytail shook his head. The third man muttered something. Jack's eyes were like flint. He watched Van, waiting.

Then he cranked the handle again.

Van lost his footing. He fell onto his backside, sliding

across the metal box to one of the far corners. His spine slammed against the bars. He stared up at the three men, at the platform, at the green-gold light that was already starting to dwindle away. His body seared with terror.

"No!" he screamed. "Somebody! Help! *Please!"*

Something flashed above him.

Something with pearly wings.

It soared across the darkness of the pit, skimming past the metal box with Van trembling inside. The pigeon landed gracefully on the handle right between Jack's clenching hands.

A second later, a woman in a long dark coat rushed onto the platform. The pigeon flapped from the handle up to her shoulder. Van recognized the sleek-haired woman from the crowd that had surrounded him in the Calendar. Sesame. She was shorter than Jack, but when she stood chest to chest with him, Van could have sworn he saw Jack flinch.

The woman whipped around, gesturing to the swinging metal box, and to Van cowering in it. Her face was irate.

"What . . . *relieve* . . . this!" she shouted. ". . . *dare* . . . who . . . *own!"*

The floor beneath Van gave another shudder.

The box rocked. Van pressed himself to the wall, bracing for another drop. But instead, the cage began to rise, swinging slowly back toward the platform.

Hands grabbed him once more. Van was too overwhelmed to do anything but flop over like a sack of wet sand. He barely noticed who caught him, or who carried him away, or where they were going, but suddenly they were stepping inside another room—a smaller, stone-walled room with a blazing fireplace and scattered rugs, and towering Nail with his rats was there, along with the sleek-haired woman and Jack and his men, and everyone looked absolutely furious.

Someone plunked Van down in a worn armchair. The adults were yelling, Sesame nose to nose with Jack, Nail and the other men right behind them. The noise made an ugly music inside Van's head. Every now and then, a word seeped through. *Betrayed . . . hear . . . only . . . know . . .*

But Van was too shaken and exhausted to even try to follow. He stared down at the floor instead.

Firelight made the stones look damp and blurry. Strange shadows scuttled at the corners of his eyes. Maybe he was dreaming. Maybe that gentle touch on his ankle was his mother sitting on the edge of his bed, waking him up.

Van blinked.

Two big black rats were climbing up his pajama legs.

Van froze. The rats scurried over his torso, up his arms, and came to rest on either side of his neck. The tips of their pointy fingernails needled his shoulders. Whiskers tickled his skin. Wet noses bumped lightly at his earlobes. Van shuddered and squeezed his eyes shut tight.

But then, with the other voices fading into darkness, Van realized that the tickle on his skin wasn't just whiskers.

It was voices.

High, tiny voices, like the tick of a watch tucked deep in a pocket.

And even without his hearing aids, he could hear every word they said.

"A Collector," the voice on the right said.

"Collecting what?" asked the voice on his left.

"Little things," said the first, slightly higher voice. "In half of a little room."

"Ah. Little room with red curtains."

Van took a shaky breath. "You mean my maquette?"

he whispered, in a voice that was almost as soft as the rats'.

Both rats froze.

"It's a miniature stage," Van went on. "With curtains."

"Ah," said both rats. They went quiet for a moment, patting at him with their paws.

"Are you . . . are you reading my mind?" Van asked.

"Can't read," said the first rat.

"Are rats," explained the other.

"No—I mean, can you tell what I'm thinking? How did you know about my collection?"

"Lemuel saw," said the lower-voiced rat. "Serafina saw."

"I don't know anybody named Lemuel. Or Serafina."

"Lemuel raven," said the rat. "And spider Serafina."

"They've been watching me?"

"*Are* watching you."

"Raduslav," warned the higher-voiced rat. "You say secrets."

"Stupid secrets," said Raduslav. "He is not liar, Violetta."

"Yes. Smells true," said Violetta, sniffing Van's earlobe. "*Seems* true."

"Um . . . Violetta? Raduslav?" Van ventured. He nodded toward the arguing adults. "What are they going to do to me?"

"Don't know," said Raduslav.

"Something," said Violetta.

Van swallowed the knot in his throat. "Are they going to hurt me?"

"No," said Raduslav. "Just keep you."

"Keep me?" Van squeaked.

"Maybe," said Raduslav. "Maybe forever. Maybe not."

"Where is your machine?" Violetta asked.

"My machine?"

"Little blue machine."

"Oh. My hearing aids. They're at home. So I can't hear what the grown-ups are saying about me."

Both rats froze again. Then Violetta jumped down and scurried across the floor to the hem of Nail's coat. Van watched her clamber up and speak into his ear.

Nail's face shifted.

A second later, Nail's tall, dark shape strode between Van and the firelight, blanketing him with shadow.

"Van Markson," said Nail. He crouched in front of

Van so that they were eye to eye. The other rat leaped from Van's shoulder back to his. "If I am close to you, can you understand me?"

"It helps if I can see your face," said Van. "And if the rest of the room is really quiet."

Nail aimed a glance at the others. "It will be." He faced Van again. Firelight fell over his features, making his cheekbones even sharper than usual. "We know what you have done," he said slowly.

The blue glass bottle. Van's stomach was a whirlpool. His head was a bomb. He glanced over his shoulder and found Jack and his men glaring back at him. There was no escape.

"I didn't—"

But Nail cut him off. "We know where you've gone. *Who you've seen.*"

Van's mind scrambled. "The baby robin? Do robins work for you too? Because I was just—"

". . . not a match," one of Jack's men interrupted. *Not a match? Knows too much?*

". . . weak and rusty," Jack growled. *We can't trust him.*

Nail stopped Jack with a raised hand. "Heavy . . . anyone . . . bout us?"

"No!" Van squeaked. "I haven't told anyone *anything*! I swear!"

"Scared," said Violetta's clear little voice.

"And a little guilty," added Raduslav. "But not lying."

"Yes!" said Van gratefully. "See? I'm not lying."

Everyone froze.

Something that wasn't actually a smile pulled at the edge of Nail's mouth. The room had gone so still that his words seemed to echo off the walls. "Who are you talking to, Van Markson?"

Van stared back at Nail, petrified.

"Say you know what we collect," Violetta whispered.

"I know what you collect!" said Van desperately. "I know about the wishes!"

The chamber had been still before. Now it was so silent, so breathless, the entire room might have been sealed inside a twinkling glass bottle.

Van realized—too late—that this was a test. And he had just passed.

Or failed.

For a long, cold, quiet minute, everyone stared at him.

"So. He knows," said Nail, in that deep voice that seemed to draw everyone in. "He hears the Creatures. And he knows."

There was another quiet minute. Van struggled to breathe. His lungs felt like two shriveled prunes wedged up against his thundering heart.

"Might it not be in our best interest," Nail went on at last, "to have someone like him—someone able to be *seen* without being *noticed*—on our side?"

The Collectors looked at one another. Then they started speaking all at once, trading words that Van couldn't catch. He shrank into the armchair, watching closely as everyone gathered around a broad wooden desk. Nail scrawled something with paper and pen. Then the crowd dispersed, and Nail glided slowly back toward the spot where Van sat.

". . . may be wrong to trust you," said Nail, bending down again so Van could see his sharp, stony face. ". . . up to you to show us. Prove that you are not our enemy." His voice grew deeper. "Or we will have to treat you like one."

"Yes," said Van desperately. "I will. I'll prove it."

Of course he had no idea how he was going to prove this. But at the moment, he would have promised to do almost anything if it would get him out of this underground room full of strange, angry people.

Nail held the folded paper out to Van. "Written

instructions. So there can be no misunderstanding." He gave Van such a long, sharp look that Van suddenly knew just how it would feel to be a peeled potato. Then Nail turned to the three burly men. "Take him home."

Jack was already at Van's side. "Rivet. Beetle," Van thought he heard him say. "Let's go."

Before Van could even begin to unfold the paper, the men had dragged him away from the firelight, through a heavy door, along a stone corridor, and back up the steep stairs to the City Collection Agency office. The flock of ravens came with them, letting out caws that sounded like the laugh someone gives when they don't think a joke is funny at all.

Jack sat next to Van in the carriage. The other men climbed back onto the bicycles, and they all whooshed off through the twisting alleys. Jack didn't speak. When Van ventured a glance his way, Jack was staring straight ahead, his black eyes glittering like tar paper. Beyond the carriage's black hood, the sky was fuzzy and deep gray, torn by one jagged hole of moonlight. The ravens' wings flashed.

The carriage whipped around a corner, and for an instant, Van thought he spotted Mr. Falborg's grand white house, with one light glowing in an upstairs window—but then they turned again, and he was thrown back against the seat. He didn't manage to wriggle upright again until they reached his own building.

The man with the raccoon—Beetle, Van thought—threw the rope and hook, sending it straight through Van's open window.

Jack sprang out of the carriage. "Claw man."

"What?" said Van.

Jack hooked one thumb toward his back. *"Climb on."*

Hesitantly, Van wrapped his arms around Jack's neck. Jack grabbed the rope and began to climb. In seconds, they were dangling above the sidewalk, Van clinging tight to Jack's back. In a few more seconds, they had reached Van's windowsill.

Jack leaned through the opening. Van tumbled down onto the hardwood floor of his bedroom, breathing hard and feeling like his bones had been replaced by cooked spaghetti.

"Be dead," murmured Jack, pointing at the paper still wadded in Van's fist. *Read that.*

Van nodded.

Giving Van one more glare, Jack slipped back over the sill and dropped out of sight.

Van staggered to his feet. By the time he reached the window, the three dark-coated men and their strange carriage had melted away into the dark.

Van closed and locked the window, even though this suddenly felt a little like closing a screen door to keep out a thunderstorm. He pulled the shades. He climbed into bed and yanked the blankets up to his chin. Then he reached for the switch of the bedside lamp.

The paper Nail had handed him was thick and yellowish, with ragged edges, and the writing on it was slanted and hard to read. With shaky hands, Van tipped the page sideways and leaned closer.

You have met a Collector of another kind. He may already have shown you some of his treasures, but there is one collection he keeps well hidden. You must get a close look at this collection. Learn what it contains. As proof that you have seen it, and that you are indeed on our side, bring a piece of this collection back to us. If you fail to do this, we will know that you are not an ally after all, but an enemy.

Van's chest squeezed. With shaking hands, he refolded the note. First he tossed it to the foot of the bed, but he could still see it lying there, watching him. He slid off the mattress, grabbed the note again, and tucked it behind the black curtain at the back of the miniature stage. He placed SuperVan in front of it to stand guard.

A Collector of another kind.

There was only one person this could mean. And if ravens and pigeons and spiders and people in long dark coats had been watching Van in his own bedroom, they could certainly have been watching him as he trotted through the door of Mr. Falborg's big white house.

There is one collection he keeps well hidden.

That dark, red-curtained room. The hidden black doors at the very back.

That unsettled feeling in the pit of Van's stomach began to bubble up again.

But Mr. Falborg was so *nice.* And now Van was supposed to spy on him, to steal his secrets and give them away.

What if he didn't *want* to be the Collectors' ally? Then again, if kidnapping was what they did to someone who only *might* be a friend, what would they do to an enemy?

That howl from deep underground echoed in Van's

memory. What dark, hidden, horrible thing had he wandered into?

Van launched himself back across the room. He dove underneath the covers. Even with the blankets wrapped tight around him, it took a very long time before he stopped shivering, and an even longer time before he finally fell asleep.

12
Unexpected Guests

VAN spent the next day reliving that horrible night, searching the entire apartment for spying spiders, and bumping distractedly into things. His mother spent it straightening the things Van had bumped, tidying the kitchen, and singing along to music on the stereo. But Van was too preoccupied to notice this.

He was kneeling on the window seat with his forehead pressed against the glass, scanning the street for dark-coated people or lurking creatures, when there was a knock at the apartment door.

His mother hurried to answer it. She was smiling before she'd even turned the knob.

"Well, hello!" she exclaimed to Mr. Grey and Peter,

who stood in the doorway with their arms full of grocery bags. "Please come in!"

Van swung his legs off the window seat.

The Greys set the bags on the kitchen counter. Mr. Grey and his mother kissed each other on the cheek. Peter stared straight ahead with his cold swimming-pool eyes.

"Shall I put the wine in the refrigerator?" Mr. Grey asked.

"That would be perfect," said Van's mother. "Giovanni, Charles is going to make us his famous risotto. Why don't you and Peter go play in your room while we cook?"

Van's chest squeezed. The stolen squirrel and the blue bottle holding Peter's birthday wish were still hidden under his bed. Having Peter close to them seemed risky—like balancing a piranha in a fishbowl on the edge of your bathtub.

"Giovanni, did you hear me?" his mother asked.

"Yes," said Van.

Wishing he could think of any way out of this, Van slid off the window seat and headed down the hall. Peter stalked right behind him.

They stepped into Van's room. Peter slammed the door.

Van backed up to the side of the bed, shielding the treasure box with his body. He reached for his hearing aids at the same time, pressing them quickly into place. "I've got some games," he said. "Or we could play Legos."

Peter stayed near the door. His eyes veered away from Van, taking in the rest of the room. He shrugged.

"Do you want to draw?" Van offered.

"I don't care," said Peter. He looked past Van, at the little stage. He stepped closer.

"I didn't know you were coming over tonight," said Van desperately.

But Peter had already knelt down in front of the stage. He reached for the SuperVan figurine, mumbling something that sounded like, "Yeah, I dineezer." He glanced up at Van. "What is this stuff?"

"It's a maquette." Van knelt beside Peter. "My father made it. He was a set designer."

Peter snorted, twirling SuperVan's head between his fingertips. "My dad doesn't make anything. He just bosses other people around."

"Well," said Van, checking the curtain to make sure Nail's note was entirely hidden, "I guess that's his job. He *is* a director."

Peter faced Van straight on for the first time. "Why are you defending him? Listen!" He tilted his head toward the door.

Van listened, but he couldn't hear anything from beyond his room. "What?"

"*Them*. This is how it *always* goes." Peter's voice was low and intent. "It's the same with every singer he picks to be his new girlfriend."

"What?" said Van again. "My mom isn't his *girlfriend*."

"What do you think's going on?" Peter hissed. "And if you say, 'They're just making dinner,' I'm going to go crazy."

"I . . ." Van trailed off.

Peter looked away. He set SuperVan back in the center of the stage.

"You said this has happened before?" Van asked, after a moment.

Peter shrugged. "Usually I just get left at home. I guess because your mom has *you*, he thought he'd drag me along." He looked at Van again. "You don't want them to be together, do you?"

Van's thoughts streaked through the pages of an imaginary calendar. He saw himself forced to spend more and more time with Peter. He pictured moving into Peter's stuffy house, being told to call snooty Mr. Grey "Dad." He imagined being left alone with Peter while his mother turned her special smile on Mr. Grey, being unable to call loudly enough or move fast enough to catch her as she drifted farther and farther away.

"No," he said.

Peter was quiet for a beat. Gently, he touched the velvet edge of the miniature curtains. "I just wish . . ."

Van smoothed the curtain so the corner of the note was out of sight. "You wish what?"

But Peter didn't finish. He tipped his head toward the door once more. "Listen."

Van tried. "I can't hear anything."

"Exactly. It's all quiet. They're probably *kissing*."

"No they're not."

"Yes they are."

"No they're not."

Wordlessly, Peter crept toward the door, beckoning for Van to follow him.

The two of them tiptoed down the hall and peeped around the corner into the kitchen.

Van's mother and Mr. Grey were bowed over a

cutting board, doing something with knives and herbs. Their hands were very close together, but their lips were several inches apart.

"I *told* you," said Van, a little too loudly.

Their parents looked up.

Mr. Grey looked faintly annoyed.

Van's mother gave a bright smile. "Giovanni!" she sang. "Why don't you and Peter come and set the table? You can show him where everything is."

Van led Peter across the kitchen to the silverware drawer. As they passed the cutting board, Van's mother gave Van a quick kiss on top of his head. Mr. Grey ignored them both.

Van and Peter arranged the knives and forks around the little table. Music was still playing on the stereo, and Van couldn't catch any of his mother and Mr. Grey's murmured conversation—although he heard his mother's bell-like laugh more than once. He snuck a look at Peter.

Peter's shoulders were slumped. His face was blank. His eyes didn't look icy any more. Now they just looked . . . watery. For the first time, Van felt something not quite as warm as liking, but much less cold and prickly than dislike, for Peter. Before Van could figure out exactly what it was, there was another knock at the door.

"I wonder who that could be!" sang Van's mother. "We're certainly not expecting anyone else!"

Van watched as she opened the door.

"Ingrid Markson?" said the deliveryman in the hallway. "Dies in fire." He handed her a bouquet of white lilies and turned quickly away.

Dies in fire? Van's mind scrambled the words. *These are for you.* That must have been what the man had said. Still, Van's heart kept beating a little too hard.

"Another admirer, Ingrid?" said Mr. Grey.

Van's mother laughed. "I'd be very surprised." She pulled a little envelope out of the floral paper. "Oh, they're from Mr. Falborg!" She smiled from Van to Mr. Grey. "You and Ivor Falborg are old friends, aren't you, Charles? He says, 'I'm delighted to be better acquainted with you and your robin-rescuing son.' Isn't that sweet? And Giovanni, he enclosed a note for you." She handed Van a second, even tinier envelope.

Master Giovanni Markson, it read, in neat, courtly script.

Van pried open the paper flap.

My friend. Let no one else see this note. Come and see me as soon as you can. YOU ARE IN TERRIBLE DANGER.

13
More Unexpected Guests

VAN did not sleep well that night.

After taking out his hearing aids, turning on the night-light, and building a barricade of pillows, he curled up in the very center of his bed and tried to switch off his brain.

But his brain kept switching itself back on.

Mr. Falborg had to be talking about the Collectors, said his brain, in a voice that sounded a lot like the china squirrel's. *They're why you're in serious danger, right?*

Of course, said Van. *Please be quiet and let me sleep.*

But what do you think it means, that you're in danger? His brain plowed on. *What are they going to do to you? Are they going to drop you into that pit? Are they going to do something worse?*

I really don't want to think about that, said Van. *Please, please, please, STOP.*

For a few seconds, his brain went still.

Then, when Van almost felt safe closing his eyes, it asked, *Remember what Nail's note said? That if you* don't *go back to the Collectors, you'll be their enemy? So you* have *to go back. But do you think it's a trap? Are you going to tell Mr. Falborg about them? And how did Mr. Falborg know about you being in danger in the first place? Maybe he knows all about the Collectors. Maybe he knows you're supposed to spy on him. Maybe he's trying to trick you. Maybe you should go into hiding. Or maybe you should run away. But where would you go?*

By this time, Van had sandwiched his head between two pillows and clenched his eyelids and his teeth. Of course, this didn't do anything to shut out the voice, which was coming from inside.

What else might the Collectors be hiding? What do you think is down in that Hold? Hey. Hey, are you awake? Hey.

Van shut his eyes tighter.

Hey! Hey, Van? Hey, Minivan? Hey. Hey. Hey.

The voice in his head seemed to have changed somehow. It was higher. Quicker. And he'd never called *himself* "Minivan."

"Hey. Are you awake? Are you awake yet? How about now? Hey. Hey, Van. Hey. Hey. Hey."

Something small and slightly damp pressed against Van's face. He shoved aside the top layer of the pillow sandwich, opened his eyes, and found himself nose to nose with a silvery squirrel.

"Barnavelt?" Van whispered. "How did you get in here?"

"I'm a squirrel," Barnavelt answered. Van realized that he'd been hearing the squirrel's voice perfectly clearly, even without his hearing aids, just like he'd heard the voices of Nail's rats. Still, he scooted back toward the head of the bed and reached for the bedside table.

"I can climb almost anything," said the squirrel, hopping after him. "Except glass. And mirrors, which are a kind of glass. And once I fell off a telephone wire, but it was icy, so that doesn't count. Hey, is this your bed?"

"Yes," said Van, putting his hearing aids in place. "It's my bed."

"It's nice." Barnavelt gave an experimental hop. "Bouncy. I bet I could—hey! Are those *spaceships* on your sheets?"

"Barnavelt," Van broke in, as the squirrel started bouncing again. "Are you here to spy on me? Because I haven't had the chance yet to do what Nail said, but—"

"Spy on you?" Barnavelt stopped bouncing. "Of course not. I'm just a wish collector, not an information collector. They're mostly spiders. I can't sit still long enough to be a spider."

"Then . . . why are you here?"

"Why am I here?" Barnavelt echoed. He stared around the room, his eyes going foggy. "Why *am* I here?"

"Did you come to warn me about something, or to get something, or—"

"Pebble!" the squirrel exploded. "Yep. That's it. She wants you."

"Wants me to what?"

"To talk. She's outside." The squirrel leaped from the bed to the windowsill, poking his nose through the opening. "See?"

Van wriggled out of bed and hurried to the window. Hunched in the shadows beside the building's front stoop was a baggy-coated girl.

"Is this a trick?" Van whispered.

The squirrel blinked. "Is what a trick?"

"This. Getting me to come outside. Is somebody going to kidnap me again?"

"I don't think so," said Barnavelt. "But I may have missed that part."

Van took another look out the window. The streetlights were on, and the glow of the moon rinsed the sidewalks, turning the pavement to silver. There was no one else in a long dark coat lurking near the doorstep—at least not as far as he could see.

"Okay," he said at last. "Just let me put on my robe."

The building's halls and stairways were deserted. No neighbors were awake to notice the very small boy in a blue robe with a squirrel riding on his shoulder. Van pushed through the building's front doors into a rush of cool night air.

Pebble was waiting for him right outside. She grabbed his arm with both hands, yanking him around the stoop and dodging behind two potted pines and a row of trash cans. There she whirled around so that the beams of the streetlamp would fall on her face.

"Thank you for coming out," said Pebble rapidly, but in the most polite tone Van had ever heard her use. "Sorry if we woke you. But I had to talk to you."

"Why?" A little shiver ran through Van's body, even though the night wasn't cold. "What is it?"

"I smell pretzels," said the squirrel, sniffing the air. "Do you smell pretzels?"

Pebble's voice dropped to a whisper. Even with the streetlights, Van couldn't follow her lips.

". . . what a pile of lies . . ."

"What?" Van whispered.

Pebble's eyes flicked over the street. "I *want* to *apologize.*"

"For what?"

"For what they did. Jack and Beetle and Rivet."

"Jack?" squeaked Barnavelt. "Where?"

Van took a little step backward. "Did they make you come here?" he asked warily. "Are you supposed to spy on me? Or talk me into doing what they said?"

"What?" Pebble looked genuinely surprised. "No! Nobody knows I'm here." She flinched as a shadow fluttered through the lamplight. "But they might be watching." She whirled back toward Van. "They shouldn't have done that. Jack and the guards. But that's their job. I hope you won't hold it against me. I mean—against all of us."

Van wondered if anyone else had ever been asked not to hold a grudge about being kidnapped. "Well, I didn't *like* it," he said. "But it wasn't your fault."

Pebble's voice was smaller than before. "So . . . you're not mad at me?"

"No," said Van. "I'm not mad at you."

Pebble's shoulders seemed to melt. She took a deep breath, her body tensing up again. "Okay," she said, almost to herself. "Good."

Van watched her closely. "Why do you care if I'm mad at you?" he asked. "Why do all of you want me on your side, anyway? Is it just because I already know some of your secret stuff?"

"No!" said Pebble quickly. "Well, partly. But it's—you're—" She threw her hands up. "You can do stuff other people can't do!"

Van had spent a lot of his life noticing that other people could do things he couldn't. They could hear things he didn't hear, and catch words and meanings he didn't catch. They always seemed to be taller and stronger and older than he was. With some effort and imagination, Van could generally keep up with everyone else. But the thought that he could do something others *couldn't* made him stop breathing for a moment. "Like what?" he asked.

"You can hear the Creatures," said Pebble. "You can see wishes. You noticed *us* in the first place."

Van shrugged. "All the Collectors can do those things too."

"Yes, but we're *Collectors!*" Pebble argued. "You're

the only one from the outside who's been able to do that stuff since . . . *ever.*"

"Really?" Van asked hopefully.

"Plus, the other side?" Pebble plunged on. "They're dangerous. *Really* dangerous."

Van folded his arms. "More dangerous than a bunch of guys who steal me out of my bed in the middle of the night and dangle me over a bottomless pit?"

"I told you," said Pebble. "Jack and the guards aren't bad guys. They just act like it."

"Doesn't that make them bad guys?"

Pebble's eyebrows rose. She was quiet for so long that Van stopped waiting for an answer.

"It might help me *want* to be on your side if I knew what that side *is,*" Van told her. "I mean, what are all of you doing down there? Why are you collecting people's wishes?"

Pebble flashed another look over her shoulders. "That's our job. We keep everyone safe."

"From *wishes*?"

"From what would happen if everybody's wishes came true."

Van shook his head. "What would be so bad about that?"

Pebble looked at him like he'd just asked what was so bad about bubonic plague. "Do you know what kind of things people wish for?" she hissed. "Do you want to get trampled by dinosaurs? Do you want an eight-year-old bully to be king of the whole world? Do you want every food in the world to taste like chocolate ice cream? *Do you know how sick of chocolate ice cream you would get?"*

"Chocolate ice cream," sighed the squirrel on Van's shoulder.

Van hesitated. "Why should I believe you?"

"Because I *know.*" Pebble's eyes were wide and exasperated. "I know both sides." She hunched over, rooting through her coat's many pockets. "Here."

She pushed something into Van's hand. Even in the semidarkness, he could see that it was a photograph, but he couldn't tell what was in it.

The light of the streetlamp flickered with another sweep of shadowy wings.

Pebble jerked back. "I have to go. Come on, Barnavelt."

The squirrel hopped from Van's shoulder to Pebble's head. "Do you smell pretzels?" Van heard the squirrel squeak again before the two of them whisked away into the dark.

Van hurried back up the stairs to the apartment. The door of his mother's room was still shut, with only darkness sliding through the gap beneath it. Van slipped into his own room and closed the door. Then he climbed back into his fortress of pillows and turned on the bedside lamp.

The photo Pebble had handed him was old and wrinkled, as if it had been kept in a pocket for a very long time. There were two people in the picture.

One was a slender older man with crinkly blue eyes, gray hair, and a neat white suit. Van recognized him immediately. Mr. Falborg.

Standing next to him was a girl of five or six years old, with big dark eyes and short brown hair that curved against her round cheeks. Mr. Falborg's hand rested on the girl's head in a familiar, playful way, and both of them were beaming at the camera.

The girl had some of the biggest ears Van had ever seen. They stuck out through the strands of her hair like . . .

Like mushrooms on the trunk of a tree.

Van held the picture closer.

The girl's eyes were exactly the color of mossy pennies.

14
A New Pet

VAN moved through the next morning like a small, silent zombie. He poured orange juice onto his cereal instead of milk, and he'd eaten half of it before he noticed that something was wrong. He put on his shirt backward. Twice. And he forgot the Calvin and Hobbes book he meant to bring to the opera house until he and his mother were halfway down the block, and he had to run all the way back home to get it.

Afterward, when he was stuck in a chair at the corner of the rehearsal room, he wished he hadn't remembered the book at all. Because what he needed wasn't a comic book. What he needed was several blocks away, shut behind the blue door of a tall white house.

Mr. Falborg's house had *everything*. The information

he was supposed to steal for the Collectors. Pebble's history. And, of course, the meaning behind the note. *Come and see me as soon as you can. YOU ARE IN TERRIBLE DANGER.* The words thumped along with Van's accelerating heartbeat. *As soon as you can. AS SOON AS YOU CAN.*

He was staring blankly at the pages of his book, crafting a plan, when a sharp voice said—

"Wad dizzy muscle doing?"

Van looked up.

Peter Grey stood beside him. His face was hard. His eyes were narrow.

"My muscle?" Van repeated.

Peter made an exasperated face. *"Your mother,"* he repeated, very, very slowly. "What. Is. She. Doing?"

Van looked around the rehearsal room. His mother was standing near the table where water and tea were set out for the singers. Mr. Grey was beside her. They were smiling, and his mother was patting at a curl of brassy hair that had slipped out of her French twist.

"She's . . . talking?" said Van.

If Peter had been a balloon, he would have looked ready to pop. "Why. Is. She. Talking. To. My. Father?" he demanded.

"Because they work together?" Van ventured.

"*No.* Look!" Peter leaned forward again. "Why is she *smiling* at him like that?"

"My mom smiles at everybody like that."

"God," Peter huffed, stalking toward the door. ". . . Russia *baby*."

Van put down his book and gazed across the room. His mother and Mr. Grey were still standing together. Suddenly they seemed very close together—and very far away from everyone else. And now that Van thought about it, he wasn't sure that this *was* quite the same dazzling smile his mother gave to everybody, from audiences to doormen. There was something different about this particular smile.

All at once, Van needed to get between that smile and Mr. Grey.

He scurried across the shiny wood floor.

"Mom." He grabbed his mother's sleeve. *"Mom."*

Mr. Grey stopped speaking in midsentence and looked down at Van with a little frown. His mother's smile stayed bright. "What is it, Giovanni?"

"Mom, I need to ask you something."

"Well." Mr. Grey took a step backward. "I'll speak with you later, Ingrid."

"Yes." His mother's smile could have lit the stage. "Until then." She turned the smile on Van, who suddenly wished he was wearing sunglasses. "What did you need to ask me?"

"Um . . . I left something at home," Van improvised. "My other book. Can I go get it?"

"Do you mean, may you walk back to the apartment right now, by yourself?" She reached down and combed a strand of hair out of Van's eyes, leaving a whiff of lily-scented lotion behind. "No, you absolutely may not."

Van veered to another path. "Then can I at least go visit Ana in the costume shop? Or see if the prop room is open?"

"Giovanni, they're unloading from the last production today. You need to stay out of the way." His mother gave him a scrutinizing look. Then her eyes brightened. "If you don't feel like sitting in here, why don't you go play with Peter? He's probably up in his father's office."

Van felt himself brightening too—but not at the prospect of playing with Peter. "Yeah," he said. "I'll go look for him!"

"Just *stay in the building,*" his mother called after him.

Van didn't glance back. Later, if he needed to, he could pretend that he hadn't heard. With his backpack over his shoulders, he ran straight up the back staircase, along a dark hall, and out onto the street.

He didn't like lying to his mother. It was hard to keep secrets from someone who knew everything about you, right down to the size of your underwear. But there was no choice.

His shoes smacked the cement as Van tore up the busy sidewalk, his backpack pulling at his shoulders as if it were trying to turn him back.

Gerda opened the blue front door. "Mr. Markson!" She gave him a pleasant but puzzled smile.

"I need to see Mr. Falborg," Van panted. "Is he home?"

"Come in." Gerda ushered him inside. Van missed a few of her words in the *creak-thump* of the closing door. ". . . Tin de parlor, and I'll tell him yer here."

Inside the fancy, ferny front room, Van tried to sit down on a white armchair. But his body wouldn't keep still. Within seconds, it had scooted back off the chair and darted toward the nearest wall. Van scanned the framed photographs and silhouettes and postcards, but there was no sign of that smaller, younger, smilier Pebble anywhere.

He was squinting up at one cut-paper silhouette when, on the window seat just to his left, something gave a twitch.

Van spun around.

The something was a cat. A large, long-haired, pale gray cat. She stretched her claws and arched her spine, rearranging herself in the afternoon sunlight.

Van had never tried to talk to a cat before. But within the last few days, he'd had conversations with a squirrel and two rats, and suddenly, *not* speaking to the cat seemed like the stupider choice. Especially when she might know everything that Van needed to know.

"You must be Renata." Van knelt beside the window seat. "I'm Van."

Renata regarded him through one half-shut hazel eye.

Van swallowed. "You know . . . if you want to talk . . ."

The tip of Renata's tail twitched.

Van leaned one ear close to her furry snoot. "If you have anything you'd like to tell me . . . maybe about a girl named Pebble, or about a super-secret collection . . . I'm listening."

The faint, fishy warmth of the cat's breath brushed his ear. Van held perfectly still, just in case, hidden in that breath, were words he'd never listened for before.

He was still crouching there, his ear pressed against the cat's nose, when Mr. Falborg glided into the room.

"Getting acquainted with Renata?" he asked pleasantly.

Van shot to his feet.

"She's a lazy old thing," Mr. Falborg went on. "But that's just what a cat should be, I suppose."

Mr. Falborg was dressed in a spotless white suit. His gray hair was neatly combed. His eyes were bright, and his smile was welcoming, and the anxious pounding in Van's chest became the tiniest bit slower.

"Oh . . . um . . . Mr. Falborg," Van stammered. "I hope you don't mind me coming over."

"Mind? I've been *expecting* you." Mr. Falborg gestured to an armchair. "Please. Sit."

Van perched on the edge of the seat.

"I'm sure my message was confusing at best, and frightening at worst." Mr. Falborg sat down in the opposite armchair. "A hidden note in a bouquet for your mother wasn't the best place for a long explanation."

"I just . . . ," Van began carefully. "I just want to know what it meant."

Mr. Falborg leaned forward. "Oh, I think you already know."

An icy wave surged through Van, almost pushing the questions out of him. *Are you watching me too? What do you know about the Collectors? How do you know Pebble? What's really going on here?* But he shoved the questions back. Keeping silent was always safer. Besides, from the way Mr. Falborg watched him with those bright, knowing eyes, Van knew he might as well have asked the questions aloud anyway.

Mr. Falborg folded his hands. "Master Markson," he said, "are you a fan of Calvin and Hobbes?"

This was not where Van had expected the conversation to start. "I've read *all* the books," he blurted. "More than once. There's one in my backpack right now."

"Ah!" Mr. Falborg said warmly. "I can always recognize a fellow collector, and a fellow Calvin and Hobbes fan. Do you remember the comic where Calvin suggests going to the zoo, and Hobbes the tiger says sure, they can go to the zoo, and then maybe they can visit a prison afterward?"

Van nodded. "I remember."

Mr. Falborg leaned an elbow on the chair's padded arm. "What do *you* think the difference is between a zoo and a prison?"

"Maybe . . . ," Van began, "that we don't know that

the animals don't *want* to be in a zoo."

"A good answer," said Mr. Falborg appreciatively. "Of course, zookeepers believe they are confining those animals for their own good, to protect them, or preserve them. Not to *imprison* them." He paused. "But why should *they* be the ones who get to decide?"

Van thought. "I suppose because people are people, and animals are just . . . animals." He threw a quick "no offense" glance at Renata. The cat just looked bored.

"That is what we tell ourselves, isn't it?" said Mr. Falborg. "But what about the especially intelligent, complex creatures? Elephants? Dolphins? Apes? The ones who can paint pictures, communicate with signs, mourn lost loved ones, who can tell us clearly that they do not *want* to be kept?"

Van felt a thump of sadness. "I don't know."

Mr. Falborg craned forward, bracing his elbows on his spotless white knees. "What if there were some creatures very much like us—in some ways even more advanced than us—that wanted only the chance to survive, to live out their natural lives without chains or cages . . . but that humans insisted on confining. Or even *destroying*. Would that be wrong?"

Pictures of lonely laboratory monkeys clinging to

stuffed animals flashed through Van's mind. "Yes," he said. "That would be totally wrong."

Mr. Falborg stared into Van's eyes. "I am so glad you think so," he said. Then, abruptly, he got to his feet. "Please follow me."

Mr. Falborg led the way through the arch and along a hallway. Van thought they'd taken this route on his last visit, but there was so much to see—an entire wall of villages carved in jade, rows of gleaming heraldic shields, an open doorway to a room where hundreds of huge, pincered beetles gleamed in hanging glass boxes—that he kept spotting things he'd definitely never seen before. They twisted around several corners and up a flight of stairs. Mr. Falborg walked quickly, without glancing back. Van scurried after him, trying not to let his eyes snag on the fantastic collections as they whooshed by.

By the time they reached the small room with the red velvet curtains, Van was so dazzled and disoriented he wasn't sure he could even find his way back out again. Mr. Falborg closed the door. He made a careful survey of the entire room, walking along each wall, examining every tiny speck. Finally he crossed toward the hidden doors, pushed back the curtains, and removed a key on a gold chain from his vest pocket. He slipped the key into the door's tiny lock.

Van's heart drummed.

The paneled doors swung open. "After you," said Mr. Falborg.

Van ventured through the doors. Mr. Falborg stepped in too, closing the doors behind them.

For a moment, the room was completely dark. The air was still and scentless. Then a light blinked on, and Van saw that they had entered a large, square, windowless room. A twisty glass chandelier hung from the ceiling like a glowing sea anemone. The walls were lined with built-in shelves. The room would have looked like a library, except that the shelves weren't full of books. They were full of boxes. Wooden and cardboard and metal boxes, some the size of a giant's shoebox, some small enough for a pair of baby booties. But Van guessed these boxes weren't for shoes.

His heart pounded harder.

Maybe it was this pounding that shut out the other sounds. Maybe the sounds were just too soft for Van's ears to catch them at first. But the moment Mr. Falborg switched on the light, from inside the boxes, a soft rustling had begun. The longer the lights were on, the louder the rustling grew, until the tapping, whispering, rattling sounds thickened around Van like shadows around a small circle of light.

"You're the first person I've allowed into this room in many years," said Mr. Falborg, drawing Van's attention back. "I hope I can trust you. I hope *we* can trust you."

Van's pounding heart gave a squeeze.

Mr. Falborg stepped toward one wall of shelves, and the noise within the boxes grew even louder. For a moment he examined the rows of boxes, brushing his fingertips over their wood and metal and enamel sides. At last he pulled down a plain cardboard box that would have been just the right size for a pair of Van's shoes.

Immediately, the other boxes went silent.

Mr. Falborg turned back to Van. "Allow me to introduce you."

He lifted the cardboard lid.

A tiny face appeared over the side of the box. It had wide, round eyes and a small, mousy nose. Ruffled ears stuck out from either side of its head. At first it reminded Van of a lemur. But there was something monkey-ish—or even human-ish—about its mouth, which Van could have sworn was giving him a shy smile.

Van inched closer.

From a few steps away, the creature looked fuzzy, like it was covered with a thick layer of dust. But as Van drew near, he could see that the creature wasn't actually fuzzy. It was *translucent*. Its body was a pale gray haze. He could see straight through it to the room's other side.

"What is it?" Van whispered.

"This," said Mr. Falborg, "is a Wish Eater." He stroked its ruffled ear with one finger, and the creature tilted its head happily. "They don't have a language of their own, so I'm afraid there's no better name for them."

"Do you mean . . . ," said Van, trying not to sound as absurd as the words that were about to come out of him, "it *eats wishes*?"

"That is their only food, yes," said Mr. Falborg. "Like pandas and bamboo, koalas and eucalyptus. They're specialized eaters." The creature tilted its head so Mr. Falborg could rub its other ear. "All sorts of things are eaten by other living beings, you know. Light. Gases. Warmth. This species happens to eat wishes."

Van stared into the Wish Eater's wide, misty eyes. "But—how does it work?" he asked. "When they eat a wish, what happens? Does the wish just . . . disappear?"

"Ah." Mr. Falborg's neat gray eyebrows rose. His smile widened. "*That* is when a wish *comes true*."

Van felt off-balance suddenly, as though everything, including the floor under his shoes, had just become a little less solid. He closed his eyes for a moment. When he opened them again, the Wish Eater was still there, gazing straight back at him.

The Wish Eater's nubby hands reached up and gripped the edges of its box. It craned toward Van, teetering slightly, sniffing the air.

"It wants a closer look at you," said Mr. Falborg. "Don't worry. They are perfectly gentle."

Carefully, Van stretched out an index finger. The creature grasped it, its hand just large enough to close around the tip of Van's finger.

Once, when he and his mother had taken a walking tour in Greece, Van had glanced down to find a tree frog riding along on his bare arm. The frog was so small, so weightless, it could have been with him for moments or hours without Van even knowing it was there. This creature's touch was even gentler.

"Hold out your hands," Mr. Falborg suggested.

Van cupped his palms. The Wish Eater climbed out of its box and into the curve of Van's hands. Even now, holding its whole body, Van couldn't feel its weight. There was only the cool, fuzzy, tickly sensation of its grippy toes and its long, misty tail.

Like he'd seen Mr. Falborg do, Van rubbed the creature's ruffly ear with the tip of one finger. The Wish Eater's eyes slid blissfully shut. It nuzzled down into Van's palms. Then, with one translucent little hand, it reached up and patted the base of Van's thumb.

Something inside Van's chest lifted up and split open. It was the same feeling he got when he walked out of school after a long day and found his mother at the doors, waiting for him. He'd never had the feeling with anyone else, but he recognized it when it came. It was the feeling of being really, truly happy to be with someone, and of being even happier because that someone wanted to be with you.

"It likes you," said Mr. Falborg. "They're such social beings. It breaks my heart to have to keep them enclosed, but it's the only way they'll be still."

The Wish Eater opened its eyes again. It gazed up at Van for a moment. Then it began to wheel around in happy little circles, its fuzzy body tickling Van's palms. Van giggled.

Mr. Falborg smiled too. "I think of myself as a

zookeeper rather than a jailor, although I wish I didn't have to be either. I keep them safe. I try to keep them fed. I do what I can." He paused, then said, in a heavier voice, "There are those who would like to kill every single one of these creatures."

Van looked up, horrified. He clutched the Wish Eater closer. "What? Why would anybody want to *kill* them?"

Mr. Falborg gazed down at Van. "You have a kind heart, Master Markson," he said. "Perhaps, in spite of your kindness, you can imagine why someone would want to possess a wish-granting creature's power. To control it. Or, out of fear, to eliminate it entirely." Mr. Falborg sighed. "And I'm afraid they are succeeding. I've been giving sanctuary to Wish Eaters for decades now."

He gestured around the room. "There are some left, the especially quick or crafty or lucky ones, living in the wild—but they grow fewer and fewer as the years go by. Many of these, when they came to me, were starving."

"Why were they starving?" asked Van, his heart squeezing. "I mean, with so many people making wishes . . ."

"Ah, but not all wishes are *real*," said Mr. Falborg.

"At least, not to a Wish Eater. A wish must be made *on* something: birthday candles, a wishbone, a coin thrown into a fountain. And when someone *else* is always watching and waiting to steal those wishes the instant they're made . . ." He gave Van a significant look. "You can see why these poor creatures have been experiencing a dire food shortage."

Van thought of Pebble snatching up the coins from the fountain, and of Barnavelt clinging to the chandelier above the birthday cake. He thought of the underground chamber with its hoard of bottled wishes. Maybe the Collectors weren't just gathering wishes in order to keep everyone safe, as Pebble had said. Maybe they were taking those wishes away from someone else. Someone who needed them to survive.

Van looked down at the little Wish Eater. It stared straight back into his eyes.

"Not only are they being starved," Mr. Falborg went on. "They are being *hunted*."

"Who . . ." Van had to stop and swallow. "Who is hunting them?"

Mr. Falborg's voice was very low, but in the sealed, silent room, Van had no trouble hearing it.

"Oh, I think you know the answer to that."

Van swallowed again.

"That is why I felt the need to warn you." Mr. Falborg reached up to a nearby shelf and grasped a tiny wooden box. "The Collectors are many. And they are dangerous."

Van's spine tingled.

Mr. Falborg opened the box's polished lid. "Come on out," he murmured. "No one here will hurt you."

A creature the size and shape of a fruit bat scrambled trustingly up Mr. Falborg's arm. It nestled against his neck, its body like a patch of mist.

"The mission of these other Collectors is to trap and starve these poor creatures until they are small and weak and helpless. Eventually, they are destroyed entirely." Mr. Falborg nodded around at the rows of boxes. "If I am a zookeeper, *they* are jailers. They are torturers. Executioners." Mr. Falborg met Van's horrified gaze. "Awful even to imagine, isn't it?" He stroked the tiny creature on his shoulder. "That's another reason the Collectors would like to keep their very existence a secret. And anyone who is unlucky enough to see a Collector at work is either enlisted to help them . . . or eliminated."

The tingle in Van's spine turned to frost.

Without disturbing the nuzzling Wish Eater, Mr. Falborg reached into his pocket and drew out a small white square. He held it toward Van on one open palm.

Van squinted down at the square. It was a photograph.

A familiar photograph.

The very same photograph that was currently tucked inside Van's own pocket. This copy was less battered and faded, but the same younger Pebble and the same Mr. Falborg smiled up at him from its surface.

It was getting hard for Van to breathe.

"My own great-niece was taken by them." Mr. Falborg's voice was soft and sad. "Five years ago. I haven't seen her since, but I still carry her with me everywhere."

I know her! Van nearly blurted. *She's all right!* But then he remembered Pebble's intent face as she'd passed him her own copy of the photograph. *I know both sides,* she'd said, as though Van would understand.

But he didn't.

Was Pebble a prisoner? She certainly didn't act like it. Was she giving him some kind of secret message? Had she been telling him the truth at all? Would it put her—or him—or *everyone* in danger if he mentioned her to Mr. Falborg now? Van didn't know what to believe. Besides, Mr. Falborg was already tenderly slipping the photo back into his pocket. Van decided, as he often did, that it might be safer to listen than to speak up.

"They will force you to join them, just as they did to her," Mr. Falborg continued. "You deserve, at the very least, to know what you'll be helping them to do." Mr. Falborg gave the tiny creature on his shoulder another stroke. He waited until Van met his eyes. "But you still have a choice. If you are willing, you can use this chance—this *very rare* chance—to help these creatures and their kind instead. This would require great risk on your part," he went on, holding Van's gaze. "I don't wish to put you in danger, Master Markson, but the truth is that you're already there."

Fear clamped like a fist around Van's throat. But then the Wish Eater climbed up his arm and nestled into the crook of his elbow, its little hands patting Van's skin, and the fist abruptly loosened again. Van took a deep breath. It was funny—having someone so small and fragile to care for made him feel bigger and stronger than he ever had before.

"What would I have to do?" he asked.

"Simply do what you already do so well," said Mr. Falborg. "Notice everything. Go back to the Collectors. See where and how these creatures are being imprisoned. How many of them there are. How badly they're mistreated. Look for weaknesses in the Collection's security. And then come and share what you've learned with me."

Van hesitated. Mr. Falborg was asking him to spy on the Collectors. Just like the Collectors had asked Van to spy on *him*. But Mr. Falborg was a kindly old man in a three-piece suit who was trying to keep a bunch of little creatures safe. The Collectors were a secret wish-stealing army. They were kidnappers. Jailers. Killers. The choice was so easy it didn't feel like a choice at all.

At least, *his* choice was easy. Mr. Falborg's choice didn't seem quite so clear.

"Are you sure you want *me*?" Van asked. "I mean, I'm—I'm not—"

"*You* are *perfect*," said Mr. Falborg, staring straight into Van's eyes. "Yes, you're small. You're unable to hear some things. You're an ordinary boy—meaning that you are not one of them. All of these things make you exactly what we need. You can do things I never could. You can move among the Collectors without being suspected. You can uncover their secrets just by watching and listening in the ways you already do. And then you can listen to your conscience and choose the path that is truly *right.*" Mr. Falborg smiled again. "You don't know, Master Markson, how very special you are."

Something warm and bright began to fill Van's body.

"Okay." Van took a deep breath. The warmth and brightness flared, and the fist around his throat disappeared for good. "Okay," he said again. "I can do that."

The look that broke across Mr. Falborg's face was like sunrise in a clear blue sky. "Thank you, Van." He held out his hand. "We *all* thank you."

Van shook it.

"Now." Mr. Falborg nodded toward the little batlike shape on his shoulder. "It's time for this one's feeding. It's quite a struggle to keep them fed, especially in secrecy." He pulled another key out of his vest pocket and unlocked a large leather trunk. He lifted out a meatless wishbone. "But Gerda's made friends with all the local butchers, which helps."

Spotting the wishbone, the batlike creature glided down from Mr. Falborg's shoulder and scampered onto the carpet.

"This Wish Eater is a very small one, so it has to be

a rather small wish in order for him to *digest* it, so to speak," Mr. Falborg went on, as the creature made an excited little twirl. "Can you think of something fairly small and simple that you want?"

"Me?" Van gasped.

Mr. Falborg held out the wishbone. "Yes. You."

"You mean . . . ," Van began. "You mean I can make a wish right now and it will definitely come true?"

Mr. Falborg smiled. "That's right. Although there are certain things that wishes cannot do. They can't control the Wish Eaters themselves, they can't kill or directly cause harm, they can't alter time, they can't force a person to do something they fundamentally would not do. And as I said, for a small creature like this one, the wish should be small and simple. This means no talking dinosaurs, no personal spaceships. . . ."

Van thought again of Pebble's desperate face beneath the streetlamps. *Do you know what kind of things people wish for? Do you want to get trampled by dinosaurs?* But not *every* wish had to be dangerous or dumb, Van reasoned. He would choose the smallest, simplest, safest wish he could. "I guess . . . I'd wish for nobody to notice that I snuck out to visit you. Is that small enough?"

"An excellent choice. Now, make that wish as *clearly*

as you can." Mr. Falborg knelt, holding out the wishbone once again. Van grasped the other end. The batlike Wish Eater hopped up and down beside their knees. Still tucked in the crook of Van's elbow, the other Wish Eater watched with its big eyes. "On the count of three, you make your wish, and we snap the bone. I'll make sure you get the larger half."

Van took a trembling breath.

"Now," said Mr. Falborg, "one . . . two . . . *three*."

I wish that no one at the opera notices I've been gone, Van thought.

The bone snapped.

A ghostly white trail dribbled from the fragment in Van's hand. If Van hadn't been watching closely, he would have missed it. The batlike Wish Eater opened its little mouth and caught the falling droplets. It looked just like the hamster in the science room at Van's last school, drinking from its wall-mounted water bottle.

The Wish Eater seemed to shimmer. A heartbeat later, that shimmering, wavering silvery-ness filled the whole room. The air felt heavy, as though a downpour was about to break. Droplets of invisible mist coated Van's skin.

And then, as quickly as it had appeared, the mist

faded. The batlike Wish Eater sank back on the floor, looking sleepy and content—and, Van thought, a teeny bit larger than it had before. Before he could be sure, Mr. Falborg had scooped it up and settled it comfortably in its box.

"Back to sleep now," he murmured. He replaced the lid and slid the box back into its spot on the shelf.

"I saw it," said Van, when Mr. Falborg turned to face him again. "I saw the wish. I saw him eat it. And then everything . . . *sparkled.*"

"Lovely, isn't it?" Mr. Falborg murmured back. "It grows rarer as the years go by. And the world grows less interesting."

"So did it . . . ," Van breathed. "Did the wish come true?"

"You'll find out soon enough." Mr. Falborg gazed down at the Wish Eater snuggled into the crook of Van's arm. "You understand now, don't you? You see why these wondrous creatures must be saved before they disappear forever?"

Disappear forever. Even the words made Van's chest ache. "Yes," he said.

"Ah." Van could have sworn Mr. Falborg's eyes filled with tears. "I am so glad."

Very gently, Mr. Falborg reached down and eased the

drowsy Wish Eater out of Van's arms. A pang of sadness laced through Van as he watched the creature disappear into its box. It had been so sweet and affectionate. Without it, he felt suddenly alone and small again.

But then Mr. Falborg turned around and placed the box in Van's hands.

"Here," he said. "It's yours."

Van's mother had had a strict no-pets rule for as long as Van had begged her to break it. She said that they couldn't move a pet from city to city and country to country, and even though Van had argued, he knew deep down that she was right.

"But . . . ," he began.

"They're simple to care for," said Mr. Falborg encouragingly. "They sleep most of the time. When they're enclosed in a dark place, they're completely passive. And it has clearly already bonded with you."

"What about the Collectors?" Van whispered, hugging the box tight. "They're watching me. Will they try to take it?"

"Keep your curtains closed. Check every corner for spiders. Always assume, until you've looked everywhere, that you are not alone. Here." Mr. Falborg reached back into the chest and took out another wishbone. "When it acts hungry, you'll be prepared." He handed Van the bone, along with a small white card. "My phone number," he added. "If you need me, just call."

And suddenly Van found himself being steered back through Mr. Falborg's winding white house, with a magical creature in a box inside his backpack.

They were nearly to the foyer when a thought hit Van like a snowball in the face. He stopped.

He was supposed to bring the Collectors a part of Mr. Falborg's secret collection. But now that he knew what it contained, and now that one small, trusting, cuddly part of it was stashed inside his backpack, he couldn't possibly turn it over to them. Not in a hundred million years.

But they would know he'd been here. A bird, or a spider, or a dark-coated Collector would have seen him walk straight through Mr. Falborg's front door. He had to bring them *something.*

"Can I use your bathroom?" Van blurted.

Mr. Falborg turned around. "Of course. Just through the front parlor, behind the door on your left."

Van rushed across the ferny front room and through the archway, glancing back to make sure he was out of Mr. Falborg's sight. Then, instead of opening the door on his left, he turned the corner into the room full of paperweights. Without switching on the lights, Van crept toward the closest cabinet.

Its door swung open easily. Van squinted in at the paperweights. He reached out and plucked one from the center, where its absence was less likely to stand out. The glass lump was cold and heavy in his hand. Before he could start to feel too guilty, he stuffed the paperweight into the zippered pocket of his backpack.

He was only doing this to save something much more precious, Van reasoned. Even Mr. Falborg would understand.

In the spotless white bathroom, Van flushed the toilet and washed his hands, just in case anyone was listening. Then he hurried back to the foyer, feeling as relieved as if he *had* just used the bathroom . . . although he wasn't quite able to meet Mr. Falborg's eyes.

Mr. Falborg flung open the front door. "Hans?" he called to a man with springy gray hair and a soft brown sweater, who was trimming a row of bushes. "Would you drive Master Markson back to the opera?"

"It's not that far," said Van. "I can walk."

"Nonsense." Mr. Falborg waved a generous hand. Then he leaned close to Van, so no one else would hear.

"It's safer this way. You're still in danger, but at least you understand why." He smiled at Van once more. "And you know that you have friends."

A few minutes later, Van was climbing out of a gleaming gray car and stumbling through the doors of the opera house.

There was no one in the lobby, or anywhere in the twisty backstage hallways. In fact, the whole building seemed oddly quiet. But as Van drew closer to the rehearsal room, he caught a new sound—not music, but the low, bubbling hum of many people talking at once.

He nudged the door open.

The opera company was packed together on one side of the room. Van caught sight of his mother clutching her bright silk scarf, and the rehearsal accompanist inching across the floor with both arms out, and the assistant director talking very quickly into his phone.

On the opposite side of the room, shifting lightly on its hooves, stood a deer.

A deer with branching antlers, black eyes, and dusty white hair.

No one else turned to look when Van pushed the door open. But the deer did. Its wide, wet eyes flicked straight toward Van. With a bound, it charged toward the open doorway.

Somebody screamed.

Van, too stunned to move, felt the whoosh of the deer's body as it leaped past. He felt the silvery dewiness of its coat. He felt the misty softness still caught on every strand of its hair. It raced past him, down the hall, toward the daylight of the lobby.

Everyone began shouting at once.

"Somebody, follow—"

"In the city?"

"—animal control!"

"From a zoo?"

"Giovanni!" His mother's louder, clearer voice clanged through the noise. Her hands grabbed his shoulders. "Are you all right?"

"Yes," said Van. "I'm fine."

But he wasn't.

He was much, much better than fine.

He had just seen a wish come true.

15
A Change of Plan

"AND Lily from the box office said that it ran straight out into the street and bounded off," said Ingrid Markson wonderingly, as she and Van strolled home in the warm twilight. "I've never seen a wild deer in the middle of the city. Certainly not an *albino* one. And it just seemed to *appear* out of nowhere, right during Michael and Sara's duet, like some theatrical effect. I swear, there should have been a puff of dry ice!" She laughed and shook her head, her hair gleaming in the last of the daylight. "I was almost sorry you and Peter weren't there to see it." She looked down at Van. "So, *caro mio*. Did you two have fun this afternoon?"

"What?" said Van, whose thoughts had jumped from the deer down to the bottom of his backpack.

He adjusted a strap, feeling the Wish Eater's box shift inside. "Oh. With Peter? It was fine."

"I wish you could have more time together," his mother continued. "But it looks like we might be heading to England soon."

"What?" said Van, more loudly. "When?"

"My contract here only runs through the end of the current show. Leola has some very exciting options lined up for me." His mother reached down and squeezed his hand. "Lined up for *us*."

Leola was his mother's manager. She was an Italian lady with lipstick so thick and bright it always left a perfect print on both of Van's cheeks.

Van pulled his hand away. "We *might* be going?"

"We *might* be going. We will *probably* be going."

"So . . . ," Van tried to push the panic out of his voice. "How soon would we leave?"

His mother tilted her coppery head to one side. "Well, if Charles doesn't surprise me with another offer, we could leave as soon as the run is finished. The show closes in just over a month."

"A *month*?"

His mother's eyebrows rose. "Why are you so astonished, Giovanni? You know this is how things work.

Sometimes we're booked years in advance, sometimes I get three days' notice."

"I just . . ." Van's mind whirled from Mr. Falborg's tall white house to the black deeps of the Collection. "I don't want to leave. Not *yet.*"

His mother's eyebrows rose even higher. "I didn't think you liked it here so much."

"I *do.* I mean—I like it more and more. Can't we stay longer?"

"Giovanni, I have to go where the job is."

Van was ready to grasp at straws. Even snooty ones.

"What about the Greys?" he blurted. "Won't you miss them?"

His mother hesitated. Van saw her face soften, and something cloudy and quiet passed through her eyes. "Of course," she said. "I would miss lots of people. I always do." She took Van's hand again. "But I have the only people I *need* right here."

This time, Van didn't pull his hand away.

He and his mother walked in silence for a moment.

"Like I said," his mother spoke at last, "it's only a possibility. A probability."

"Okay," said Van softly. "Only a probability."

Inside the apartment, Van trudged down the hallway.

"I'll be in my room," he said over his shoulder. If his mother answered, Van couldn't hear.

He shut the bedroom door behind him. Then he pulled the shades, closing out the lavender evening light. He scanned the corners. He peeked under the bed. He opened the closet. He checked every piece of lint and fleck of dirt, making sure they weren't secretly spiders. Finally, when he was certain that everything was secure, Van sat down on the floor, unzipped his backpack, and drew out the cardboard box.

He lifted the lid. A tiny, hazy face peeped out at him.

A burst of joy shimmered through Van's chest. The Wish Eater was as real—and as adorable—as he remembered.

"Hello again," Van whispered.

The Wish Eater blinked. It craned over the side of the box, looking timidly around.

"You can climb out." Van held out one hand. "It's safe. I promise."

The Wish Eater inched onto his palm. Van felt cool, whispery lightness as it crouched there, looking up at him with big eyes.

Van raised his hand to give the Wish Eater a better view.

"This is my room," he told it. "For now, anyway. That's my bed. You'll sleep underneath it, with my collection, where it's safe. And this is my miniature stage."

Van tipped the Wish Eater gently onto the stage floor.

"That's SuperVan," he explained, as the Wish Eater blinked shyly at the figurine standing at center stage. "He's a good guy. He tries to help everyone who needs him."

Van dragged out his collection box and rummaged through the miniatures. He pushed aside a helicopter, a purple elephant, and a tiny Santa Claus in a reindeer-drawn sleigh. At last he uncovered a wizard made of molded white plastic.

The Wish Eater watched, wide-eyed, as Van pushed the wizard across the stage.

"SuperVan!" cried the White Wizard. "We need your help! You are the only one who can save us!"

"I want to help you," SuperVan answered. "But I've been called away on another quest."

"Please, SuperVan," the White Wizard pleaded. "The entire species of Wish Eaters depends on you!"

The Wish Eater's eyes flicked from one figurine to the other.

"I have no choice," said SuperVan. "The mother ship is about to take flight."

"Then use your powers!" said the White Wizard. "Act fast! You must find a way!"

Van sat back on his heels.

The White Wizard was right. SuperVan *would* find a way.

He had to help the Wish Eaters. And now he had even less time.

Van glanced at the window. The light tinting the curtains was deepening from lavender to violet. Soon it would be dark. He couldn't sneak out of the apartment until his mother was asleep anyway, by which time it would be *really* dark, and he'd have to venture out into the huge, shadowy city all alone, heading straight into the grasp of potential danger. . . .

Van swallowed.

Onstage, the Wish Eater glanced back and forth between SuperVan and the White Wizard, as though it was waiting for them to speak again. With one tiny, hazy finger, it reached out and gave SuperVan a tap. SuperVan toppled forward and hit the stage floor with a smack.

The Wish Eater reared back. It took a terrified leap into Van's lap.

"It's all right," said Van, wrapping his arms around the weightless, shivering thing. "Don't be scared. I've got you."

The Wish Eater lifted its head and blinked up at him.

And that's when Van knew, with solidifying certainty, that he *was* going to help this creature. This one, and every other poor little creature like it who was trapped in the darkness deep underground.

He rubbed the Wish Eater's ruffled ear. If only he had SuperVan's powers. Then he could get to the Collection quickly and safely, and—

Wait.

Van paused, mid ear rub.

He *did* have powers.

And he had a very good reason to use them.

An hour later, after a hurried round of toothbrushing and a soft kiss on the forehead from his mother, Van closed his bedroom door for the night. He flicked on the night-light and switched out the others. He slipped Mr. Falborg's paperweight into his left pants pocket. Then, with his hearing aids still in place, he climbed into bed, pulled the covers up over his clothes, and settled back against the pillows to wait.

After what felt like ages, the light beneath his bedroom door winked out. His mother had gone to bed at last.

Van slipped out of the blankets. He crouched beside the bed, pulling the cardboard box out of its hiding spot.

The Wish Eater stared eagerly up at him from beneath the opening lid. The glow of the nightlight made its whole body shimmer.

"Everything all right in there?" Van whispered.

The Wish Eater leaned over the side of the box, reaching out with both nubby hands.

"I can't just keep calling you the *Wish Eater*," said Van, as the creature clambered up his arm. "You need a name. You look kind of like a lemur, so what if I call you Lemmy?"

The Wish Eater's ruffly ears twitched.

"Lemmy," Van repeated. "Do you like it?"

The Wish Eater didn't answer, but its ears twitched faster.

Van reached for his backpack, which lay on the floor where he had dropped it, and unzipped the front pocket. He drew out the wishbone.

Instantly, the little Wish Eater straightened. It sniffed

at the air like a cat that smells an opening tuna can.

"All right, Lemmy," Van whispered. "I've got a wish for you."

He grasped the wishbone's fragile ends.

But there Van hesitated. When he'd made his last wish, he'd had Mr. Falborg to guide him. If anything had gone wrong, he would have had help in fixing it. Now he was completely alone. The Wish Eater gave an eager little bounce in his lap. Well—not *completely* alone. He had Lemmy's help, and he was going to help Lemmy in return. He *had* to help. And the night was already sliding past him. There was no time to waste on fear.

I wish to get to the Collection as quickly, and safely, and secretly as I can, Van thought.

Snap went the wishbone.

Something pale and delicate dribbled from the bone's broken edge. Lemmy craned upward, mouth open, to catch it. The air swirled with mist. Van felt it dampening the ends of his hair, coating his skin with its softness. When the mist cleared, Lemmy was leaning back in his lap, looking contented, and everything was quiet.

Van held his breath.

He looked around. He listened.

Nothing.

Van let out the breath.

Maybe the wish hadn't worked. Maybe it had been too big for little Lemmy to handle. Maybe he hadn't been specific enough, or clear enough . . . or maybe all of these magical, impossible things were just as impossible as they seemed.

Then, as Van started to lose hope, something shot out from under his bed.

Van turned. The thing had already flown straight behind him, its velocity rippling his hair. He turned again. Whatever it was still hovered just out of sight. But a little voice near his left ear exclaimed, "Ho, ho, ho!"

Van whipped around. A few feet away, outlined by the glow of his night-light, was a flying miniature sleigh drawn by flying miniature reindeer. A tiny chuckling Santa grasped the reins. Van let out something between a gasp and a laugh.

He glanced down. Lemmy leaned back in his lap, wearing what looked like a sleepy smile.

The sleigh flew on, bounding over invisible hills. It sailed across the room, lifting higher and higher, heading straight for the curtained window. Before Van could make a move, it hit the covered pane with a *THWACK.*

"Careful!" whispered Van, not sure if he was talking to the tiny plastic Santa or his tiny reindeer, and realizing that neither seemed believable anyway. "My mother will hear!"

The reindeer smacked against the window again.

Van slid Lemmy into the cardboard box and jumped to his feet. "Shh!" he hissed, as the sleigh struck the curtained pane even harder. "We have to be quiet!"

Thwack thwack thwack, went the sleigh against the window, like a fly trying desperately to get out.

"Please!" Van begged.

THWACK THWACK THWACK.

Van dove the last few feet to the window. Before the sleigh could strike it again, he whipped the curtains apart and shoved the pane upward. A cool river of air poured into the room. Santa and his sleigh sailed out into the night.

Van stared after it, expecting to see the escaping toy dwindle into the distance.

But the sleigh didn't dwindle.

It grew.

It hung in the night air just outside his bedroom window, twinkling with a haze of pearly mist. It swelled and stretched until it was the size of an actual sleigh, and the plastic reindeer were as big as real reindeer, and the plastic Santa that turned its cheery smile toward Van was just the right size for a jolly old elf.

"Ho ho ho!" said the Santa, patting the space beside him on the red plastic seat.

A laugh that Van couldn't hold back burst out of him. He'd imagined flying like SuperVan hundreds of times. He'd never imagined flying like Santa Claus. Was he really going to climb out of a fourth-floor window into a floating plastic sleigh, in the middle of *July*? He glanced at the row of hovering reindeer, and at the seat that Santa patted invitingly once more. Yes, he really was.

He *absolutely* was.

Van climbed up onto the windowsill. The sleigh waited just inches away. With a deep breath, Van plunged over the sill and half stepped, half fell into it. It rocked under his weight like a carriage on a Ferris wheel. Before Van could settle into the seat, Santa twitched the plastic reins. The reindeer shot forward.

They all whooshed out into the city, Van clutching

the side of the sleigh with both hands. They threaded between tall buildings that melted around them into a soft gray smear. They dove over rooftops and whipped around corners. One instant, the reindeer were climbing, and Van was staring straight up at the fuzzy purple sky. Then the reindeer plunged, and the sleigh tilted after them, and he was staring down at the glinting black street below.

"Ho ho ho!" announced the plastic Santa.

Van heard himself laugh too.

He probably should have felt afraid. But he didn't. He felt electrified. He was part of something magical and impossible and odd, wrapped up inside it, carried through the dark in its speeding weightlessness.

And then, long before Van was ready for the ride to be over, the sleigh came to a gentle stop. Van peered over the side.

They were hovering above the pavement of a quiet street. The sidewalks were empty, the nearby buildings sleeping for the night. The only streetlights were far-off and dim—but just ahead, around the corner, Van spotted the familiar neon sign of an exotic pet shop.

The sleigh dropped until it had touched down on the deserted sidewalk. Van climbed out. Before he could say "Thank you!" or give the reindeer a grateful pat, the sleigh zipped back to miniature size. It fell over onto the sidewalk with a little *click*.

Van picked it up and put it in his pocket. He smiled to himself for a moment, letting the weightless, electrified feeling fade. He had a job to do. A serious, dangerous one.

With a last quick look around, he scurried to the corner and bolted down the street, straight toward the City Collection Agency.

16
Down to the Dark

THE office of the City Collection Agency had been dim in midafternoon. Now, in the middle of the night, it was *black*. Van padded across the empty room as though it was a box full of tar, both hands stretched out in front of him. He'd just opened the hidden door, letting loose the smell of smoke and dust and a faint haze of green-gold light, when he felt something moving through the darkness behind him. Van whipped around. No one was there. No one *human*, anyway. On the carpet, trundling toward his feet, was a portly raccoon. Something small and pale was clutched in one of its front paws, making its gait extra wobbly. A packet of French fries dangled from its teeth.

"Oof," it said, in a raspy voice. "Would you mind holding that door?"

Van held it politely.

The raccoon waddled by. "Much obliged."

Van started down the stairs behind the raccoon. They'd taken only two steps when the raccoon spoke again. "How rude of me," it said. "Would you like a French fry? They're nice and cold."

"Um . . . no, thank you," whispered Van.

"Are you sure? They're fresh out of the Dumpster behind Pete's Barbeque," the raccoon went on chattily. "Great spot for wishbones *and* cold French fries. Of course, if you prefer stale breadsticks, the Dumpster at LaMama is *perfection*. Or, if you like noodles with your wishbones, you have to try the Dumpster at Izakaya Ito. The best in the city. The *best*. Don't listen to what other raccoons might tell you about that place Zen-Zen. Their Dumpster isn't even worth the climb." The raccoon stopped to tug a fry out of the packet with its spare front paw. "Mmm. *Mmmm,*" it said, munching. "You're sure you don't want one?"

"That's all right," said Van.

"It's all right with me too." The raccoon scarfed down another fry. "Mmm. Well. Have a good night!"

The creature scurried forward, leaving Van to tiptoe down the rest of the flight on his own.

The air grew colder. The scents of dust and smoke grew stronger. The green-gold light seeped up over his feet, and then over his legs, and finally flooded the rest of him.

Just as Van reached the final step, something small and furry pounced onto his shoulder—something that *didn't* smell like French fries.

"Hey!" squeaked a familiar voice. "I know you!" Barnavelt's damp nose poked at his cheek. "Look! Pebble! It's Vanderbilt Maximillian!"

Pebble's hands were already clasped around his arm. Both of them had appeared so fast, Van wondered if they had been waiting there, at the bottom of the stairs, just for him.

"I *knew* you'd come back!" Pebble beamed, practically jumping up and down. Her mossy eyes were bright. "You've decided, right? You'll help us? You're on *our* side?"

Van had never seen Pebble's smile before. It transformed her entire face, the way a ray of sunlight changes a dark room. Van couldn't help smiling back. For an instant, he almost forgot that this *wasn't* why he was here. He was here as a spy—to learn about and help the Wish Eaters. But Pebble didn't need to know that. She *couldn't* know that.

He let his face mirror Pebble's eager expression. "Right," he said. "I'm on your side."

Pebble's smile grew even more brilliant. "Come on!" She wheeled around. "I'll bring you to Nail. Everybody will be so happy!"

Pebble raced to the end of the massive entry chamber, with Van running right behind. Their shadows streaked over the green stone walls. At the chamber's end, Pebble turned down a narrow corridor, and from there into another corridor, and from there into a small, familiar room with a big desk and an even bigger fireplace.

Nail stood before the fireplace, speaking with sleek-haired Sesame. One of the big men from the other night—Beetle, Van thought—stood guard near the door. Everyone turned as Pebble and Van charged inside. Even the pigeon on Sesame's arm and the rats on Nail's shoulders sat up, boring into him with their quick black eyes.

A shudder climbed the bumps of Van's spine. He forced it back down again. He had a mission to fulfill. He wouldn't fail before he'd even begun.

"He's here!" Pebble shouted.

"I'm here!" agreed Barnavelt, from Van's shoulder. "Here I am! Right here!"

"Van Markson." Nail moved swiftly around the desk. Van flinched instinctively, but Nail's eyes, like Pebble's, were warm. "Welcome back." He reached out to shake Van's hand. "We are so glad that you've made this choice."

"Me too," said Van, as brightly as he could manage.

"Please." Nail opened his hands. "Tell us what you have learned so far."

Everyone waited.

"Well . . . ," said Van, very slowly. "That's the thing. I'm not sure I learned what you wanted to know."

The warmth in the atmosphere faded slightly. One of Nail's eyebrows rose. The pigeon on Sesame's shoulder cocked its head.

"I mean," Van went on, when no one else spoke, "I didn't see what you said. I looked, I promise. But I didn't see anything strange."

Pebble sucked in a breath. One of the rats climbed off Nail's shoulder. It scurried down the length of his black coat and across the firelit stone floor, straight toward Van's feet.

Nail folded his arms. "Are you telling us you saw no other Collectors?"

"Not really," said Van. The rat put its front paws on the toe of his shoe. "I mean, not like *you*."

"Certainly *not* like us," said Sesame.

"Did you not meet a man named *Ivor Falborg*?" Nail demanded, his voice quick and firm. "And did he not invite you into his home? For the *second time*?"

A chill gusted through Van's chest. He fought to keep his tone light and his body still as the rat climbed up his pants leg. "Oh—Mr. Falborg? Our neighbor?" he said. "You mean *that* kind of collector? Yes, he showed me some things. They weren't like your collection. But I did what you asked, just in case."

He pulled the paperweight from his pocket and held it out on his palm. Firelight lapped at the bubble of glass, ruddying the bouquet of flowers sealed inside.

Nail's eyes moved to Pebble. She gave a little nod.

"He didn't show you anything else?" Nail asked, his eyes flicking back to Van. "Nothing more *unusual*?"

Nail clearly suspected something. But there was no way Van was going to tell the Collectors about the hidden room, or about all those helpless little Wish Eaters waiting to be let out of their boxes for a tiny bit of food and company.

Van swallowed hard. The rat had reached his shoulder. He could feel its whiskers against his neck. "Not really," he managed. "Unless you mean those hair wreaths. Those were pretty weird."

The rat craned upward, sniffing at Van's chin. "Smells scared," it said softly. Van recognized Violetta's tiny voice.

Van wasn't sure if the whole room could hear her, or if she had spoken only to him. But no one else answered, and there was no point pretending he couldn't hear the Creatures anymore anyway.

"I *am* scared," he answered. "I just sneaked through the city by myself in the middle of the night."

"I don't smell *scared,*" said Barnavelt. The squirrel shoved his nose into Van's cheek. "I smell spaghetti."

"I had spaghetti and garlic toast for dinner," said Van.

The squirrel's eyes glazed. "Garlic toast. With butter," he whispered. "And a nice crunchy crust. And—"

"You know," Sesame said, staring down at Van with clear, steady eyes, "it's very unusual for anyone who's not a born Collector to be able to hear the Creatures."

Van gazed up at her.

"You say you're ordinary. You even tell us that you're *hard of hearing*. But you hear them." Sesame's eyes narrowed slightly. "Why do you think that is?'

"I don't know," said Van honestly. "I think . . . maybe I'm not great at hearing, but I'm good at listening."

Sesame inclined her head. She stared at him for a long moment. Then she said, "Good answer."

"Good answer!" cheered the squirrel.

Pebble threw Van a pleased smile. A trickle of relief, warm and steadying, washed through him.

Nail kept quiet. He surveyed the room, taking in Sesame's cool expression, Pebble's smile, and Beetle's chilly stare, before finally turning back to Van. "It looks like you get another chance, Van Markson," he said at last. "You will keep a close eye—a *closer* eye—on Mr. Falborg."

"I will," said Van quickly. He dropped the paperweight back into his pocket. "But . . . can I ask why?"

Nail didn't blink. "Because he poses a serious threat to us. To our work. To our existence."

Van thought of the spider smashed in Mr. Falborg's handkerchief. He couldn't imagine kindly Mr. Falborg being a threat to anything else. "Mr. *Falborg*?" he asked. "Are you sure?"

"Very sure. We know him well." Nail's eyes slashed to Pebble again. When they came back to Van, they were softer. "This must be confusing to someone from the outside. But you will understand more once we bring you *in*." Nail stepped toward Van. "It goes without saying that the things we're about to show you, and tell you, and teach you must be kept entirely secret. But I am going to say it anyway." He bent down. The rats on his shoulders snuffed at Van with matching whiskered noses. "Do not tell *anyone* what you are about to see."

"I won't," said Van quickly. He hoped the rats couldn't smell a lie.

"Pebble will guide you," said Nail, straightening up again. "Kernel is waiting for you in the Collection."

"Colonel?" Van murmured to Pebble. "Like in an army?"

"Like in a corncob," Pebble murmured back.

Barnavelt snapped to attention. "Popcorn?"

Nail strode to the other side of his desk. "You may go," he said, sweeping one long-fingered hand toward the door. Then he added, his words slow and precise, "And thank you for your honesty, Van Markson."

Pebble's face warmed back into a smile. "Come on!"

She bolted toward the door. Van tagged behind,

Barnavelt still clinging to his shoulder. Beetle, standing guard, didn't move as the three of them brushed past. But his eyes followed them into the corridor, through the chilly shadows, until they were out of sight.

"Now we can tell you *everything*!" Pebble shouted over her shoulder as they raced back through the cavernous entry chamber. She pointed toward another hallway that branched off into the dimness. "If we went that way—a certain stair—observatory—"

"Observatory?" Van repeated, trying to catch up. "Like . . . for observing stars?"

"*Falling* stars," said Pebble. "We have to know exactly when meteor showers are coming."

She plunged ahead of him down the massive staircase. "You've already seen the Atlas," she said, speaking very fast but very loud, as they approached the first archway. "Sesame's in charge of it. It's where we track wishful locations. Like wells and fountains and ponds. Coin-tossing spots," she added, as they charged through a flock of pigeons that flapped and flittered out of the way. "Of course, people can blow out birthday candles or break wishbones pretty much anywhere, so we keep track of apartments and houses and other addresses too."

Van watched one of the pigeons take wing, soaring out over the pit's bottomless blackness. In a place so massive, something as small and quiet as a Wish Eater would be awfully easy to hide. How was he going to find them?

"I know what you're thinking," said Pebble, coming to an abrupt stop on the landing. She whirled around to face Van head-on.

"You do?" squeaked Van.

"Oh, good," said Barnavelt, from Van's shoulder. "Because I can't remember *what* I was thinking."

"You're wondering how we get inside restaurants and houses and apartments without people noticing." Pebble gave Van a knowing smile. "That's where the Creatures come in."

"That's where we come in!" crowed Barnavelt.

"There are thousands of them," Pebble rattled on. "All the creatures people don't usually notice. Pigeons, raccoons, rats—"

"And squirrels," interrupted Barnavelt.

"Spiders, ravens, bats, mice—"

"And squirrels!" Barnvelt added.

"And squirrels," Pebble finished. "Every kind of little city-dwelling animal. Especially the nocturnal ones.

And *especially* the ones who already like to collect shiny little things."

Van's mind leaped to the box full of shiny little things under his bed. Was he just another creature for the Collectors to use?

Pebble's expression faltered. Her customary frown began to creep back. "I'm talking really fast, aren't I?"

"Well . . . ," said Van.

"I am. I'm sorry. I just—I've never gotten to tell anybody any of this before." Her smile returned, a little more cautiously this time, pushing the frown out of place bit by bit. "Ready to keep going?"

"Ready," said Van.

They hurried on. Through the archway, beneath the carved letters spelling THE ATLAS, Van caught a glimpse of the room papered with maps and charts, the knots of Collectors and Creatures scurrying between the long tables. Then his feet hit the next set of steps, and the chamber slid out of view.

"You've . . . Calendar too . . . ," said Pebble, bounding down the flight ahead of him. Half of her words dissolved into the sound of other voices. A flood of Collectors gushed in and out of the Calendar's archway, accompanied by flapping birds and running rodents. They jostled Van as they rushed by, throwing him quick, curious looks and a few small smiles.

"Grommet . . . the head of the Calendar," Pebble shouted back. ". . . Pin and Caraway . . . names and birth dates. Today's a really popular one!"

By now Pebble was speaking so fast, it was like a rush of water through an open spigot. Each new word rinsed the last ones away. Van tried to follow her voice, her feet, and her pointing hands all at once, but with the noise of the crowd, it was getting hard to do.

Besides, she wasn't telling him what he needed to know. Van scanned the area. There was no sign of Wish Eaters through the archway, in the long black bookshelves of the Calendar. And he knew they weren't hidden in the twinkling jars of the Collection below.

The Wish Eaters had to be somewhere else.

Somewhere deeper.

"Come on!" Pebble called, beckoning him onward. "Kernel will . . ."

Her voice faded as she leaped down the next flight. Van, lagging behind, let it fade. He moved slower and slower, until the gap between them was wide enough that even Pebble's keen ears wouldn't hear him.

Then he glanced at the squirrel perched on his

shoulder. "Barnavelt?" he whispered. "Where do they keep the Wish Eaters?"

Barnavelt's bright eyes blinked. "The Eaters?" he repeated in a small voice. "We're not supposed to talk about them."

"But you know about them. Don't you?"

"Maybe. No. Yes." The squirrel blinked again. "I mean—what's a Wish Eater?"

"Are they down there, in the Hold?" Van asked. "Is that what it's for?"

"It's for holding them," blurted Barnavelt. "Wait. What was the question?"

"What are they doing to them?" Van hurried on. Below, Pebble had already reached the end of the flight. "Are they trapping them? And what's that awful noise? Is something hurting them?"

"I don't . . ." Barnavelt flicked his tail anxiously. "Oh, look! A hawk!"

"You don't have to tell me," said Van. "If I'm right, just say nothing."

Barnavelt stared back at him. "Nothing," he whispered.

"Hurry up!" Pebble stood on the landing, looking up at them impatiently. Just beyond her, through the massive arch, Van could see the towering double doors of the Collection.

He trotted down the rest of the steps.

Pebble waited until he'd reached the landing. "Kernel . . . tell . . . thing . . ." she said, turning toward the double doors.

But this time Van didn't follow her.

This was his chance.

Van charged across the landing and barreled down the next flight of steps. His feet slapped the cold stone. Barnavelt's paws dug into his shoulder.

"Where are you going?" the squirrel squeaked. "Where are *we* going?"

Van didn't answer.

He finished that flight and raced onto the next. The darkness grew even thicker. Soon Van could barely make out the edges of the stairs and the squirrel's eyes glittering beside him. The air grew colder, clammier, until it seemed to stick to his face like wet leaves.

Without enough sight and sound, Van had to rely on touch. And all he could feel was cold and hard and damp. His heart rattled in his chest.

Far behind him, he thought he could hear Pebble shouting. But he didn't stop. He *couldn't* stop. Not now.

The thought of other creatures like Lemmy, small and scared and starved, pushed him onward. Faster. Faster. Down, down, down.

Before long, there was no light at all.

Van couldn't sense the shapes heading up the stairs. He couldn't hear their quick, heavy steps.

And he couldn't see a thing until a sudden flare of lantern light revealed the blade, silver and hooked and viciously sharp, flashing straight toward him.

17
Razor

THE blade stopped just inches from Van's face.

It was attached to a long, thick pole, and that pole was clenched in the hands of the most frightening person Van had ever seen.

The man was so tall that even though Van stood two steps above him, his head barely reached the man's chest. The man's hair was dark and long and tied back with a leather cord. He was dressed in a long black leather coat. Another metal hook on a pole glinted in the straps that crossed his chest and wrapped over his back. Behind the man stood other dark-coated people, some holding blades, some holding flaming glass lanterns.

By the uneven light of the lanterns, Van could

see that something like a huge silver fishing net was wrapped around the big man's shoulders. And his face . . . Frost bloomed in the pit of Van's stomach. The man's eyes were so dark, they were practically black. One small scar twisted the corner of his mouth, and another, much bigger scar, like a slash cut in a loaf of bread, curved down from his lower eyelid all the way to his jaw.

Van let out a shriek.

He staggered backward—straight into Pebble.

"Razor!" Pebble exclaimed. She dragged Van behind her body, out of range of the glittering blades. "I'm so sorry. He got away from me." She shot Van a look that was both desperate and commanding. "Van, go up to the landing and wait for me."

Maybe it was Pebble's tone, or maybe it was the blades, or maybe it was the man's scarred, shadowy face, but Van didn't even pause. He scrambled up to the landing as fast as his legs would carry him.

From below came the murky sound of voices. Van could hear Pebble speaking, and someone else replying, but he couldn't decipher a single word.

"Who was that?" he whispered to Barnavelt, who was still clinging tightly to his shoulder.

"That was Pebble." Barnavelt blinked at him. "Haven't you two met?"

"No, that man. The huge one with the hooks and the nets."

"Oh." The squirrel blinked again. "That's Razor. He's master of the Hold."

Van's frosty stomach turned to a solid lump of ice. "*That* guy—that guy with all those weapons—is in charge of the trapped Wish Eaters?"

The squirrel flicked his tail. "Right. I mean—left. I mean—what's a Wish Eater?"

A shape came jogging back up the stairs toward them. A second later, Pebble grabbed Van by the sleeve. Her big, bright smile had vanished so completely that Van could barely remember what it looked like.

"*What* was *that*?" she hissed into his ear. "What were you *doing*?"

"I just . . . I guess I made a wrong turn," Van said lamely.

"You are *so lucky* I was there," she growled. "Come on." She headed up the steps, keeping a tight grip on Van's sleeve.

Van glanced into the darkness over his shoulder. Razor and the flickering lantern light had disappeared.

Apparently getting down to the Hold wouldn't be easy. And maybe, considering those silver blades, he *had* just gotten awfully lucky.

Pebble pulled him through the Collection's double doors.

Even though he'd seen the huge, softly twinkling room once before, for a few seconds, Van could only stand on the threshold, paralyzed. The rows and rows of shelves, the webs of staircases and platforms, the silvery glass ceiling, and the thousands of bottles, each one alive with its own mysterious wish, were too much to take in all at once. It was too big, too beautiful, too wondrous to fit into a single look.

"Ah!" said a voice.

A short, portly man—the penguin-shaped man Van had spotted behind the podium at the center of the Collection during his first visit—came waddling swiftly toward them. Silvery light twinkled on his round spectacles.

"There you are!" The man held out both hands and grabbed one of Van's, giving it a swift shake. "I am Kernel, head of the Collection. We are *most* pleased to have you joining our efforts."

"Me too," said Van.

"Let us step out of the way." Kernel gestured toward one corner of the chamber, where a twisting flight of stairs formed a nook. "The Collection in this location dates . . . over . . . hundred years . . . ," he began, leading the way. His voice traveled back to Van in dribbles. "Collections . . . over the world . . . wherever wishes are most dense . . . many centuries. We protect . . . in secrecy. *Well.*" Kernel reached the nook and whirled around to face Van again. He smacked his hands together, and Van couldn't help but think of flippers. "If you are to work with us, you ought to understand the importance of that work. What questions do you have?"

A pileup of questions threatened to rush out of Van's mouth. *Where are the Wish Eaters? What are you doing to them? Why are you hurting them?* But Van bit the inside of his cheeks until he knew those words would not slip out.

"So . . . ," he said carefully, as a Collector climbed the steps above them, a blue bottle glimmering in her hands, "anytime anyone makes a wish, it's your job to collect it?"

"Not just *any* wish," said Kernel. "It must be a *viable* wish. A living wish. An authentic wish. A wish with its roots in the magic of millennia."

"Some kinds of wishes are just words," said Pebble. "Only certain kinds of wishes actually *exist.*"

"Oh, like—" Van stopped himself from blurting out "like Mr. Falborg said." "Like wishes on wishbones, and birthday candles . . ."

"Birthday cake?" said Barnavelt hopefully.

"That's right," said Kernel. "Broken wishbones, birthday candles, falling stars, and coins tossed into fountains or wells provide viable wishes—as long as an underground freshwater source is within close distance, that is."

"So if you blow on a lost eyelash, that isn't a real wish?"

"*Eyelashes.* Hmph." Kernel shook his head. "I don't know where that specious idea began. No, those are not viable wishes."

"What about wishing when the clock says 11:11?" Van asked.

"A waste of time, frankly. And literally."

"What about when a ladybug lands on you?"

"Unless your wish is for an aphid-eating beetle to use you as a landing strip, utterly useless."

Van gazed out into the chamber, where the millions of green and blue bottles stretched away into the distance. "Once you collect them, do the wishes just stay here forever?"

"As long as there are Collectors to preserve them," said Kernel. "That is to say: yes."

"But if you've been collecting these wishes for more than a hundred years," Van said thoughtfully, "some of the people who made them must be long gone. Can those wishes still come true?"

Kernel's tufty eyebrows twitched. "An excellent question," he said. "No. Those wishes—dead wishes—cannot come true. Not exactly."

Something in Kernel's expression made Van's neck prickle. "Then why do you keep them?"

Beside Van, Pebble stiffened.

"Because," said Kernel, "dead wishes are the most dangerous of all."

"Dangerous?" Van repeated. "Why?"

"Allow me to explain how a wish works." Kernel clapped his hands together. "When a wish is made, the wisher determines *what* will happen, but not *how* it will happen. For instance, say you were to wish that you didn't have to go to school."

Van had no trouble imagining this. He nodded.

"Say that you made a viable wish, perhaps using a

coin, or a falling star," Kernel continued. "Say that wish went uncollected by us, and it ended up being granted. *Now.*" He patted his hands again. "Perhaps you would come down with a mild case of pinkeye, resulting in excusal from school. Or perhaps you would become terribly ill. Perhaps a severe blizzard would strike the city, bringing everything to a halt. Or perhaps your school would collapse under a hail of falling fish."

"Fish?" Van repeated.

"It is possible. *Anything* is possible." Kernel's voice grew lower, but he spoke slowly and clearly. "Wishes are extraordinarily hard to control. And once a wish becomes a *dead* wish, once no limitations remain, once that wish is nothing but magical energy—it becomes an exceedingly powerful thing. It becomes pure chaos."

Van glanced around the chamber again. The glimmer of the bottles seemed different now. More daunting. More like a flame just waiting for fuel.

"If the wishes themselves are so powerful," he said slowly, "might somebody try to get in here and take them?"

"Oh, they could *try.*" Kernel gave a dry smile. "Fortunately, the Collection is well protected, by means both magical and . . ."

But Van had stopped listening. The floor beneath his feet had started, very slightly, to shiver. On the nearest shelf, bottles were trembling, streaks of light reflected on their sides beginning to flash and waver.

Van turned back to Kernel. But before he could ask what was going on, the little man had charged straight past him.

"STATIONS!" Van heard him bellow as he rushed away. *"STATIONS, EVERYONE!"*

The chamber burst into action. Collectors raced to the shelves. Owls and pigeons and shrieking ravens wheeled above. Furry Creatures skittered everywhere, dodging the Collectors' running feet.

The floor shivered harder. Now Van could catch the sound of thousands of bottles jingling together, as high-pitched and brittle as a scream. And beneath that sound was a roar—the loudest, most powerful roar he'd heard yet.

Someone grabbed Van by the sleeve. He was flung against a shelf, his back pressed tight to a row of trembling bottles. "Stay there!" Pebble shouted into his face. Van nodded. Pebble threw herself against the shelf beside him, spreading her arms to brace as many wishes as possible. Barnavelt hopped off Van's shoulder and clutched two bottles in his little paws.

For a few heartbeats, the chamber shook. Van pulled his shoulders toward his ears. His teeth were clenched so tight he could feel his pulse in his jaw. He could almost see the shelves beginning to crack and tumble, a million bottles plunging toward the stone floor, the explosion of shattering glass. . . .

. . . when, with a last huge *HUFFFffffffff,* the roar died.

The floor stilled. The clinking bottles went quiet.

There was a beat, like the moment of silence between changing TV channels.

And then, as one, the Collectors and Creatures went calmly back to work.

Barnavelt hopped onto Pebble's shoulder. "What were we talking about?" he asked. "Birthday cake?"

But Van wasn't going to be distracted. He grabbed Pebble's arm. "What is doing that?" he demanded. "You can't tell me you didn't hear it this time! What's going on down there?"

Pebble didn't answer. But her eyes led Van to the center of the room, where Kernel was waddling rapidly toward the doorway.

Before Kernel could reach them, the double doors slammed open.

A man in a long black leather coat stood on the threshold.

Razor.

Somehow, in bright light, Razor looked even more frightening than he had on the lantern-lit staircase. The straps crisscrossing his body held more weapons and tools than Van had spotted before. Without the softening shadows, his scar-twisted face looked like something made of stone.

Razor's eyes scanned the room as Kernel spoke to him, never blinking, never stopping. Then they landed on Van.

And stayed there.

Van felt himself become several inches shorter.

Razor bowed his head. He spoke to Kernel for a moment. Kernel nodded. Then the huge man whirled around and stalked back through the doors. The hooks on his back glinted viciously. The doors banged shut.

Kernel hurried back toward the spot where Van and Pebble stood. "My apologies," he puffed. "As I was saying—"

But Van wasn't listening. Years ago, he and his mother had toured a medieval German castle, and the things on display in the dungeon—the torture devices and the chains and the deep, narrow pits where prisoners had been tossed—had filled his nightmares for months. Razor's hooks and nets dragged those nightmares back. If that was what the Hold was like, Van had to know. He had to know *now.*

"What do they do down there?" he burst out. "In the Hold? With the hooks and the nets and the knives? Are they hurting them? Are they *killing* them?"

Behind their twinkly spectacles, Kernel's eyes went cold. "That's all the time I can give you," he said abruptly. "Pebble will show you out. Good night, Van Markson."

Pebble grabbed Van by the sleeve. She yanked him along, back through the doors, into the dimness of the corridor.

Van could hear Barnavelt, perched on her shoulder, saying, "I like carrot birthday cake, personally. Oh hi, Pebble! Where've you been all this time? I like carrot cake with walnuts in it. And cinnamon. And cream cheese frosting. And walnuts . . ."

Pebble started up the steps. Van staggered behind.

"Wait!" he called, trying to wrench his sleeve out of her grasp. "Why can't we go down to the Hold? Why won't you even tell me what's happening down there?"

Pebble tightened her grip on Van's sleeve until it crunched his bones. "Nobody is allowed in the Hold."

"Why *not*? Because they're doing something awful down there?"

Silently, Pebble yanked Van along. The farther they got from the depths, the clearer Lemmy's trusting little face became in Van's mind, and the harder and heavier grew the lump of horror in Van's stomach.

"Please tell me," he begged. "I have to know. Just tell me!"

But Pebble didn't answer.

She dragged him up the long, twisting staircase without turning back again. She climbed faster and faster, pounding up the final flight of steps, hauling Van along the corridor so quickly that the walls on either side became one long gray smear. She pulled him through the office, out the front door, onto the moon-lit street. And still she didn't slow down.

She ran until they turned a corner, and the dingy gray lump of the City Collection Agency faded out of sight. Then she spun around so suddenly that Van jumped back.

"Hey! It's Van!" squeaked Barnavelt from his perch on Pebble's shoulder. "Where have you been?"

Pebble stared straight into Van's face. "He showed you the Wish Eaters." She almost spat the words. "Didn't he?"

Van's mind whirled. The lump in his stomach knocked against his pounding heart. What did Pebble already know? How much truth could he tell her? And if he told—or *didn't* tell—would Razor come looking for him with those glinting metal hooks and—

"He showed you," said Pebble. "You don't have to say it. I can tell."

Van gulped.

"You saw all the little boxes in his hidden room," she went on, "and you think that Wish Eaters are these cute little fluffy things—"

"Oh, thank you." Barnavelt patted his whiskers modestly. "I suppose I *am* pretty fluffy."

"And you think they're all sweet and tiny and helpless." Pebble stepped closer to Van. "But do you know what *locusts* are?"

Van was pretty sure a locust was both a kind of tree and a kind of bug. His mind offered him a picture of a leaf with legs. "Kind of."

"Okay," said Pebble. "How about termites?"

"Well, I've never *seen* one—"

"But you know what they do. You know that they're swarms of little, tiny, helpless, hungry things that can destroy an entire house." Pebble's eyes went dark. "Uncle Ivor isn't a bad person," she said firmly. "But he's the kind of person who would keep a swarm of pet termites."

Van realized how chilly the air had grown. He shivered. He wished that he was home, safe under his own blankets, with his mother in her bedroom just down the hall. He glanced at Pebble. In her bulky coat, she didn't *look* chilly—but it was far, far colder than this in the underground chambers of the Collection. Van wondered how she slept down there, in the cold and the damp and the darkness. Did those awful roars ever wake her? Did she have a bedroom somewhere? Did she even have a bed?

"Don't you miss Mr. Falborg?" he asked. "He misses you."

Pebble looked almost surprised. She leaned back, her mossy eyes blinking. It took her a few seconds to reply—as if she had to think hard, or to dig out the answer from someplace where it had been buried. "Sometimes," she said at last. She gave Van a funny look. "But once you pick a side, you can't go back."

Van looked down at the pavement. If he met Pebble's eyes any longer, she'd be able to see straight through him, down to the spot where his secrets waited like a bunch of pennies in a pool of rippling water.

Pebble turned and walked on, down the deserted sidewalk. Van trotted beside her. They passed under a streetlight, and Van noticed that Pebble was rolling something small and glittery between her fingers. He had to squint to see it, but he was pretty sure that it was the marble he'd given her beside the fountain in the park, the very first time they'd met.

"Couldn't you be on both sides?" Van asked, watching Pebble turn the tiny glittering ball. "Maybe the Collectors would understand. Mr. Falborg *is* your family."

Pebble pointed back in the direction of the City Collection Agency. "That is my family."

"I mean your *real* family." Van studied Pebble's profile. "You must have had other people in your family too. What about your parents? What happened to them?"

Pebble glanced at Van, very quickly, from the corner of her eye. "I don't have them," she said. "I never had them."

"Everybody has a parent," Van argued. "Even if you don't know them. Even if they go away. You had to have them to be born."

"I wasn't born." Pebble stopped so suddenly that Van walked several steps without her. He turned and jogged back to the spot where she had flopped down on a broad stone stoop. Weak light from the glass doors above outlined her coat with threads of gold.

"Uncle Ivor wished me," she said.

Van was pretty sure he'd heard this wrong. *"What?"*

"That's how Collectors are made," said Pebble. "That's why we're . . . how we are. We're not like normal people. We see things normal people don't see and hear things they don't hear. We live longer than normal people can live. We don't get born. We're wished."

For a few terrifying seconds, Van's mind somersaulted backward through his entire trove of memories. He could see things other people didn't see, and he could hear the Creatures. But he had parents. And he'd been born. He was sure. He'd seen the hospital pictures.

"Oh," he breathed. "So all the other Collectors . . ."

"They came from wishes too," Pebble finished. "It takes a big wish to make a person. It can go wrong in a lot of ways. It's really risky. That's why Collectors only do it when they absolutely *need* to. That's why, right now, I'm the only young one."

Van knew what it was like to be the only kid in a world full of grown-ups. There weren't a lot of other children hanging around at opera houses. But to never see any other kids at all, and to have no family of your very own. . . . "That sounds lonely," he said.

Pebble shrugged her baggy shoulders. "That's why Uncle Ivor wished me." She turned the marble around and around in her fingertips. "He wanted company. Not just people who worked for him. Someone like him."

"No," said Van. "I meant—lonely for you."

Pebble shrugged again, a smaller, slower shrug. "Sometimes. But being different just has to be that way. Sometimes."

On her shoulder, Barnavelt was unusually quiet. Van noticed that the squirrel had pressed himself close to Pebble's cheek.

"I know I'm not exactly like you," Van began. "But I'm not *not* like you. So if it would help to have a friend, or something . . ."

"Well, it's not that I *need* it," said Pebble, still not looking at Van. She passed the marble from hand to hand. "But I guess it wouldn't hurt to have one."

"Right," said Van. "It wouldn't hurt."

Pebble closed the marble in her fist. "So, we are, then?"

"We're friends?"

"Are we?"

"Yes," said Van. "We're friends."

Pebble didn't answer this. But Van saw her give a small, hidden smile, her whole face transforming once again, as she dropped the marble back into her pocket.

They hurried the rest of the way to Van's street.

Pebble stopped at the corner, beneath the rustle of a big, dark tree.

"We'll come back for you soon," she told him. "Until then, just don't do anything stupid." She flashed him a last tiny grin before turning and racing off into the shadows.

"Goodnight, Minivan!" Van heard Barnavelt call, as both of them slipped out of sight.

Van tiptoed into the building, along the sleeping hallways, through his own apartment door. He couldn't hear his mother breathing behind her closed bedroom door, but he could sense her there—her warmth, a wisp of her perfume. He stepped into his own room. After closing the curtains and double-checking every corner, he pulled Lemmy's box out from under the bed.

The Wish Eater was fast asleep. It had curled into such a tiny lump that it looked like a tennis ball made of lint. But when the light of Van's bedside lamp hit it, it stirred. It blinked up at Van, its little face surprised and anxious, its eyes wide. Then it seemed to recognize him. Its face relaxed.

"Hi, Lemmy," Van whispered.

The creature gave a small smile. Then, with a shiver, it curled into a ball again.

"Are you cold?" Van asked. "You look like you might be cold."

Van dug through his drawers until he found his softest sweater—one his mother had bought in Italy, made from shaggy, silvery wool. He tucked it into the bottom of the box. The Wish Eater sidled carefully onto the sweater. It patted and sniffed at it for a moment before snuggling down and closing its eyes.

Van thought of Razor and his hooks, and the Hold's deep darkness, and that awful, stone-shaking howl. He thought about Pebble and Mr. Falborg and the little creature nuzzled in the box in his lap.

Maybe he could help them all somehow. Maybe, once he knew the truth, he could use it not just to free the Wish Eaters, but to show Pebble how unfair the Collectors could be, and to bring her safely back to someone who missed her so much. The thought filled him with electric warmth. At least he could try.

Gently, he shut the lid of Lemmy's box.

He slid the box back under the bed. He took out his hearing aids and placed them in their spot on the bedside table. He set Mr. Falborg's paperweight beside them. After changing into his pajamas, he switched off the bedside lamp and settled down into the pillows, softness and silence falling around him.

But his mind wasn't ready to shut off quite yet. It carried him back through the night, back to that moment when he'd stepped out of his window into the flying sleigh and glided off into the dark. Van smiled, wiggling his feet under the blankets. Kernel had been full of warnings about wishes and their powers, but he'd never mentioned how wondrous they could be.

Maybe the Collectors didn't want anyone to know. Maybe this was one more glittering, beautiful secret they were keeping hidden.

But now *Van* knew.

He nestled deeper into the pillows and closed his eyes.

In his dreams, he soared through forests leaping with silvery creatures, his long black cape billowing behind him, over hills and rivers, into a world where anything he hoped for could come true.

18
Hot Dog with the Works Pizza

VAN followed his mother up the sidewalk to the opera house. The day was bright and clear, the streets busy and the sidewalks bustling—but Van was too tangled in the memories of last night to notice anything else. The fact that he'd only gotten four hours of sleep didn't help either. He didn't spot the twenty-sided die in the opera's back entryway, or the snapped bracelet of purple glass beads that sparkled on the carpet in one corridor. He didn't even realize that his mother had turned left instead of right, and that they were heading away from the rehearsal rooms past a row of larger and larger offices, until suddenly his mother's ringing voice exclaimed, "Hello, Peter! How are you?"

They'd arrived at the doorway of Mr. Grey's office.

Inside, sprawled on one of the fancy leather couches, frowning at a video game, was Peter Grey. He looked up at them with his chilly, swimming-pool eyes.

Peter mumbled something Van couldn't quite hear—it sounded like *mine,* or *why,* or *die*—but he'd probably just said "Fine."

"Charles and I thought, as long as you're both stuck here during rehearsal, you'd have more fun *together.*" His mother's hand steered Van firmly into the room. "Have a good time!"

She swished quickly back out of the office.

Peter stayed where he was.

Van let his backpack thump down to the fancy rug. "I brought a comic book," he began. "So if you want to just keep playing your game, I can . . ." But Peter had gotten to his feet. He crossed the room so suddenly that Van took a flinching step back. "Come on," Peter muttered. A second later, he was disappearing through the door.

Van tagged behind him.

He was starting to feel like he spent all his time tagging behind someone. His mother. Pebble and Barnavelt. Peter. But he couldn't even ask Peter where they were going. He couldn't see Peter's face, and Peter always talked to him in such a mumbly, clenched-jaw way that it was hard to understand him even when they were face-to-face. So he just hurried after Peter's back, feeling more and more like a dog whom no one wanted to walk.

Peter led the way down two flights of stairs, along a back hallway, and out a metal door onto the sidewalk.

A rush of noise blasted around them. Garbage trucks roared by. Motors revved. Horns squealed.

"Wait," Van finally spoke up. "I'm not supposed to . . ." Ugh, he sounded like such a baby. Not at all like an important double agent. Not like SuperVan. "I promised I wouldn't leave the building."

Peter shrugged one shoulder. He kept walking. "Urgent . . . run . . . lock . . ."

"What?" Van shouted.

Peter stopped at last. He turned to face Van. "We're JUST going AROUND the BLOCK," he said, in such a loud, slow voice that every word sounded like an insult. Then he turned away again, striding fast enough that Van couldn't catch up.

Van chased Peter around the corner, past the plaza where rows of fountains shot spears of water into the air. Throngs of people wandered there, sipping from paper cups, talking on phones, taking pictures. Van tried to see if any of them were tossing coins into the pools of water—or if any black-coated figures were lurking nearby, watching, waiting. But Peter was already veering into a shop with a sign reading PAVAROTTI'S PIZZA—EVERY SLICE A TRIUMPH!

Van followed him through the swinging glass door.

The shop was one long, narrow room. A row of glass cases, all filled with pizzas and hot golden lights, ran from one end to the other. Each pizza had a little tag beside it, like a painting in an art museum. Van leaned down to look. There was Hot Dog with the Works Pizza. Mama's Homemade Lasagna Pizza. Spicy Chicken Curry Pizza. Peanut Butter and Jelly with Marshmallow Sauce Pizza. Van leaned even closer, and a barrage of strange and wonderful smells rushed up his nose and all the way down to his stomach.

"The MACARONI and CHEESE PIZZA is my FAVORITE," said Peter, still speaking in that slow, loud voice. "But they're ALL pretty GOOD. Except for the SCOTCH EGG one."

"Good to know," said Van.

"WHAT KIND do you WANT?"

"Oh." Van touched his pockets. "I don't have any money."

"I do." Peter nodded at the cases. "Just PICK."

"I guess . . . the macaroni and cheese one sounds good."

Peter ordered two slices. The man behind the counter passed them their pizza on paper plates, and Peter led the way to a tiny table in the corner.

"SEEEE?" said Peter, drawing out the word, after they'd both taken a bite. "It's GOOOOOD."

Van nodded, chewing. Then he took a deep breath. SuperVan would speak up. He would be calm and brave. "You don't have to talk like that."

Peter frowned. "Like what?"

"So loud and slow. I can understand you."

"Oh." Peter actually looked—was it *embarrassed?* He shoved a hand through his hair. "I just thought . . . because of your—"

"If I'm in a loud place, or outside, it's harder," said Van. "But if I'm near someone, and I can see their face, and there aren't too many other noises, it's usually okay."

"Oh," said Peter again. "Sorry."

There was a little pause.

"You're right," said Van. "The macaroni and cheese is really good."

They ate for a while. Then Peter lowered his slice and said, in a normal voice, "My dad and your mom had lunch alone together three times last week."

"What?" said Van.

"My DAD and YOUR—"

"I heard you. What do you *mean*?"

"I mean, they had lunch. At a restaurant. Three times. Just them." Peter stared impatiently into Van's face. "Like, a *date*."

Van, who had been picturing his mother and Mr. Grey sitting at a lonely, quiet table in a school cafeteria, suddenly saw the picture change. Now there were tablecloths. Candles. Little bottles of flowers. His mother and Mr. Grey leaning closer to each other, laughing, clinking their glasses together over and over, as he imagined people did on dates.

"How do you know?" he asked.

"I saw his calendar."

"But . . . when? I'm always with—"

"Once on Saturday," Peter interrupted. "When you weren't around. Twice during the week before that, when you were with the costumers or the prop people or something. It happened. Three times." Peter shrugged impatiently. "Why do you think your mom came to rehearsal so early today? Where do you think they are *right now?*"

Van swallowed a mouthful of pizza that suddenly tasted like Styrofoam. "Maybe they're just talking about work stuff," he said. "We might be going to England, so—"

Peter cut him off again. "Today my father told me I should *get used to being with you*. They're trying to make us be friends." Peter's eyes got even chillier. "You know why, right? If they keep dating, they'll probably get married. And then we'd be . . ."

The word fell out of Van's mouth like a bite of half-chewed food. "Stepbrothers."

Both boys went silent.

Van didn't know what Peter was thinking, but his own mind was leaping from one awful image to another. Sharing a bedroom with Peter. Snotty Peter and stuffy Mr. Grey sitting at the table at every meal. No more traveling alone with his mother, helping her navigate through new cities, finding the best ice-cream shop in every neighborhood. No more just the two of them.

"I just thought you should know," said Peter at last.

Van set down his pizza crust.

Peter met his eyes. "You don't *want* it to happen, do you?" he asked. "Them getting married?"

"No," said Van. "No." And then, just in case, *"No."*

Peter's eyes got a little less icy. "Me neither," he said. "On my birthday, I even wished . . ."

Van's ears pricked. *Peter Grey. June 8. Twelfth birthday.* But Peter didn't finish.

"You wished what?" Van prompted.

"Nothing," said Peter. "It's stupid."

"What was it? Did you wish your dad would get crushed by a giant macaroni and cheese pizza?"

Peter gave a snort that might actually have been a laugh. "No."

"You can tell me," said Van. "Or is it something really embarrassing? Like, did you wish you were a mermaid, so you could swim away from all of us?"

Now Peter gave something that was definitely a laugh. "No. I just . . ." He paused. "They say if you tell somebody your wish, it won't come true."

"They didn't tell *me* that," said Van, without thinking.

"What?"

"I mean—I've never heard that." Van took a last bite of pizza and tried to look casual. "Who really believes in *wishes*, anyway?"

"Fine." Peter let out a loud breath. "I wished my dad would stop dating your mom."

"Really?" said Van. "You didn't—maybe—wish that something *bad* would happen to my mom, or—"

"No," said Peter quickly. "Your mom's fine. I just don't want them to get married. That's all."

Van nodded. "Me neither."

"Maybe it won't even happen," said Peter, after a quiet moment. "Like I said, I just thought you should know."

He stood up and shoved his paper plate into the trash. Van followed him into the noise of the street, back to the doors of the opera house, with the macaroni and cheese pizza bubbling queasily in his stomach.

Van's mother was in a wonderful mood that night. She hummed throughout the whole walk home. Van tuned out the sounds of her voice and the traffic and the breeze and stared hard at the sidewalk instead.

Gum wrappers. Bottle caps. Lost buttons. Nothing good.

His mother gave his hand a tug. Van looked up. She was wearing her stage-lighting smile. "Giovanni," she began, "what would you think about staying here permanently?"

Van's heart launched upward like a rocket. He could feel it smash against the roof of his mouth. "What?" he choked. "I thought we were going to England!"

"That was just a possibility." His mother's smile got even brighter. "Charles has some ideas that would keep me here for the next few seasons. Maybe longer."

Van tried to control his voice, but it still came out sounding like a shout. "Opera ideas?"

"Yes. Mostly. I've been thinking that it might be time to settle in one spot. I could take a few students. Do some recording, work with small ensembles and new composers. There are lots of possibilities." She gave him a quizzical look. "What's wrong, Giovanni? Last night, you didn't want to leave, and now I tell you we might stay, and you look utterly miserable!"

"I . . ."

"You said you were starting to like it here. You're getting to know people. Am I wrong?"

"No," Van managed.

"Well then?" His mother's smile returned. "This is

just a new possibility. A new *probability.* Let's leave it at that for now."

They walked the rest of the way up to the apartment without speaking, Ingrid humming, Van drifting along behind her in a small, silent fog.

The moment his mother locked the door behind them, Van hurried down the hall and shut himself inside his bedroom.

He flopped down on the floor. He *couldn't* leave now. Not without helping the Wish Eaters. But he didn't want to stay if he'd have to do it as Peter Grey's step-brother. He was stuck between two painful things, like a piece of skin caught in a zipper.

Van reached for his collection. Maybe acting out the scene with Pawn Girl and the White Wizard and SuperVan would help. And maybe Lemmy would like to watch.

The little shoebox was just where Van had left it, nestled against the box of treasures. Van pulled it out and set it in his lap.

But when he lifted the lid, no misty little face appeared in the crack. No big eyes blinked up at him.

Fear jolted through Van. For an instant, he was sure that the box was empty.

He flung the lid aside.

And there—thank goodness—was Lemmy, still curled up in one corner.

The Wish Eater was trembling. Its misty body seemed fainter than before. It looked like condensation on a cold window, something a hand could smear away without even trying. Van reached out with one finger and brushed Lemmy's ruffly ear. Slowly the Wish Eater opened its eyes. It stared up at Van. It made a weak, groping gesture. Then, as if even that little motion had taken too much effort, it sagged back into the corner.

"Lemmy!" Van gasped. "What's wrong?"

The Wish Eater shivered. Then it gestured again, scooping one nubby little hand toward its mouth.

"You're hungry?" Van asked. "Is that it?"

The Wish Eater grasped Van's finger. Its grip was weak. Its eyes were pitiful.

"But I just fed you yesterday!" whispered Van. "Was that wish too tiring for you?" He leaned closer to the little creature. "You need to eat again? Is that right?"

Lemmy didn't answer. Its misty body trembled a little bit harder.

Panic started to slosh in Van's chest.

Could Lemmy really be hungry again so soon? And

why had he already used that stupid wishbone? What was he going to do?

There was only one person who might be able to answer any of these questions.

Van bolted out of his bedroom.

"Mom, can I use your phone?" he panted.

His mother glanced up from a musical score spread out on the table. Her arching eyebrows rose. "Why do you need it?"

"Um . . ." Van groped for a good answer. "I was just going to call Peter."

The surprise on his mother's face brightened into delight. "Really? Of course you can!" She held out her phone. "The Greys' home number is in my contacts."

Van rushed the phone back to his room and shut the door.

As a rule, Van hated the telephone. The flat, faceless voices were hard to understand. But now there was no choice. Tucking the phone under one arm, he dug through his treasure box until he'd uncovered the little white card printed with Mr. Falborg's phone number.

"Hallo?" Gerda's voice answered on the second ring.

"Um . . . hello?" Van stammered. "Um—Mrs. . . . Gerda? This is Van Markson. Is Mr. Falborg there?"

"Sorry . . . noction . . . won't be back . . . dayofter tomorrow . . . off raid."

"He's at an auction?" Van repeated. "He won't be back until the day after tomorrow?"

". . . Zit emergency?"

The last word was perfectly clear. Van halted. It certainly felt like an emergency. But could he trust Gerda? How much did she know? And how could he explain the awful mess he'd already made?

"Um . . . ," he swallowed. "No. I'll just—I'll talk to him when he gets back."

". . . Airy way. Nye, Mr. Markson."

Gerda hung up.

Now the panic in Van's chest was starting to freeze into a dry, cold lump. What could he do? What would SuperVan do?

Van dug through the treasure box again.

The blue glass bottle was still there, wrapped in its drawstring bag, at the very bottom. Van lifted the bottle to the light. The glass glimmered. The silvery wisp twirled inside like a dreamy ballet dancer. *Peter Grey. June 8. Twelfth birthday.*

Peter had said he wished that his father would stop dating Van's mother. If Van had had another wishbone, he might have made the very same wish. But what if Peter hadn't told him the whole truth? Van remembered the way Peter had glared at him from the other side of the birthday cake just before blowing out the candles. What if he had wished for Van and his mother to disappear? Or worse?

Van paused, feeling the lump of panic grow even icier. What if Peter's wish really *shouldn't* come true?

Van glanced down at Lemmy's box. The Wish Eater was still crumpled in one corner, but it followed every twinkle of the blue glass bottle. Van saw hunger and hope in its foggy little eyes. It couldn't wait. Not for days, until Mr. Falborg came back. Not even for the next few hours, while Van tried to come up with another plan. It needed him.

He had to take the risk. He had to hope that Peter had told the truth. And he had to hope that the way the wish came true was as unterrible as possible.

Maybe Mr. Grey and Van's mother would have an argument. Maybe Mr. Grey would find another girlfriend. Maybe Van's mother would realize that Mr. Grey was an obnoxious snob, and that she would rather not spend time with him anymore, and that she and Van should do fun things alone together again instead. That wouldn't be terrible at all.

"You're going to be all right," Van whispered to Lemmy. "I'll take care of you."

Like he was trying to scoop up a soap bubble without popping it, Van gathered Lemmy into one hand. He'd never held anything so light.

With his other hand, he tugged the cork free. The bottle opened with a little pop. The wisp of smoke twirled out of the glass and straight toward Lemmy's mouth, like a chilly breath in reverse.

Van felt a shimmery softening in the air. In his hand, the Wish Eater stopped shaking. Its fuzzy outlines already looked firmer. Its face wasn't fearful and hungry anymore. It turned toward Van with a tiny, grateful smile.

"Did it work?" Van whispered.

As if in answer, his mother's cell phone began to flash. Van set Lemmy on the floor and jumped to his feet.

"Mom!" he called, rushing the phone down the hallway before his mother could come to get it. "Your phone is ringing!"

"Ah. It's Leola," said his mother, glancing at the screen. "We need to discuss extending my contract here. Thank you, *caro mio*."

"You're welcome!" called Van, streaking back to his room.

By the time he stepped inside, Lemmy had climbed onto the floor of the miniature stage. The Wish Eater clambered around the figurines Van had left there: SuperVan, the china squirrel, the White Wizard. Its nubby fingers patted playfully at the wizard's robes.

"You look like you're feeling better, at least," said Van, as the Wish Eater hopped to the wizard's other side. And it was true. Lemmy looked more solid—and perhaps slightly larger—than just a minute before. The Wish Eater's happy little face sparkled like dew in sunlight. "*Are* you feeling better?"

The Wish Eater didn't answer. But a moment later, the tip of the wizard's white plastic staff began to glow.

Both Lemmy and Van stared as the glow brightened, forming a ball of lightning-bug gold that lit the whole stage. The glow fell over the little china squirrel, who sat up, grooming its whiskers and flicking its tail, and over SuperVan—who raised both arms and took off into the air.

Van let out a gasp.

SuperVan spiraled toward the ceiling. His tiny black cape billowed behind him. Before his little plastic fists could hit the plaster, he turned and sailed back down to hover just in front of Van's face. When Van reached out to touch the figurine, it zipped out of reach. Van laughed out loud. SuperVan circled his head, performing a series of perfect barrel rolls, one after the other.

Van glanced at Lemmy. The little creature crouched on the glowing stage, looking back and forth between the enchanted toys and Van's face. Each time Van smiled, it smiled too.

This was too much fun, Van thought. *Lemmy* was too much fun. Not only could the little creature grant wishes, but it could make this kind of playful magic. How could Mr. Falborg resist letting them scamper around, making magic, all day long? Of course, Mr. Falborg had said that feeding them all was tricky. And Van was now completely out of food.

"Lemmy," said Van. "Don't wear yourself out. I don't have—"

Before he could finish, the bedroom door flew open.

Van felt the gust of air. He whirled around to see his mother coming in.

The squirrel froze. SuperVan plummeted onto Van's bed. The wizard's staff went dark. Lemmy ducked behind the stage's velvet curtains.

"Giovanni!" His mother's face was incandescent. "Such amazing news! They want me for the next opera at *La Scala*!" Van's mother shouted those words the way most people shouted *"Disney World!"*

Van blinked. "What?"

"It's *very* short notice." His mother waved her hand. "Someone got sick, and someone *else* got fired, but that's supposed to be a secret. Anyway . . . La Scala! That gorgeous opera house! Summer in Italy! Gelato!"

"But . . ." Van felt as though time had picked him up, dragged him backward, and plunked him down in the middle of a problem he'd just solved. "But—when would we leave?"

"As soon as possible. Charles will *not* be happy." His mother's sunny face clouded. "But our arrangements weren't official yet. I think he'll understand." She waved her hand again. "I'll speak with him tomorrow, and then we'll pack up and go!"

Van wanted to seal both hands over his ears and scream. But he could only gape up at his mother, trying to look like he wasn't crumbling into a pile of panic. "What about what you said—about settling down here for a while?"

"Giovanni . . ." His mother bent down and ruffled

his hair. "This is an opportunity I can't pass up. There's no telling what doors it will open." She straightened up again. "Italy! Gelato!" She paused beside the door, her fingernails tapping the frame. "If Charles is really, *really* unhappy . . . it might be just a few days."

Something cold and hard clunked through Van's chest.

His mother threw him one more smile, and blew a kiss to go with it. "Don't stay up too late, *caro mio.*"

The door thumped shut.

Van slumped against the side of the bed. He wrapped his arms over his head.

What had he done?

Peter's wish had come true. Van's mother and Mr. Grey weren't just separating. Soon they would be an entire ocean apart. And Van would be crossing that ocean too. The chance to save the Wish Eaters, to help both Pebble and Mr. Falborg, to be part of the magic of the Collection, would be over.

The wish had ruined everything. He was back where he'd started, with no wishes to spare. And now he had even less time.

Lemmy peeped around the curtain.

Van dropped his arms. "Why did you make it so

we'd have to *leave*?" His voice threatened to become a shout. "I can't take you *with* me! And now all the other Wish Eaters will still be stuck, and I'll be—" His throat clenched. "I'll be gone."

The Wish Eater cowered. It stared at Van around the strip of velvet. Its foggy eyes seemed to shimmer with tears.

Maybe it was those tears that did it, because Van's anger suddenly sizzled out. This wasn't Lemmy's fault. It was *his*. Pebble and Kernel had warned him about how unpredictably wishes could come true. And he hadn't listened. Or he hadn't cared. He sagged down to the floor, bringing his eyes to the creature's level.

"I'm sorry, Lemmy," he murmured. "You didn't try to make things worse. You just did what you do." He leaned over and buried his face in his arms. "But now what do *I* do?"

Van stayed like that, head bowed, holding himself, for a very long time. The room grew darker. The night beyond the windows grew quieter. At last, Van felt a pair of dewy little hands on either side of his neck. Lemmy was holding him too.

And Van made up his mind.

19
Footsteps in the Dark

VAN lay in bed, staring at the ceiling, as wide awake as he'd been two hours before.

Thoughts fizzed inside of him like soda pop. His brain whirred. His toes twitched. His hearing aids lay in their nighttime spot on the table, and still his head was full of an impatient buzz.

He rolled onto his side. In the gap beneath his bedroom door, he could see a yellow band of light, which meant that his mother hadn't yet gone to bed.

Van counted the breaths that whooshed in and out of his body. He felt the rumble of his pounding heart. He pressed a hand against Lemmy's box, tucked under the covers beside him.

At last the yellow light winked out. The hall went dark.

Van slid out of bed. He wedged Lemmy's box under one arm and shoved his feet into a pair of loafers. He dropped a penny into his pajama pocket. He left his hearing aids on the table. He didn't want the distracting blur of sounds in his head tonight. He needed his eyes to be sharp and his mind to be clear.

Slowly he inched the bedroom door open. His mother's door was shut. Van tiptoed out of his bedroom and slunk along the hallway, through the kitchen. He'd had practice at this now. He felt like an actual spy: stealthy, confident, senses honed for a secret mission. He slipped through the apartment door.

"Giovanni?" his mother's drowsy voice called.

Van didn't hear it.

He pattered down the stairs, across the lobby, through the big brass-handled doors, and out into the night.

The air was cool and dewy. It slid under his cuffs and into his sleeves like the water in a shallow stream. Holding Lemmy's box tight, Van broke into a run.

In daylight, the streets around the park bustled with shops and sidewalk cafes. At night, the same streets looked abandoned. The shops were dark, with cages pulled across their windows and doors. The café chairs had been piled up and put away. There were no noisy, strolling, jostling crowds—just one boy in plaid pajamas, racing down the sidewalk.

Van slipped through the gates. It was damper and darker here inside the park. The scents of earth and water and blooming flowers wound around him with the breeze. The fear thumping in his chest began to fade.

Of course he couldn't hear the footsteps padding through the darkness behind him.

Van hurried across the cool grass. Thorns snagged on his pajamas as he cut through a rose bed. A stem scratched his ankle, but Van didn't look down. Collectors could be watching him at this very instant. If he was about to be grabbed by Jack and his men, at least he would make his wish first.

In the blackness over Van's shoulder, a twig snapped.

Van didn't hear it.

He pressed close to the basin of the fountain. Falling droplets spattered his hands. He set Lemmy's box on the basin and lifted the lid. In the dimness, he could just make out the misty little creature craning up, sniffing at the breeze.

Van fished the penny out of his pajama pocket.

He needed this wish to come true and stay true. He needed his mother to remain in the city, and the longer the better—but not because of snooty Mr. Grey. And he needed her not to change her plans if a better job came along. Could he squeeze everything he wanted into one little wish?

Van closed his eyes. He clasped the penny so hard that its edges left dents in his palm.

I wish that my mother and I would stay here for a long time.

Van opened his eyes and threw. The penny hit the water. Now, glowing around the coin, Van could see the green-gold light of the waiting wish.

Lemmy pawed after it like a bear cub catching salmon. Its nubby fingers grabbed the glowing disk. The coin, stripped of its light, sank to the bottom of the pool, and the Wish Eater sat down in its box again, its hands wrapped around the luminous disk. It opened its mouth.

The air stilled. Everything shimmered. The wish disappeared into Lemmy's mouth.

At the same instant, out of the corner of his eye, Van saw the bushes shiver.

A tall, dark shape—a shape dressed in a long dark coat—lurched toward him.

Van's heart shot upward.

He crammed the lid onto Lemmy's box. A tiny part of his brain, somewhere far in the back where panic hadn't quite swamped everything, realized that the lid could barely close. Clutching the box, he darted away from the fountain, away from the shape in the long dark coat that was already running after him.

Van raced across the grass. He steered for the shadows, even though they could hide roots to trip on and trees to crash into and things with staring, sharp black eyes. He knew he couldn't outrun a Collector—not a grown-up one, anyway. But maybe he could outmaneuver one.

Van lunged through a row of shrubs. A twig flicked his left eye. His vision bleared. Wincing and blinking, he stumbled onward—straight into a wrought-iron fence.

He'd reached the edge of the park. There was no time to find a gate. Pinning Lemmy's box under one arm, Van climbed up onto the crossbars. His feet were narrow enough, and his body was light enough, that he could use the iron whorls near the top for another foothold. From there, he jumped down to the pavement on the other side.

His feet hit the sidewalk with a painful *thwack*. Van almost lost his grip on the box. He straightened up, his eye burning, his legs throbbing. Bushes and shadows rippled behind him. The Collector was only a few steps away.

Van lunged across the street. Maybe he could hide in an alley. Maybe he could make it around the corner and disappear before the Collector saw where he'd gone.

He pounded up onto the opposite curb. The sidewalk was deserted. No one was there to notice one small boy tearing down the street. No one was there to save him.

Behind him, he thought he heard someone shout.

But his blood was thundering in his ears, and he knew his imagination was running away with him.

His burning eye refused to stay open. Shutting it made Van lose his balance. And his good eye was behaving strangely too. He could see his reflection in the dark windows beside him, looking small and terrified—but he could have sworn his reflection was dressed in a superhero's bodysuit, with a long black cape flying out behind. Van ventured one quick glance down at

Lemmy's box. The Wish Eater's head was thrust out below the lid, its eyes wide, a tiny smile on its face.

Van skidded to an intersection. The cross street was a busy one. Cars zoomed past, their headlights leaving streaks on his watery vision. Without waiting for the light to change, Van plunged out into the street. He felt the whoosh of a car just behind him, and saw the glint of another car just in front of him, and then he was staggering safely onto the sidewalk.

He'd just had time to let out a breath when, through the blur and the pounding and the darkness, there came one clear, powerful scream.

Van knew that scream.

He spun around.

His mother lay beside the curb. She'd thrown a long dark coat over her silk pajamas. Coils of coppery hair spilled around her face. Her leg was bent at an impossible angle. A taxi rolled to a stop beside her, its driver's door already swinging open. More cars slowed. People began to appear, popping out of doorways, collecting like ants around a spilled ice-cream cone.

Van inched nearer.

His mother was still screaming.

"Giovanni!"

Her voice seemed to come from very far away, even while Van tiptoed closer and closer, until finally she could reach out and grab the hem of his pajama pants. He didn't hear the sound of the sirens until he and his mother and the box in his arms were all washed with the pulses of blue and red light.

20
They're Coming

"WHY on earth did you *DO* that?" Ingrid Markson was shouting. "Couldn't you hear me calling you?"

"I wasn't wearing my hearing aids," said Van, who still wasn't. But shut inside a tiny, brightly lit hospital room, he had no trouble understanding his mother at all.

"Why did you leave the apartment in the first place?" Her voice made the walls ring. "Why, in the name of everything that makes *sense,* would you go running *out of the house* into the city *alone* in the *middle of the NIGHT?"*

Van knew opera singers were supposed to be able to shatter champagne glasses with their voices. He'd never seen his mother do this, but he was pretty sure he saw the glass in the door tremble.

"I don't know," he said.

"You don't *know*?" his mother repeated. "You're not even going to tell me a story about a stray cat or dog or some other creature you saw out the window?"

Van glanced at the windowpane. It wouldn't have surprised him to see a squirrel or bird or other creature staring in at him through the blinds, watching his every move.

"I think," he began, "maybe I was having a bad dream."

"Oh, *Giovanni*!" His mother's head flopped dramatically back onto the hospital bed. Except for the bulky white cast covering one leg, she would have looked like she was playing a tragic opera scene. "What am I going to do with you?"

"I don't know," said Van again. A painful lump swelled in his throat. "I'm sorry, Mama."

He wanted to throw himself onto her bed and let her wrap him up in a big, lily-scented hug, but he wasn't sure if that would hurt her even more, or if she was too angry to hug him anyway. So he stayed where he was.

A nurse and a doctor bustled in. The bumpy blur of their voices filled the room. Van rubbed his sore eye. He was suddenly exhausted, slumping there in an armchair, in his pajamas, wrapped in a blue hospital blanket. Lemmy's shoebox rested in his lap, hidden by the blanket's folds. Everyone had been too worried about his mother to notice it. Van pulled the blanket tighter.

In a twisted, terrible sense, his wish had worked. His mother couldn't take a job in Italy now. But the *way* that the wish had come true . . .

Van shuddered.

It was just a broken leg. His mother would be all right. It could have been worse. When Van imagined how *much* worse, he felt like he might throw up. He clamped his hands around Lemmy's box. He wouldn't make another wish for a very long time.

Maybe ever.

The blanket started to warm him at last. Van's head drooped. His eyes were halfway shut when the door swung open yet again.

Charles and Peter Grey strode into the hospital room.

Mr. Grey wore a long trench coat over a pair of slacks. Peter was dressed in his pajamas: dark gray pants and a matching thermal shirt. Cool pajamas. Not like the plaid ones Van was wearing. Van pulled his legs out of sight.

His mother's face brightened. One hand flew to her hair. She straightened her shoulders. "Oh, Charles," Van heard her voice through the fog. ". . . So *sweet* of you . . ."

"Well . . . sibling . . . *alone* . . . ," Mr. Grey's voice murmured back.

Peter's eyes moved around the room. They landed on Van like the smash of an ice-cold water balloon. Van's chest squeezed.

He made a little wish that he knew wouldn't come true. He wished that Peter could know what he was thinking; that just by looking at him, Peter would see that none of this was what Van wanted.

Peter's chilly eyes flicked away again.

The doctors and nurse talked, and Van's mother talked, and Mr. Grey talked, their voices filling the room with noisy fog. Minutes later, Ingrid Markson was settled into a wheelchair, and the whole group squeezed out the door into the hall.

A van and driver waited outside the hospital lobby doors. Some orderlies helped Mr. Grey fold Van's mother and the wheelchair into the middle of the van. Peter climbed into the back. Mr. Grey took the front passenger seat.

"*Climb in*, Giovanni," called his mother's voice from

inside, as though she'd already said this more times than she wanted to.

Van squeezed inside next to his mother. Somebody slammed the door after him, and they all rolled away through the nearly dawn darkness.

His mother and Mr. Grey spoke, but Van didn't even try to follow. He held Lemmy's box tight and leaned his head against the window. The hum of the motor and the vibration of the glass erased everything around him. He let his eyes slide shut.

When the van rolled to a stop some time later, Van sat back, blinking. He gazed through the window.

This wasn't the right building. This wasn't the right street. This was a block of stuffy stone houses. And the one right before them was Peter's stuffy stone house.

"Why are we here?" Van asked, realizing from the way that Mr. Grey turned to frown at him that he had already been speaking.

"Mother . . . elephant . . . someone to . . . aisle . . . ," said Mr. Grey.

Van stared at his mother's face.

"Charles and Peter are so incredibly kind, they're letting us stay with them for a while," she said clearly. And pointedly.

"But—"

"Just until I can get around with crutches. Isn't that *kind* of them, Giovanni?" Her stare was like a shove.

"Yes," said Van.

The driver of the van helped Mr. Grey hoist Van's mother out of her seat and back into the wheelchair. They boosted her up the steps to the front door. Peter and Van followed. Van clutched Lemmy's box. Peter glared straight ahead, not looking at anyone.

Once they were shut inside the big stone house, words began to swim through the fog.

"Emma, the nanny, go to your apartment . . . things . . . tomorrow . . . ," Mr. Grey was saying. "List . . . exactly . . . chew on . . . to bring back."

"Really, Charles," said Van's mother. "This is too much."

Mr. Grey reached down and took her hand. "It's nothing."

Van saw Peter's face tighten.

"For now . . . comfortable as we can. Ingrid . . . bed for you downstairs . . . sitting room. Giovanni, you . . . RED GUEST ROOM. Peter . . . shoot ache him there."

Without speaking, Peter turned and stalked up the

curving staircase. He didn't glance back, not even when they reached the upper hall.

They stopped at the third door on the right.

"Here," mumbled Peter.

He shoved the door open. Inside was a guest room with red walls, one big window, and a gray-blanketed bed.

Peter started to walk away.

"Wait, Peter," Van called. "I'm sorry. I mean—I didn't want this to happen. I wanted the *opposite* of this to happen."

Peter glared at the floor. His mouth moved, letting out words Van couldn't catch.

"*I* don't want to be here," Van went on, in what he hoped was a loud, but not *too* loud, whisper. "I don't want my mother to be here. I don't want this."

Peter's eyes snapped up. He stared at Van for a second. Then he said, very clearly, "But it's *your fault*."

Van couldn't argue with that.

He stood in the guest-room doorway, clenching Lemmy's box in both arms, as Peter stalked into his own room and slammed the door.

Sleeping in a strange bed, no matter how soft and pillowy and well blanketed that bed is, and no matter how exhausted you are, is never as easy as sleeping in your own. And Van's body buzzed with so many furies and fears that he could barely hold still.

His mother's scream as she lay in the street. Mr. Grey's hand on his mother's shoulder. Peter's ice-water eyes. Van tucked Lemmy's box under the blanket beside him. Then he untucked it again and lifted the lid for a peek.

Lemmy was sleeping sweetly, wrapped up in its own misty arms.

Van felt a tiny bit better.

They might be in a strange house, but the people he cared about would be all right. His mother's leg would heal. The Wish Eater would be safe in its shoebox, loved and watched over by Van—at least, until it got hungry again. But he would think about that problem later.

He tucked the box back in.

The blankets on the guest room bed smelled like lavender sachets. The sheets grew warmer and softer as Van's weight settled into them. He shut his eyes. Silence and lavender grayness surrounded him.

He couldn't hear the tapping at the guest-room window.

He couldn't hear it growing louder and faster as whatever was tapping tapped harder.

He couldn't hear the *shush* of the window sliding open. The feet hitting the carpet. Padding toward his bed.

He only knew that something had gotten inside when it landed on his chest.

Van shot up, barely stifling a scream.

A squirrel was clutching his pajama collar. Van looked past Barnavelt, into Pebble's pale, panicked face.

"They're coming," she whispered.

21
Hold on Tight

VAN wormed back against the headboard.

"What?" he gasped. "Who's coming?"

Pebble's face was gray in the predawn light. Van could catch only one of her words, but that word was enough. *"Razor."*

Van's skin prickled. "Why?"

Pebble gave her head an impatient shake. *"Because.* They *know."*

"They know what?"

"About the *Eater,"* Pebble practically growled. "Somebody . . ." Her lips moved faster, and Van lost the thread of the words.

"What did she say?" he asked Barnavelt.

"She says, 'Somebody saw you because you made

a wish in a public park with an Eater right beside you, you *moron*.'" Barnavelt tilted his head. "Oh. Sorry."

"What are they going to do?" Van asked.

Pebble said something else fast and forcefully.

"She says, 'They're going to put it where it belongs,'" squeaked Barnavelt. "Hey, what happened to your spaceship sheets?"

"Are they going to put it in the Hold?" Van's throat was tight. "Will they hurt it?"

Pebble paused. Van thought he heard her say "no" or "don't know." He hugged Lemmy's box tighter, hoping the creature couldn't hear.

"What should I do?" he whispered.

"Nothing," said Pebble firmly. "Just give it to them."

Barnavelt nodded in agreement. "Just give it to them," he echoed. "That will be the very best thing for everybody. Well—*almost* everybody."

Van tried to picture himself handing Lemmy over to Razor, with his scarred face and his gleaming hooks, and his mind switched off like an unplugged TV. He couldn't do it. Not even in his imagination. There was no way he could place tiny, trusting Lemmy in the Collectors' hands.

"If you think I should just let them take it," said Van, "then why are you warning me?"

"Because." Pebble leaned very close to him, her face intent. She grabbed his hand. Van had the feeling that, for once, Pebble wasn't about to drag him somewhere—she was just holding on tight. *"Don't try to fight them.* Please. You could get hurt. And I don't want . . . I don't want *that."* Her eyes flicked to the window. "Better go."

"Wait!" Van scrambled to his knees, still holding the box. "When are they coming?"

Pebble shrugged. "Soon," Van thought she said, though it might have been "noon" or "two." She threw a leg over the sill. *"Barnavelt."*

The squirrel stopped nosing the blankets. "Oh! Hi, Van!" he exclaimed. "Fancy meeting you here! What a small world!"

"Barnavelt!" said Pebble.

The squirrel leaped to her shoulder. "Pebble!" he squeaked. "So good to see you! It's been ages!"

Pebble gave Van a last look before disappearing over the windowsill. "Just . . . be safe," she said.

Be safe. Or "be brave." Or "face it." Van wasn't sure which.

Then he was left alone, crouched in the middle of the guest-room bed, holding tight to the little cardboard box.

He peeped inside.

Lemmy was still asleep. As the box opened, the creature turned over. It gave Van a sleepy smile.

That smile landed on Van like one last drop of water in a sink about to overflow.

Certainty flooded through him. So what if he got hurt? There was no way he could *let* Razor take his defenseless little friend. No way at all.

Van kicked his legs out of bed. With Lemmy's box under one arm, he grabbed the pillows and the soft gray blanket.

The guest room closet was empty except for a white bathrobe and an extra set of sheets. Van shoved these aside. He spread half the blanket on the floor, arranged the pillows, crawled inside, and shut the closet door behind him.

No one was going to sneak up on him here.

With his body curled protectively around Lemmy's box, Van lay down. He honed his senses, feeling the soft vibration of water pipes in the floor, watching the thread of moonlight beneath the door, smelling the dusty lavender of the blanket. After minutes, or hours, he finally fell asleep.

There was light slipping under the closet door.

It was brighter than the peachy glow of morning, so Van knew he had been sleeping for a while. Or that someone had turned on the light in the room outside.

A shadow flickered across the strip of light.

Van froze. Without his hearing aids, he couldn't catch any sounds from beyond the door. But someone was there. Someone tall. Moving slowly.

Van held his breath, and Lemmy's box, as hard as he could.

The light in the gap disappeared, blocked by someone's body—or by the edges of a long, dark coat. The shadow halted there. Waiting. Listening.

Van's heart banged like a marble in an empty tin can.

He pressed himself into the closet's corner, trying to hide behind a hanging bathrobe. The closet door inched open.

Desperately, he shoved Lemmy's box out of sight behind his back.

Daylight poured in. Van squinted up at the silhouette in the doorway.

It was Emma, the nanny.

"Well, hello," he saw her say. ". . . who . . . ride?"

"Yes," Van gasped. "I'm all right."

"How . . . breakfast?"

"Oh," said Van, wishing both that his heart wasn't pounding so hard and that he wasn't crouching at the bottom of someone else's guest-room closet. "Sure."

Van kept Lemmy's box in his lap as he ate a bowl of cereal in the Greys' kitchen, and afterward, he left it within reach while he changed into a borrowed set of Peter's too-large clothes. He brought it along when he and Emma went to the apartment to fetch a few important things, including Van's hearing aids. He held it during the taxi ride back to the Greys', and while he and Emma played a game of Scrabble with his mother, and while Peter came down the stairs, glared into the living room at the three of them, and then stomped back up to his own room.

He even kept the box in his lap when they all sat down together at the dinner table.

Mr. Grey gave him a funny look before finally asking, "What's in the box, Giovanni?"

"Just . . . part of my collection," said Van.

"Nobody wants to steal your stupid collection," muttered Peter.

"Peter," said Mr. Grey.

"What?" Peter frowned at his father. "He probably couldn't even hear me."

"I could hear you," said Van quietly.

But nobody seemed to hear *him*.

After dinner, Peter charged back up to his room. Emma cleared plates, and Mr. Grey and Van's mother lingered at the table, finishing their desserts and telling stories about opera friends. Van slunk away. He carried Lemmy's box upstairs to the guest bathroom. He peeked under the lid, just to be sure—Lemmy was drowsing peacefully—and arranged the box on the counter before taking out his hearing aids, undressing, and climbing into the shower.

Van had washed in hundreds of apartments and hotels, and it didn't take him too long to figure out how to turn on the Greys' fancy shower nozzle. Under the spray of warm water, Pebble's warning started to rinse away. Maybe she had been wrong. Maybe no one was coming after all. Or maybe it had just been a trick to scare him—something to make him hand Lemmy over, or reveal Mr. Falborg's secrets.

He would just have to be smart, and careful, and not let them see that he was afraid.

He *wasn't* afraid.

Dun da dun DUN, dun da dun . . .

Van hummed to himself under the hiss of water. He closed his eyes and scrubbed his face. A patch of darkness fluttered over the shower curtain.

Van's eyes flew open. Soap stung them, but he didn't blink.

"Hello?" he whispered.

If there was an answer, Van couldn't hear it.

He waited. There were no more shadows.

Van counted to thirty, never blinking, not even when droplets splashed into his eyes.

Nothing.

Finally Van let his body relax. He turned back to the showerhead, scrubbing the soap away and picking up the shampoo.

Dun da dun DUN . . .

Another shadow slid over the curtain. The fabric gave an almost imperceptible ripple. From the corner of one bleary eye, Van thought he saw a patch of darkness receding, like a spill pouring backward into a bottle.

He grabbed the shower curtain and whipped it aside, hoping—too late to do anything about it—that Peter or

Mr. Gray or Emma *wouldn't* be standing there, staring back at him.

But the bathroom was empty. His hearing aids sat, undisturbed, by the sink. Lemmy's box was safely shut.

Van took a deep breath. It had been his imagination. Again.

He finished showering as speedily as he could. Then he dried off with one of the Greys' cushy towels, wriggled into his least-embarrassing stripy pajamas, and put on his slippers.

He padded down the hall to the red room with Lemmy's box securely in his arms.

Once the door was shut behind him, he pulled the shades, checked the corners, and sat down in the middle of the bed.

He lifted the lid.

The box was empty.

22
Another Broken Bone

VAN rushed to the bedroom door. The hallway was deserted. He tore back across the guest room, ripping the shades apart to stare out the window. But there was no one in the yard below, or in the alleyway beyond the vine-coated brick wall, or anywhere, as far as he could see.

Van clenched his hands. His pulse pounded. His veins were full of stinging bees.

What could he do? He couldn't tell anyone—at least not anyone *here*—what had just happened, not without having to explain too many other impossible things. And he couldn't let the Wish Eater go, either. Not when he knew who must have taken it. Not when he knew where they were headed.

Van shoved the window up and craned out.

A wide stone ledge ran below the guest-room window. The ledge ran all the way across the back of the house, sticking out in a wider spot over the windows of the dining room.

Before he could worry himself out of it, Van swung one leg over the windowsill. He set his slippered foot on the ledge, just like Pebble must have done the night before. And if Pebble had done it, why couldn't he?

He dragged his second leg through the window and balanced on the ledge, his back pressed hard against the wall. The ground was dauntingly far away. Only the thought of tiny, terrified Lemmy being jostled through the city, not knowing what lay ahead, kept him from climbing straight back inside.

Leaning against the wall, Van shuffled sideways until the ledge widened. There he turned around, crouched on his hands and knees, and inched backward toward the edge. If he held on to the ledge with both hands until the very last second, the drop to the ground wouldn't be *that* far. At least that's what Van told himself.

He dangled one leg, and then the other, over the ledge. Clamping his hands around the stones, Van pushed backward. There was a short plunge, and Van found himself hanging like a wet wind sock just outside the tall windows of the dining room, where Mr. Grey and his mother were seated.

Fortunately, they were facing away from the window.

Van took a deep breath. Then he let go.

He hit the ground with both feet. A painful jolt lanced up through his slippers into his shins, and Van couldn't help letting out a little *oof.* Before the pain had faded away, he was scrambling across the grass and using the big stone planter to climb over the yard's back wall once again.

He raced out into the twilit city.

Block after block after block streaked by. Van didn't think about his tired legs, or his aching lungs, or all the trouble he might find himself in when he finally got back to the Greys' house again. He didn't think of anything but little Lemmy.

So it wasn't until he was panting up the walk to the big white house that Van remembered Mr. Falborg wasn't at home.

His pounding heart sank into his stomach.

But there must be something he could do on his own. Especially if he had the help of a wish or two.

Van veered off the walkway into the hedges. Through the leaves, he could see the glow of lights in a few of the house's windows. Maybe Mr. Falborg had come home early. And even if he hadn't, maybe Van could sneak in through a back window and make his way up to the hidden room where—

Van's feet flew out from under him. His body tilted backward. His spine hit the lawn with a painful smack.

Someone craned over him.

In the dimness, Van could just make out the features of a craggy face.

Hans.

Hans's lips moved. A trickle of sound worked through Van's pounding heart and panting breath, but he couldn't make out any words. Because, as Van remembered with a sinking feeling, he'd left his hearing aids on the Greys' bathroom counter.

"I—" Van gasped. "I need *help.*"

Hans held out a warm, calloused hand. He pulled Van to his feet, saying something else in his rumbly accent. It was too dim for Van to see his lips, but he knew what it meant when Hans gestured to the front door.

Van followed him into the house.

Gerda sat in the big black-and-white kitchen, drinking tea and sorting mail at a square white table. Renata lay on a stack of envelopes beside her. They both looked up as Hans and Van entered. Gerda's eyes widened with surprise. Renata looked as bored as ever.

Gerda rose from her chair. She gestured for Van to take it, saying something that ended with ". . . do for you?"

Van stayed on his feet. "I forgot Mr. Falborg wouldn't be here," he said carefully. Gerda and Hans exchanged a look as Van went on. "He let me borrow something. But somebody stole it. I'm afraid they're going to hurt it." A hard, sticky lump was forming in Van's throat. He swallowed. "I just thought, maybe . . . if I could use *another* of Mr. Falborg's things, I might be able to get it back."

Gerda and Hans traded another look. Then Gerda leaned closer to Van.

"Choose a small box," said her lips. "And wish very carefully."

Van gave a start.

Gerda's mouth curled into a small smile. "We don't yest take care of de *house*, you know."

Hans ushered Van swiftly up to the hidden room.

"We would go with you, Gerda and I," he said, stopping to face Van after unlocking the doors. "But we would be recognized."

"Recognized?" Van repeated. "Do the Collectors know you?"

"Oh, yes," said Hans. "They know all about us. To our misfortune."

Hans reached through the doors and turned on the light.

Van watched Hans pause, surveying the room—probably checking for spiders or bats or missing boxes—before striding across the floor to the locked trunk. He opened it, pulling out two wishbones.

"Take an extra bone with you," he told Van. "In case."

Then he handed Van the bones, gave the room one last glance, and went out, shutting the doors behind him.

Van was left alone.

. . . But not *really* alone.

Van turned in a slow circle, surrounded by the rows and rows of boxes. He could feel the quiet, misty breathing of the hundreds of contained creatures. He lifted one of the wishbones. Instantly, he sensed the air change, as if all that misty breathing had gotten a bit faster. The Eaters were awake. They could smell food. And they surrounded him on every side, waiting, hungry . . . Van remembered Pebble's words about a swarm of termites.

But *one* Wish Eater wasn't dangerous. And he only needed one.

Putting the spare wishbone in his pocket, Van grasped the very smallest box on the very lowest shelf.

He sat down on the floor and lifted the lid.

At first glance, the box looked empty. But then Van spotted something curled up in one corner—something long and snakelike. As Van watched, it began to uncurl itself, revealing many pairs of short legs along its body, and a wolfish, sharp-featured face. It raised its head to look at Van. A tiny, misty tongue dangled out of its mouth. It panted softly.

"Hello," whispered Van. "I have a treat for you."

The wolf worm panted harder.

Van couldn't quite bring himself to let the creature climb into his hands. Imagining all those stubby legs crawling across his palms made him feel like he'd just swallowed a mouthful of lemon juice. He set the box down and craned over it instead, holding the wishbone in snapping position.

And then he halted.

He thought of all the wishes he'd made, or helped to make. Half of them had worked beautifully. Half had gone wrong. And the last one had almost gotten his mother . . . Van couldn't even think the next word.

He would have to be careful. *Incredibly* careful. He'd make the smallest, most limited wish he could think of. A wish more like his first two. Maybe then everyone would be safe.

Van tightened his grasp on the wishbone.

I wish to get into the Hold without anybody noticing me.

The bone cracked.

A white wisp trickled from its end. The wolf worm lapped it up like a dog drinking from a garden hose.

The air thickened. Van felt the brush of dew on his skin, a cool little tingle on every hair. Something sparkled on the ends of his eyelashes.

The dew faded.

Van didn't feel any different. He glanced around the room. Nothing had changed. There were no reindeer-drawn sleighs waiting to take him away this time. Maybe—like with the white deer—he'd find evidence of the wish later. He certainly *hoped* so. He slammed the lid over the wolf worm and shoved the box back into place. He hustled toward the door. But on the threshold, he halted again.

Van had never wished for perfect hearing. That would have been like wishing for more teeth, or an extra hand. He had what he was used to. He knew how it worked, and he knew how to use it.

But tonight, without his hearing aids, in the tarry darkness of the Collectors' lair . . .

He turned back. In two steps, he'd crossed to a shelf. He pulled down a small cardboard box.

The creature inside was shaped like a bear cub. As it turned to blink up at Van, he saw that it had large, almost human eyes, and a muzzle that looked like a pig's snout. Van tugged the spare wishbone out of his pocket. The creature sat upright, snuffling eagerly.

Van grasped the wishbone by both delicate ends. He didn't want anything too big. He didn't want any special powers. He just wanted, for a single night, to hear like an average eleven-year-old boy.

Snap went the bone.

And, Van realized, he had actually heard it snap.

Instinctively, he raised his hands to his ears. But the little plastic bumps of his hearing aids weren't there. Van could hear the brush of his fingertips against the whorls of skin. He shivered. When he turned his head, he heard the rustle of hair against his pajama collar. His own startled breathing was annoyingly loud. *Distractingly* loud.

Something jingled overhead. Van glanced up. The big glass chandelier had started to spin. Van looked around, but nothing else in the room was moving—just the chandelier, which was now twirling and rocking from side to side.

The Wish Eater stared up at the ceiling too. It gave a little shimmy, the fur of its bearlike body puffing mistily around it. An instant later, as both Van and the Wish Eater watched, the light from the chandelier began to change color. It darkened to aqua blue, then paled to green before blossoming into splashy fuchsia. The jingling grew louder. Below the jingles, a rhythmic song started to play.

Bump-bumbum-BUMP-bum, bum-bumbum-BUMP-bum . . .

Van flinched. The noise grew larger, pressing down on him like a prickly blanket. When he glanced down, the Wish Eater looked larger too.

With a nervous rush, Van tried to shove the lid onto the box. The Wish Eater struggled, pushing back with its dense little body. The chandelier flashed to purple.

Jing-jing-JING! went its glass arms. *Bump-bumbum-BUMP-bum!* said the music, which seemed to come from everywhere at once. And then, swiftly, smoothly, the chandelier began to drop downward. Its chain lengthened behind it, like the thread of a descending spider. The music grew louder still. When it was just a few feet from the floor, the chandelier stopped falling and began to sway. It swung back and forth, faster and faster, making widening arcs across the room. *Jing-jing-JING! Bump-bumbum-BUMP.* Its light seared from purple to red.

The chandelier swung harder, its fragile glass arms nearly hitting the shelves on either side. It sliced straight over Van's head, close enough that he could hear the *whoosh* as it ripped through the air.

"Stop it!" Van hissed to the Wish Eater. "It's going to smash!"

But the Wish Eater went on shoving against the lid, its smiling little face following the light.

The chandelier swooped toward the opposite wall, missing the shelves by inches, dragging warped shadows after it. It roared back toward Van. He dove to the floor just as the chandelier met the spot where his head had been an instant earlier.

Van leaned against the lid of the box with all his weight. "Stop!" he begged, as the Wish Eater pushed back with its fuzzy arms. Just as Van was about to scream for help, the Wish Eater lost its footing. It tumbled sideways, and Van crammed the lid back onto the box.

The music ceased. The chandelier faded to white. After one more swing, it went still. With a soft clicking sound, its chain retracted into the ceiling, and the chandelier rose, and everything was as it had been before.

Van shoved the Wish Eater's box onto its shelf. He slumped back on the rug. His own heavy breathing clogged his ears.

He hadn't wished for that to happen. Just like he hadn't wished for the toys on his miniature stage to come to life. Mr. Falborg's fancy chandelier could have shattered into a thousand pieces. It could have sliced Van with a thousand little shattered-glass cuts. Then he would have had to use another wish to repair the damage, and who knew where that would have led? Kernel's words whispered in his mind: *Wishes are extraordinarily hard to control.* Watching Lemmy play with SuperVan had been fun. But this had been frightening—like climbing onto a carnival ride and then looking down to find no one at the brakes.

A bit nauseated now, Van wobbled to his feet.

But the reality of what lay ahead stopped him before he could reach the door. Without a spare wishbone, he was unarmed. Unprotected. Even more alone.

He wouldn't use another wish—absolutely not. Not unless he absolutely had to.

But what if he absolutely had to?

Van darted back to the leather trunk, hoping he could jimmy the lock somehow. But as soon as he pushed the lid, it flew open. Hans must have forgotten to lock it again, Van realized. Or maybe he'd left it unlocked on purpose.

Van reached in and chose one perfect, pointy-tipped wishbone. He slipped it into his pajama pocket. Then he scurried out of the room, through the winding halls, and down the main staircase of the big white house. As he was dashing around one corner, Van thought he spotted—out of the corner of his eye—a flash of a figure in a white suit. But when he glanced back, the flash was gone, or it had never been there at all.

He was halfway through the hall when he thought of something else. "Hans? Gerda?" he asked, skidding back toward the kitchen. "Do you have a flashlight I could borrow?"

Moments later, with a small flashlight clicking against the wishbone in his pocket, Van burst through the front door into the night.

23
The Beast

THE City Collection Agency huddled in its dingy spot beneath the night sky.

Van tugged the door open and slipped inside. For a second, he leaned back against the wall, panting, letting the quiet of the office envelop him. His head was pounding. The roaring, whooshing sounds of the street still ricocheted inside his skull. Hearing this way made him feel uncomfortably fragile, like he was walking around with one less layer of skin.

He'd spent the whole trip hoping that some magical ride would show up—a friendly dragon, maybe, or a bumper car. Apparently his wish wasn't going to come true that way. Besides, he'd only wished to get into the Hold. He'd have to do the rest himself.

Once the pulse in his ears had quieted, Van tiptoed to the inner door.

There was no one on the stone staircase. Even the flocks of pigeons and scurrying rats seemed to have cleared the way. He raced down the steps into the green-gold light.

But when he peeped out into the entry chamber, Van's skin went cold.

There were Collectors *everywhere*. Maybe, thanks to the thick cloud cover shutting out any falling stars, it was an unusually calm work night. Crowds of people in long dark coats milled around, talking, laughing together. Van ducked into a shadowy nook a few steps beyond the staircase.

This was a lucky move. An instant later, a raven flew down the staircase and shot past Van's hiding spot, its caws drilling into his ears.

Another voice—a human one—followed it. *"We need help here!"*

All the Collectors turned to stare.

A dark-coated man dashed from the staircase into the main corridor. A small mound of fur and blood lay in his arms. "Get Nib! It's bad!"

Several Collectors came running. Their footsteps

thundered in Van's head. "Who is it?" someone shouted.

"It's Ruddigore," the first man panted. "A dog got him."

There were gasps. "A dog?"

"A big German shepherd. We were watching the Venti Park fountains . . ."

The crowd closed around the man, rushing him toward one of the branching corridors—but not before Van caught a glimpse of a raccoon's striped tail dangling limply over the man's arm.

His stomach wrenched into a knot. There was no way of knowing if the injured raccoon was the same one who had offered him a French fry. But it certainly could have been.

Had his wish done this? Was a poor, injured raccoon providing the distraction that would get him down to the Hold?

Van swayed on his feet.

What could he do? It was too late to prevent the injury. He couldn't help save the raccoon. All he could do was try to save another other poor little creature. And this was his chance.

Van charged as fast as he could toward the massive staircase.

He ran down, down, down, past the Atlas and its maps, past the Calendar and its heavy black books. He could hear the distracting slap of his own feet against the stones. He raced past the landing that led to the Collection's grand double doors, down into thicker and colder darkness.

At last Van's steps began to slow. When the darkness grew so dense that he could barely make out the next step, he pulled the flashlight from his pocket and flicked it on.

Its beam was small and narrow. Aiming it straight ahead showed him nothing at all. It was like trying to reach the bottom of a well with a chopstick. That was all right, Van reasoned. He didn't want to give a signal to Razor or his assistants. He aimed the beam straight downward instead. It made a small, pale splotch on the stone steps. Van followed it, stepping from one bright place to the next, keeping his eyes and ears sharp. No one was going to sneak up on him this time.

He'd just reached the end of another flight when a roar ripped through the darkness. It was closer than it had ever been before—and, to Van's ears, a thousand times louder. The noise vibrated through the steps straight into his bones. His skull throbbed. His thoughts popped like fireworks. Instinctively, he reached up to pull his hearing aids away. But there were no hearing aids. There was no escape from the awful, obliterating noise. Van clenched his teeth, gripped the banister, and waited.

The roar died away slowly, softly, like a cloud of smoke spreading out over a dark sky.

Van didn't get angry very often. In fact, it happened so rarely that he almost didn't recognize the feeling. But now, all at once, he was filled with something fast and fiery and hard. He felt like he could punch a brick wall and crack it into a zillion pieces.

It was a little like being SuperVan.

How dare the Collectors bring helpless little creatures like Lemmy to a freezing, dark pit full of roaring monsters? *How dare they?*

Van charged down the steps into blackness that didn't scare him at all anymore. He switched off the flashlight and stuffed it back into his pocket. Checking each step was just slowing him down. He flew across another landing, down one more flight, and staggered forward onto a broad stone floor.

There was no light. The air was as cold and damp as the spray from a waterfall. With both hands out,

Van ventured straight ahead, his ears ringing. His toes landed on something small and brittle. It broke with a snap. Van crouched, patting at the floor.

Bones. He was certain. The floor was littered with bones. Van tugged out the flashlight and flicked its little beam over the floor. His guess had been right. These weren't wishbones, but tiny, straw-thin bones, left behind by mice or rats or birds and long ago picked clean. They clicked beneath his fingertips. Van looked over his shoulders. It was too dark to see, but he thought he heard the whistle of huge wings.

Another muffled roar shook the darkness. Van could feel it in his teeth. The floor below him shuddered.

He was very close now.

His stomach twisted. His throat clamped.

But someone had to know the truth. Someone from the outside. Someone who could collect and carry that truth out into the light.

Van straightened up. From somewhere in the blackness, not far away, there came a thin band of light—the kind of light that slips under a closed door. Pushing the flashlight into his pocket, Van lunged through the blackness. His palms struck an icy metal surface that trembled with the waves of another roar. It *was* a door.

It had to be. Van's fingers touched a metal latch. He pulled it.

The door creaked open.

Van found himself staring down a wide, winding corridor. Lamps with oily orange flames sputtered along each curving wall. At first Van thought the walls were made entirely of stone, but as he inched inside, he saw that many of the stones were actually doors—gray metal doors, painted to blend into the walls themselves. Some were as small as an envelope. Some were as big as a washing machine. All of them were latched with thick metal bolts, and each was fitted with a tiny glass peephole.

With a shiver buzzing inside his ribs, Van bent and put his eye to a bread-box-sized door.

Inside was a tiny stone chamber. Something small and foggy was curled up in one corner.

It wasn't Lemmy. Its body was too long, more weasel-ish than lemur-ish. But it had Lemmy's misty fur. And it was about Lemmy's size.

The creature barely had room to turn around. It had no toys. No food. No windows. It didn't even seem to notice Van's eye pressed to the peephole, or to hear him when he whispered, "Hello?"

Van moved on to the next little door. Something small and fuzzy was balled up on the floor of this tiny cell too.

Because that was what they were, Van realized. Cells. This place was built for imprisoning hundreds—maybe thousands, maybe more—of sad, lonely, hungry little Wish Eaters.

And Lemmy had to be there somewhere.

Van rushed to the next door, and the next, and the next. But the more he checked, and the farther he rushed, the more doors he saw stretching out ahead of him. He'd never have time to check them all. He'd only wished not to be noticed until he reached the Hold, and here he was, vulnerable, alone, and all too noticeable. He moved even faster. Ten more doors. Twenty more. Still no sign of Lemmy. His pulse was fast and painful now, thrumming in his ears. He barely noticed the floor below him beginning to slope steeply downward, or the doors on either side growing larger and larger.

From somewhere at the corridor's end, there came another roar. Van froze as it blasted past him, quaking the stones so hard he nearly fell off his feet. No wonder there were tremors in the Collection above. With no walls or stairs to muffle it, the roar sounded not just louder, but *different,* somehow. It sounded angrier. Rougher. Almost like a word.

The roar died away. Van lunged onward, stumbling as his foot slipped over a ledge. He threw out both arms, catching his balance just in time.

The sloping floor had become yet another flight of stairs. Beyond Van's toes, shallow stone steps led down to a huge, round, open chamber.

Van and his mother had visited the Colosseum when they were in Rome. The chamber below reminded him of that ancient arena. But this arena was underground, and its sides weren't lined with archways and stone benches. They were lined with doors. Monstrous doors. Doors large enough for two semitrucks to squeeze through side by side.

A dozen Collectors formed a circle on the stone floor. They held sharp spikes and open, silvery nets. In the center of the circle, with his back to Van, stood a huge man with glinting hooks in each scarred hand. Razor.

And rearing up in front of Razor was the most terrible thing Van had ever seen.

It was a giant, roaring, rippling beast. It was shaped like a stretched-out crocodile, with a thrashing tail, a triangular head, and a long . . . long . . . *impossibly* long snout full of jagged, needle-shaped teeth. Its skin was a dead, cloudy gray. It was larger than a city bus. It made the people around it look like tiny plastic toys.

The beast let out another ear-piercing roar. Van heard it again: a word.

The word *NO.*

The beast lashed its tail.

Three people in the ring fell backward.

Razor lunged to one side, swinging his metal hook.

The beast edged back. It gave an angry growl.

"To my left!" Razor shouted. "Stitch! Key! Back it up!"

But the monster had gone still.

It sniffed the air.

The Collectors crouched, watching.

The beast's huge head swung and snuffled across the arena, toward the steps, straight up to the spot where Van stood. Van stopped breathing. For an instant, the monster froze too. Its eyes were two balls of white smoke, but Van could tell they were staring at him. *Into* him.

Then, with a bellow, the monster charged.

Van whirled around. His slippers pounded up the sloping corridor. He could hear himself shrieking, not caring if everyone else could hear him too.

Behind him, the beast charged up the staircase. Its running feet shook the floor. Van could hear its huffing, hungry breath. Pumping his legs faster, faster, he glanced over his shoulder. The monster's cloudy body filled the entire corridor. It was gaining on him. Cell doors rattled as it charged by. Burning lamps flickered.

Van ran faster than he'd ever run before. Now he could hear and *feel* the monster coming closer, the wet chill in the air that wrapped around his heels. He shoved the Hold's outer door just as a massive force threw him forward, launching him straight out into the blackness beyond.

Van landed on his stomach. He slid through grit and splintered bones, his palms stinging, the wind crushed out of him. The pocketed wishbone jabbed him in the thigh. His heart hammered. His breath hissed. Somewhere behind him, the monster growled again. There was too much noise; it was making him sick. He wanted to rip these terrible sounds back out of his ears, along with every memory they left behind. He flipped onto his back, trying to breathe, trying to see through the fireworks that exploded across his vision.

The beast lumbered through the open door. It glowed against the dark like static on a black screen. Its teeth glimmered. Its smoke-white eyes didn't blink. Van scrambled backward, but there was no place to hide, and not enough time to get there anyway. Something frigid and sparkling filled the air. Through the freezing mist, Van watched the beast barrel closer. Its needle-nosed jaw opened wide.

"Now!" shouted a voice.

Someone lunged in front of him.

Lamplight glittered on a swinging hook.

Van stared as the hook scraped straight through the beast's translucent body, releasing a trail of smoke. The creature let out a roar.

"Nets! On my right!" the voice shouted.

Dark-coated figures flew through the shadows, forming barricades of bodies and rope. The beast wheeled, but the figures closed in, driving the beast back through the Hold's open door. Someone grabbed Van by the arm, pulling him along.

In a knot, the Collectors forced the beast along the corridor, past the sputtering lamps, to the top of the staircase. The hand let go of Van's arm.

"All together!" shouted the deep voice. "Forward!"

Van wobbled at the top of the steps, gasping, as the line of Collectors charged. The beast backed down the staircase to the stone floor, with the Collectors in pursuit. Hooks whizzed through the air. The monster roared. The stones trembled.

The beast spun. Its whipping tail knocked several people off their feet. Its teeth snapped at two others, catching and tossing them backward. It came to a stop, snorting, head low. Its bone-white eyes homed in on Van.

The monster rumbled low in its throat.

Van could have sworn he heard another word within that rumble.

MINE.

Once more, the beast surged up the staircase. Van stared, petrified, at the opening jaw coming closer and closer.

Just before its teeth could close around him, a black silhouette flew into its path. There was the *whoosh* of a swinging hook, followed by one more skull-crushing roar, and the beast skidded back down the steps. The knot of people tightened around it, forcing it into the open cell, and the huge metal door thundered shut.

Van let out a gasp that was almost a sob.

He was alive. He was safe.

The black silhouette in front of him turned around.

Maybe he was safe.

Razor towered over him. He was breathing hard, but his scarred face was calm. His voice was deep and surprisingly gentle.

"Are you all right?"

"I . . ." Even with his sharpened hearing, Van couldn't catch the word over his own pounding heartbeat. "What—what *was* that thing?"

Someone in the crowd below let out a short laugh.

Razor's face didn't change. He gazed down at Van as he slid the hooks back into their shoulder straps, his eyes black and bright.

Inside its cell, the beast gave a last muffled growl.

Razor tilted his head toward the door. "That?" he said. "That's a Wish Eater."

24
Predators

"THAT—that's a *Wish Eater?*" Van choked. "But they're—I thought they were *tiny!*"

"The more they feed, the larger they get," said Razor. "And the hungrier." His eyes glinted with reflected lamplight. "What's in your pocket?"

Van gave a jerk. "My . . . ?"

"Your pocket." Razor pointed to Van's pajama pants, his voice still calm. "*That* pocket."

Shakily, Van drew out the flashlight and, after another second, the wishbone.

Razor nodded. "That's what it was after." He glanced down at one of the other Collectors. "Eyelet, take care of it."

A woman with a tight black braid climbed the steps.

She whisked the bone out of Van's hand and strode away.

Van watched her go, feeling suddenly small and silly and dangerously lucky all at the same time.

Razor crossed his arms. "You're the boy Pebble brought down here."

"I'm Van." Van swallowed. "Van Markson."

"And you see us."

"Yes. I see you."

"And you see *them*."

"Yes." Van swallowed again. "But I—I've never seen one that big."

"They start out small. Like everything else." Razor looked steadily into Van's eyes. "If they don't feed, they shrink back to manageable size." His mouth shifted with the hint of a smile. "Eventually."

"So . . . you put them in cells until they shrink?" said Van.

Razor nodded at the others. "That's our task, as Holders. We contain them. Keep everyone safe."

"You mean—you're *starving* them?"

Razor didn't blink. "Are you starving a fire if you don't let it burn you?"

Van's mind turned this question around. "I don't . . ."

"We don't hurt them," Razor went on. "Unless we have to." He touched one of the hooks. "Eaters hate sharpened iron. And they can't get through spiderweb. That's what these are made of." He gestured to the nets slung over his arm. "We use tools to confine them. Once they're completely enclosed, they get groggy and docile. But we don't kill them. They can't die."

Van's head was starting to feel like an overstuffed suitcase. The noise and the panic and all the things he'd seen and heard were smashed inside together, and he couldn't find anything he needed amid the mess.

"So all those roaring sounds were . . . ," Van began. "I didn't think they could make any sound at all."

A few of the Holders laughed. Razor grinned back at them, his scar twisting. "Oh, they can. When they want to."

Van shivered. "What else can they do?"

"When they've just fed, almost anything."

"Can they hurt you?"

Razor's grin lingered. He gave the scar a playful tap. "They sure can."

Van's mouth went sour. "The one that was chasing me . . . What would it—would it have—"

Razor's hand landed on Van's shoulder. It was heavy

but comforting, and Van suddenly realized he'd been shaking.

"Why don't we take a little walk?" said Razor.

Razor steered Van along the corridor, keeping that steadying hand on his shoulder. When they were out of sight of the arena, halfway down the hallway of doors, Razor stopped. He turned to face Van again.

"We know why you're here," he said.

Van's stomach, which had just started *not* to feel like a sack full of fighting weasels, suddenly started twisting again.

"We know you were keeping one of the Eaters," Razor went on, saving Van from having to confess. Or lie. "We had to confiscate it, for your safety. For everyone's safety."

"But Lemmy is so *little*." The argument flew out before Van could bottle it. "He's just a tiny lump of fuzz. He wouldn't hurt anyone."

"You think he wouldn't. But nobody can predict exactly what an Eater will do. Not how they'll grant a wish. Not how they'll change. Not what they'll do when they're fed and full of power." Razor's black eyes stared into Van's. "You've seen what they do then. Haven't you?"

Van remembered SuperVan zooming around his

bedroom. He remembered Mr. Falborg's swinging chandelier.

"The longer they're free, the more they feed, the larger and more dangerous they become," Razor went on. "They get vicious. Volatile. Impossible to control."

A lump was forming in Van's throat. "*All* of them?" he managed.

Razor gazed back at him. There was nothing cruel in his black eyes. He pointed to a small door just over Van's shoulder. "Look."

Van put his eye to the peephole.

Inside a cell just a bit larger than a shoebox, a small, fuzzy shape was curled up on the floor. It was sleeping peacefully, its tail curved around its body. Wide, ruffly ears folded around its face.

"Lemmy!" Van gasped.

The creature didn't wake.

"You can see for yourself," said Razor. "We just keep them safe."

Van placed his hands against the cold metal of the door. Every impulse in his body told him to yank it open. But Razor stood right behind him. "So . . ." His eyes prickled. "Once you've got them, what happens?"

"We let them sleep," said Razor. "It's hibernation,

really. They can stay in that state for years. Centuries. With time, they shrink until they finally disappear."

Van stared at the little gray ball. "That's what will happen? To Lemmy?" He couldn't meet Razor's eyes. He didn't want the big man to see that his own were blurry with tears. "It will just be here until . . . until it isn't anywhere?"

"Think about what would happen if we *didn't* keep it here," said Razor, instead of answering. He nodded toward the arena. "On the loose, it would grow into something like *that*. It's their nature. Cubs grow into grizzlies. Kittens become cats. Predators eat."

Van let out a long breath. Even if Razor was right—and Van had the horrible, confusing feeling that he might be—he had still failed. He had promised to keep Lemmy safe. And he hadn't. He felt empty and sore inside, like his body had been hollowed out and scraped clean.

"It was brave of you to come here."

Now Van looked up at Razor, even though one tear had leaked out and was starting to dribble down his face. "What?"

"You could have just let it go. But you put yourself in danger instead. Even more danger than you guessed."

Razor smiled. "You're brave. And you're loyal. You would make a good Collector, Van Markson."

Slowly, a small and watery glow began to fill the emptiness inside of Van. Having a man like Razor call him brave had never happened before. For a second, Van wished that Razor would put a hand on his shoulder again.

Instead, a howl tore through the air.

Both Van and Razor whirled toward the Hold's outer door.

The door swung open. "We've got a big one!" a woman shouted into the corridor. Beyond her, Van could make out a flock of birds whipping through the darkness, wheeling and screeching around the stone staircase. "They're lowering it now!"

"Holders!" Razor's voice boomed through the corridor. "Everyone to the stairs! We've got an arrival!"

Before Van could ask any questions, Razor steered him out the door into the dimness. He positioned Van against the wall, far from the foot of the staircase.

"Stay right here," he said firmly. *"Don't move."*

Van nodded.

Razor turned and strode away, his black coat flaring behind him.

One of the other Holders was lighting lanterns that

hung all around the huge, empty chamber. By their flickering light, Van could see the cyclone of dark birds—owls, ravens, crows—that filled the air, screaming as though they'd spotted a fresh carcass. More Holders came pounding through the metal door behind him; others were racing down the stairs above. In the center of the spiraling staircase, something was plunging through the shadows: something silvery and huge, wrapped in a bundle of nets and lowered by ropes.

The Holders formed a tight circle.

"In position!" Razor called. "Open the net!"

Two men pulled at the ropes. A giant Wish Eater surged out onto the stone floor.

This one was shaped like a bull, with hulking shoulders and a body like a freight train. Two long, tapering horns curved out from its head. Instead of hooves, its legs ended in paws like a lion's. It bellowed, and the entire cavern shook.

"Back it up!" Razor's slashing hook left a trail like a comet across Van's vision. "Stitch! Move inward!"

The beast lowered its head and charged. Razor and two other Holders leaped out of its path.

"Over here!" called another—the woman named Eyelet, who'd taken the wishbone. She waved her arms, drawing the Wish Eater's attention. When it charged again, she stepped aside, sending it straight through the Hold's door.

"Nets!" called Razor. The Holders whipped out their knotted ropes, forming a cage behind the creature. "Guide it down!"

Van watched as the Holders forced the Wish Eater out of sight. One more bellow rang along the corridor. When its echo had finally died away, Van tiptoed after it, back into the Hold.

Without the horrible roaring to fill it, the broad corridor actually seemed peaceful. Lamplight glimmered over the walls. All the closed doors reminded Van of a hotel hallway late at night, when everyone is asleep in their matching rooms.

He crept back to the peephole in Lemmy's door.

The Wish Eater had turned slightly in its sleep, so that Van could see its little face. It looked peaceful. Just like it had looked in its shoebox under Van's bed.

Maybe Razor was telling the truth. The Wish Eaters didn't seem hurt or sad or scared—at least, not once they were contained. They weren't being mistreated or abused. They were just . . . *safe.* It wasn't so terrible, Van told himself. In fact, it wasn't so different from the rows and rows of boxes in Mr. Falborg's hidden room.

Van pressed his palm to the door.

Even if what he really wanted was to open the door, hide Lemmy inside his pajama shirt, and smuggle him straight back to the apartment, he knew he couldn't. Someone would be sure to see him. And then they would both be caught. Even if the Holders weren't cruel to the Wish Eaters, he wasn't sure what they'd do to a traitor. Furthermore, if Razor was telling the truth, Lemmy would eventually grow into the kind of huge, dangerous beast that had just almost chomped Van like a sandwich.

At least he could tell Mr. Falborg what he'd seen. The Wish Eaters weren't being hurt. They were secure. They were safe.

Van swallowed hard. He pulled his hand from the door.

"Bye, Lemmy," he whispered.

Chest aching, he turned away.

The air around him began to shimmer.

He turned back.

Far away, in the sunken arena, the Holders were herding the bull-like beast into a waiting cell. Their shouts and bellows faded into nothingness.

Enclosed in a twinkling fog, Van reached for the door of Lemmy's cell. His hand turned the metal bolt.

Van stared at the hand.

He hadn't told it to do that.

He hadn't told his fingers to pry open the metal door, or his body to step back as it swung open.

Lemmy woke.

Its big eyes blinked at Van. Swiftly, it crawled out the door and floated down to the stones. It gazed up at him, beginning to smile.

Panic speared through Van's chest. What was he doing? Why was he doing it? And how was he doing it without even trying?

Van bent down to scoop Lemmy into his hands, but his body jerked back, mid-motion. He tried again. His hands refused to reach for the Wish Eater. Instead, they turned the bolt on another nearby door. And then another. And another. And another.

Something else was controlling him. Van realized it with a dizzying jolt. Something else was moving him, like a marionette on an invisible stage.

Four more little Wish Eaters clambered down from their cells. Then six. Ten. More.

Van's hands flew from cell to cell, twisting locks,

opening doors. Finally, when a herd of tiny Wish Eaters—some like furry lizards, some like winged squirrels, some like animals Van had never seen or imagined—had joined Lemmy, filling the corridor from wall to wall, Van's body stopped.

The Wish Eaters turned toward the Hold's entrance, their noses and ears and little foggy bodies all craning intently in the same direction. Then, like a bunch of dandelion seeds being blown from a stem, they whooshed out through the huge metal door.

Van stood very still.

His body felt strangely heavy, as if the strings that had held him up had suddenly been cut. His head ached. His legs wobbled. Even his arms hurt, like he'd been shoving back against something much bigger and stronger than he was. He felt ill.

Van threw a glance back toward the arena. What would Razor and the other Holders think when they learned what he had done?

They would think he was a traitor.

And maybe he was.

He had to get out of here.

Van lunged out of the Hold.

The shadows of the stairwell closed around him.

Even in the dimness, he could tell that the Wish Eaters were not in sight. Where had Lemmy gone? His hand gripped the icy stone banister. He'd raced up only two flights when he heard the sounds.

They were coming from above—shouting, thumping, crashing sounds. They grew thicker around him as he climbed. For the hundredth time that night, Van wished he could reach up and pull out his hearing aids. A ball of dread settled in his stomach. He could guess where those sounds were coming from—and when he reached the next landing, he knew for sure.

The Collection's double doors hung open. Inside, the chamber was in chaos.

Many bottled wishes had already fallen—or been pushed—from the high shelves. Fireworks of shattered glass pocked the floor. Collectors were shouting. Hawks and ravens screeched. Rodents scurried everywhere, darting out of the way of running feet. As Van watched from the threshold, a green bottle plummeted from halfway up one wall, exploding with a burst of emerald shards and a flash like a tiny shooting star. The flash cometed upward, straight into the open mouth of a creature the size of a Great Dane that hung from a spiral staircase. The creature had long limbs—Van counted six of them—and feet with prehensile, monkey-ish toes, and a mouthful of smoky, pointed fangs.

Two Collectors armed with iron spikes rushed up the staircase toward the long-limbed beast. Out of thin air, a red cloud appeared above the Collectors' heads. It released a torrent of bloody rain, sending the Collectors tumbling back down the coiling steps. Van could have sworn he saw the beast laugh.

Another Wish Eater, this one already the size of a pony, charged toward a low shelf where a row of Collectors stood guard. At the last moment, the Wish Eater veered to one side, its snakelike tail lashing over the Collectors' heads and striking the bottles on the shelf above. The Collectors ducked. Glass pelted them as it smashed to the floor. Dozens of silvery wisps whirled up from the broken bottles. Some wisps were snagged again by desperate Collectors, but more were sucked straight into the Wish Eater's open mouth.

The creature swelled. A flock of shadows seemed to burst out of its body. The shadows wheeled through the air, all sharp beaks and talons and pointed wings, before diving at the Collectors, scattering them in every direction.

"Keep your positions!" Kernel shouted over the

cacophony. "Don't let their magic distract you! Someone sound the alarm!"

Another noise added itself to the fury. It was a mechanical wail that grew louder as it climbed, until Van felt like his skull would pop from the pressure of containing it. Covering his ears, he scanned the Collection again. He could only count four Wish Eaters. This meant that more—*many* more—must have climbed even higher. Lemmy had to be one of them.

He staggered back toward the staircase.

From below, he could hear the thumping footsteps of the Holders.

"Nets ready!" Razor was shouting. "When we reach the doors, we form a wall. Stitch, Tick, Bullet, you stay in the main chamber. The rest—"

Van didn't wait to hear more. He pounded up the steps as fast as his legs would lift him. The alarm's amplifiers hung all around the hollow square of the staircase, so as he climbed, the wail grew louder and louder. Van's eyes watered. He clenched his teeth so hard he thought they might crumble.

The staircase was getting crowded. Collectors rushed in every direction, nearly knocking Van off his feet.

Everyone was too focused on the emergency at hand to give him a second glance. . . . That is, until something with beady black eyes and a beak like a sharpened pencil landed on his shoulder.

The raven stared at Van, its talons digging straight through his pajamas and into his skin. Van recognized Jack's raven. And it recognized him.

Van's blood turned to ice water.

The raven took flight, swooping out into the darkness. Van broke into an even faster run.

He scrambled up the steps, tripping once and bashing his knees against the rough stone. No matter how fast he ran, he couldn't outpace a raven—a raven who had probably already flown to Jack. He had to hide.

At the next landing, he veered through the archway, into the Calendar.

Chaos had reached this chamber too. Several bookcases had toppled like dominoes, scattering heavy black volumes across the floor. Voices shouted. Creatures squealed.

Clambering over a fallen shelf, Van rushed into a corner just past the arch and pressed his back against the cold stone wall. He sank down into a crouch, making himself as small as possible. He had to catch his breath. Once he felt sure that Jack and the guards had lost his trail, he would slip back out again.

On the landing, several pairs of footsteps came to a stop.

"Near here, Lemuel?"

That deep, hard voice. Jack's voice. Van stiffened.

"Heeeerre!" cawed the bird.

"Beetle, you head up. Rivet, you go down. I'll take this floor." The voice tightened. "That little idiot. I swear, when I find him, I'll throw him straight over the banister."

Two sets of footsteps faded away.

A third set came closer.

Van held his breath as Jack strode through the archway. The big Collector paused with his back to Van, scanning the chamber. On his shoulder, the raven scanned the room too.

Keeping tight against the wall, Van sidled past the fallen bookshelf. If he could slip out through the arch while Jack's back was turned, he might be able to get away. Of course, Rivet was hunting for him above. Van slowed. Who *wouldn't* be hunting for him as soon as they knew he was to blame?

But he *wasn't* really to blame. Someone else had

made him unlock those cells. Someone who—Van's foot bumped a fallen book. It rasped against the floor.

The raven's head spun toward him.

Before Jack could turn around too, Van shot out through the archway.

He tore up the stairs, hating that his short legs would only let him take one step at a time, too scared to even glance over his shoulder. His heart thumped against the roof of his mouth. His slippers slapped the stone faster and faster—but, Van realized, he couldn't hear them anymore. At first he thought his heartbeat had drowned out everything else. But even that heartbeat was growing fainter. His wish was wearing off.

At the next landing, he skidded toward the archway into the Atlas. Maybe he could find another hiding spot.

But there, in the middle of the room, shoving tables aside, was Rivet. Van ducked behind a pillar just as Rivet turned. At the same moment, something smoky and winged soared up through the middle of the central staircase. Van felt the gust of wind over his shoulder. He whipped around. A beast that looked like a cross between a dragon and a vulture hovered above the pit, its massive wings beating the air. The Wish Eater let out a puff of green flame, which dissolved an instant later into a hail of plummeting marbles. Collectors screamed on the staircases below.

Van turned back just in time to meet Rivet's sharp black eyes.

With a little gasp, Van flew through the arch and toward the next staircase. He skidded across a patch of marbles, catching himself on the banister to keep from plunging over. A glossy black wing swept in front of his eyes.

"Heeeerrree!" Lemuel's voice pierced through the blur. *"HEEEEERRRREEE!"*

Van glanced down. Two landings below, he could see Jack staring up at him, his eyes like arrows.

Van reached the entry chamber at a full-tilt run. The space had never seemed so huge, the floor so endless. He dodged knots of Collectors, catching sight of Nail at the center of one distraught group.

"He may already—" Nail was saying as Van dashed past, his deep, clear voice sinking back into the noise.

Van looked over his shoulder at last.

Both Jack and Rivet had reached the top of the staircase. Their eyes were honed on Van. And they were getting closer.

Van pelted for the final staircase, the one leading up to the office, and to escape.

He veered around its corner.

A crowd of Collectors stared down at him. They filled the staircase from wall to wall, top to bottom, all of them armed with iron bars and sticky ropes to catch any escaping Wish Eaters.

Or any treacherous boys in flannel pajamas.

"Hey!" Van heard one of the Collectors shout, her voice sounding muted and very far away. "Isn't that the boy who—"

He didn't catch anything else.

Because at that moment, something snagged his arm and hauled him backward, into perfect darkness.

25
The Fall

HE couldn't hear.

He couldn't see.

The sudden, total darkness wrapped him like a cocoon, winding his exhausted body inside. He knew he was in a small space—the air had the stillness of enclosure—and he knew that he was not alone. And that was all.

Van held as still as he could, hoping that whoever was with him couldn't see or hear either.

Something furry brushed against his neck.

Van jumped. His shoulders bumped the cold stone wall.

"Hey! Van de Graaff Generator!" squeaked a voice. "What are *you* doing here?"

Van fumbled the flashlight out of his pocket. He clicked it on. A slashing light cut the darkness, falling on a silvery squirrel and Pebble's familiar—and desperate—face.

Van watched her lips. ". . . Need . . . out of here," they said.

"No kidding!" Van exploded. "That's what I'm trying to do, but—"

Pebble's hand clamped over his mouth. "Ears . . . way . . ." Her voice was barely a buzz. ". . . Back . . . you . . ."

Van shook her hand off his face. "The stairs are blocked," he said desperately. "Jack's after me. Everybody thinks I released the Wish Eaters, but I *didn't*. I mean, I didn't do it on purp—"

Pebble's hand smacked over his mouth again. She said something—it might have been "No!" or "I know!" or "Now!"—before grabbing him firmly by the arm and dragging him behind her, into denser darkness.

The beam of Van's flashlight bounced ahead of them, bleaching tiny plots of a narrow, twisting hall.

Barnavelt's voice chirped brightly in his ear. "*I* know the back ways too. I know *all* the ways. Front ways, sideways, anyways . . ."

"Barnavelt," Van whispered. "Is Pebble turning me in?"

"Turning you into what?"

"In to *Jack*."

"Is Pebble turning you into Jack?" The squirrel sounded confused. "I don't think she can do that."

"Then where are we going?"

"Up," said the squirrel.

They had reached a massive black spiral staircase. Pebble tugged the flashlight out of Van's hand. She aimed its beam up the metal coil. Before Van could see where the stairs ended, Pebble started to climb, pulling Van after her.

The stairs twisted up and up, in a tight, dizzying spiral. The metal steps shivered under their feet. The railing felt as steady as a piece of dental floss. Van did his best not to look down, even though he knew he would only have seen darkness.

After dozens of steps, Pebble slowed. Van clung to the railing, panting, as she stepped onto a small platform, dropped the flashlight into one of her many pockets, and pushed open a door.

A second later, she whisked through it, dragging Van behind her.

Van blinked.

They had arrived at the edge of a great, round room, dimly lit by strings of twinkling lights. The walls were made of metal, and the floor was strewn here and there with worn rugs and saggy armchairs. On a platform in the center of the room, a few people were gathered around the base of what looked like a giant telescope. A handful of others stood at tables nearby, busy with charts and instruments. No one seemed to notice Van or Pebble creeping stealthily by.

"Is this the Observatory?" Van whispered to Barnavelt. "What are we doing here?"

"What?" The squirrel shook his head. His eyes focused on Van again. "Hey! Van Gogh! What are *you* doing here?"

"That's what I just asked *you*."

Pebble's head whipped around. "Shh!" Van saw her hiss. She pointed straight ahead, toward a set of curved metal rungs that led straight up the wall.

Van's stomach flipped.

Pebble grasped the rungs and began to climb. She glanced back, jerking her head for him to come along.

"Okay," Van whispered to himself. "Here we go."

"Hooray!" cheered the squirrel. "Here we go! We're going! Let's go!"

The rungs were cold and firm. But Van's sweaty palms turned them warm and slippery in no time. The thin soles of his slippers bent around the bars, hurting his feet and making him wobble. And the top of the ladder was still nowhere in sight. Van pinned his eyes to the wall between the bars, trying not to think about how much of that wall was waiting above him. Or dwindling away below him.

"Good climbing!" cheered Barnavelt. "We're almost there!"

"Really?" gasped Van.

"No. Not really." The squirrel leaned closer to his ear, dropping his voice to a whisper. "And your climbing isn't very good either."

Higher. Higher. Higher.

Van's arms ached. His hands burned. His feet felt like they'd been hammered into horseshoes from carrying his weight up all those metal bars.

Something fluttered the ends of his hair.

He looked up.

A few rungs above him, Pebble had pushed open a hatch in the metal wall. Through it, Van could see a slash of purple sky spotted with stars.

"Almost there!" squeaked Barnavelt, hopping up

and down on Van's shoulder. "Really, this time!"

The hem of Pebble's coat disappeared over the rim of the hatch. A second later, her face poked back through the opening. She said something Van couldn't hear.

Blood thundered in his ears. He hoisted himself up the final rungs and lifted his head out into the night air.

They were somewhere high. Somewhere very, very high. The air felt thin, woven with threads of powerful wind. A breeze battered him. He clutched the ladder tight.

Pebble held out a hand. Reluctantly, Van let go of the rung to take it, and she half helped, half hauled him through the hatch onto a tiny platform. Van moved his grip from Pebble's hands to the railing at the platform's edge. Then, at last, he took a look around.

The entire city spread out below them.

Van gazed down at the rooftops of tall buildings, at the streets' interlacing slices of light, at the tiny glints of moving cars. A few skyscrapers reached even higher than their platform, spearing their tips into the violet sky. He turned in a slow circle, and saw that he and Pebble were perched on the roof of a water tower—one of those huge, round, pointy-topped tanks that stood atop the city's older buildings. The observatory's round, metal-walled room suddenly made sense. What a perfect place to hide and stare up at the stars. The sky seemed so close, Van could have reached up and smeared it with his fingers—if he hadn't been too afraid to let go of the railing, anyway.

"And now we go down!" Barnavelt sang, leaping from Van's shoulder to Pebble's.

"Down?" Van glanced over the railing.

There, along the outside of the water tower, was another set of metal rungs.

His stomach started to churn.

Pebble threw one leg over the railing. She paused for a moment, steadying herself in a gust of wind. Then she crouched down and set her feet on the rungs. Before Van could speak again, she'd climbed out of sight.

Van wavered.

He looked up at the sky once more, as if a handy plastic sleigh might come sailing past and scoop him up. But there was no sleigh. There was only the huge, purple, nighttime sky, and the giant twinkling city, and the hidden lair full of furious Collectors waiting below him, like a nest of wasps.

There was no other choice.

Van slid one leg over the railing, like Pebble had

done. His foot couldn't quite reach the rungs. Balancing his torso on the rail, he inched sideways, until his foot hit a solid surface. He dragged the other leg over. Now he was holding tight to the outside of a tiny ledge, with nothing between him and the city far, far below except for the whipping night air.

Slowly, never letting go of the railing, Van bent into a crouch. He locked his right hand, and then his left, around the top rung. The wind puffed, shoving him sideways. Van let out a little shriek. His arms went rigid. After what seemed like ages, the wind softened again, and he shuffled his feet downward, through the darkness, onto the waiting rungs.

Don't think about how many rungs are left, Van told himself. *Don't think about how far you are from the ground. Just move one step at a time. Be calm. Be brave. Be like SuperVan.*

Of course, SuperVan could have just flown away.

Don't think about that, either.

The metal rungs were icy and slick with condensation. Even Van's sweaty hands couldn't warm them. He clenched each rung so hard, his knuckles gleamed through the skin. The soreness in his feet deepened into rubbery numbness. Only the pressure lancing up his shins told him when he'd settled on another rung.

He crept down another step. Another. Another.

He was moving so slowly, it would take him forever to reach the bottom. But he was too terrified to go any faster.

He threw a brief glance downward.

Pebble was many rungs below him—so many that he could barely make out her face in the dimness. Her bulky coat whipped around her. Spreading out beneath her was the world of miniature trees and miniature buildings and tiny toy cars. Everything was so small that it looked pretend, like the set on a gigantic model stage.

Van lowered himself down another rung.

He was never going to reach the bottom.

He could hardly remember how he'd gotten here in the first place. He had been stuck, clinging to a narrow metal ladder high above a city, forever. And this was where he would stay. Because there was absolutely no way he would get down from here in one Van-shaped piece.

He was doomed.

His knees locked.

Panic flooded him. It poured through his stomach.

It filled his mouth. It shorted out the wiring in his brain. For a long, empty moment, Van hung there, eyes closed, the wind dragging through his hair.

Something else brushed his cheek.

Van looked up.

A glossy black bird hovered beside him. Then it landed on the rung just above, its eyes boring into Van like the tips of two pins.

Lemuel.

Van sucked in a gasp.

The bird took off. *"Hee's heeeerrrre!"* Van heard the bird shriek, as it wheeled upward and out of sight. *"Heeeeeeeerrre!"*

Van forced himself to move again. His sweaty hands scrabbled at the rungs. He glanced up, but there was no sign of Jack or the other guards making their way down the ladder.

Not yet.

He looked down. Still so far to go.

And as he was looking, his slipper skidded. His heel dropped backward. In less than a breath, Van was dangling from the ladder by one cold, exhausted hand.

For an instant he hung there, the wind grabbing at his pajamas like hungry teeth. He clenched his fingers as hard as he could. But every muscle in his body was ready to give in. Van felt his elbow go slack, and then his wrist, and then, one by one, each of his freezing fingers.

And then there was nothing left.

Van fell.

He caught a flash of Pebble's horrified face as he plummeted past her, Barnavelt's smaller, wide-eyed face on her shoulder, and then they were both shrinking upward, and he was still falling down, down, down.

He missed the rooftop of the building below the tank by inches. Van wasn't sure if this was a worse or a better thing; if the smash might or might *not* have killed him—but it didn't really matter. He was still falling, and now the building's sheer stone wall was streaking past him, and he knew that the smash had only been delayed.

Everything slowed. His body flipped over, shifting and kicking. He watched one of his slippers sail away into the dark. The air was as thick as water. Van could feel it pushing back as he plunged through it, growing warmer, damper, dewier. . . .

A shimmering filled the air.

Something vast, with wings that nearly spanned the street, dove after him.

Van cringed.

But there was no shelter in midair, and the vast thing seared toward him with the speed of a comet. For a second Van wondered if it actually *was* a comet, and then two huge, smoking paws closed around him.

Wind rushed in all directions at once. Van couldn't tell if he was falling or flying, or if it was just the beating of the creature's massive wings that pulled the air straight out of his lungs. He squinted up, his eyes blearing, and saw a body like a lion's, with a bat's face and leathery wings, and a tail that seemed to stretch to the other end of the city block.

A Wish Eater.

A *gigantic* Wish Eater.

It plunged toward the pavement.

Van closed his eyes, bracing for the smash.

But the smash didn't come.

His body hit something firm but stretchy—something that tossed him upward again, like a gymnast on a trampoline. He opened his eyes just in time to see the Wish Eater soaring off above him, its tail vanishing into the distance. Van's body hit the peak of its bounce and dropped gently down again. A poof of striped fabric ballooned around him, and then he was rolling off a wide canvas awning into a planter full of petunias.

Van lay there for a long time.

Nothing—not the Greys' guest-room bed, not the king-size bed with a zillion pillows that he'd slept on at the Covent Garden Hotel in London, not his own cozy twin bed with the spaceship sheets—had ever felt quite as comfortable as that planter full of petunias.

His heart thunked steadily in his chest.

His breaths whooshed in and out.

He stared up at the slice of purple sky peeping through the towering buildings, now looking very, very far away—

—until a squirrel's face popped up in front of it, looking very, very close.

"It's Vanderbilt!" cheered Barnavelt. "He's alive!"

Pebble's face appeared over Barnavelt's little shoulders. Even in the dimness, Van could tell that her face was red, and she was out of breath, as though she'd just run down several dozen flights of fire-escape stairs.

"It was a Wish Eater!" Van exclaimed, before she could speak. "It saved me!"

Pebble pulled a hand out of her pocket. She held up the halves of a snapped wishbone. "I know."

26
Unwelcome Wishes

VAN sucked in a gasp. "Where did you get that?"

It was hard to see Pebble's lips in the predawn dark. "Ocarina . . . case . . ."

"What?"

"She said, 'I carry it with me, just in case,'" Barnavelt piped in.

Pebble grabbed Van by both hands and pulled him out of the planter.

Van swayed on the sidewalk. His knees felt watery. The rest of his body was full of such relief and joy, it could have dissolved into a thousand floating bubbles.

Pebble glanced to both sides, scanning the nearly deserted street. Then, still holding him by the arm, she broke into a run.

"Where are we going *now*?" Van asked, as Barnavelt scampered up Van's pajamas and perched beside his ear.

If Pebble answered him, Van couldn't hear or see it.

"I smell doughnuts," said Barnavelt dreamily. "Do you smell doughnuts?"

As a matter of fact, Van *did* smell doughnuts. A moment later, he realized why.

Scattered over the stoop of a building to their right were dozens and dozens of doughnuts. As Van watched, more doughnuts plopped onto the steps. They seemed to be falling straight out of the sky, like glazed and sprinkled hailstones.

"What . . . ," Van started to say, before he found his own answer.

Of course. The Wish Eaters. How many of the Collection's wishes had they eaten and granted? How much other magic had they made? How many of them were now on the loose?

Van was still watching one sprinkled doughnut bounce off a handrail when a herd of creamy white horses galloped past. Van turned to stare as the horses ran down the street, manes and tails flying, and disappeared between the rows of sleeping buildings.

Over her shoulder, Pebble shot him a look.

"She says, 'See?'" squeaked the squirrel in his ear. "'People wish for stupid things.'"

Pebble dragged him faster, around corners, down blocks that grew leafier and quieter, until they were racing down a familiar street.

Several sudden thoughts collided in Van's head.

Pebble had made a wish. She had always seemed so firmly opposed to wishing—but maybe she was only opposed when the wishes were for 'stupid things,' not for life-and-death emergencies. Maybe she thought the risks of wishing didn't apply to her. Or maybe, Van thought, as she rushed ahead of him toward Mr. Falborg's tall white house, there was something else going on here.

Pebble flew straight past the walkway that led to the blue front door. She dragged Van along the manicured hedges and whipped into a narrow side path that ran between high walls of shrubbery. Above the hedges, Van could see the windows of Mr. Falborg's house staring down at them like dark, empty eyes. They came to a planter spilling with vines. There Pebble turned again, pulling Van through a gap in another hedge, opening a wrought-iron gate, and stepping through it into a large, sunken, completely enclosed backyard.

Mr. Falborg's backyard was as grand and beautiful as the house itself. Blossoming plants scaled the brick walls. Moonlit statues posed on pedestals. Sturdy trees, some heavy with fruit, some with flowers, waved their limbs in the nighttime breeze. In the center of the yard stood a huge stone fountain. Pearls of water fell from bowl to bowl before splashing into a pond flocked with lily pads. Van spotted soft, peach-hued fins sculling in the water's shadows.

And seated on a little bench beside the pond, his white suit glowing in the darkness, was Mr. Falborg.

He didn't look surprised to see a girl in a too-large coat, a boy in pajamas, and a wild-eyed silver squirrel come tearing into his backyard.

In fact, he looked pleased.

Or even—maybe—*relieved.*

Mr. Falborg got to his feet. "Ah," Van saw him say. "There you are." But it was too dim and too muddy, with the breeze and the fountain and his own rasping breath, to catch more.

Pebble finally let go of Van's arm. She strode toward Mr. Falborg, speaking fast. Van heard only a stream of sounds falling one on another like the drops in the fountain. He glanced over at the splashing water.

That was when he noticed it.

Past the fountain, beyond a cluster of trees, something smoky and silvery and very, very large was coiled in the shadows. Van made out two wide eyes. Ruffled ears. Jagged, foot-long teeth.

The branches of a maple tree stirred. Van looked up.

Something with leathery wings and a long, whipping tail perched in the branches, its body nearly as large as the tree itself.

He checked the corners. More faces. More smoky claws. More teeth. More huge, cloudy eyes—all of them staring hungrily down at the splashing fountain.

Van's mouth went dry.

He jerked his gaze back toward Pebble and Mr. Falborg. He couldn't tell if they were arguing or just talking—but at the moment, he got the sense that they were talking about *him*. Mr. Falborg gestured in Van's direction. Then he glanced up, perhaps waiting for Van to reply.

"What did he say?" Van whispered to the squirrel on his shoulder.

"He says, 'Haven't you?'" Barnavelt whispered back.

"Haven't you *what*?"

Barnavelt blinked. "Haven't I what?"

". . . can't hear us," Van thought he heard Pebble say.

Mr. Falborg's eyebrows rose. He reached into his vest pocket. His palm emerged, covered with glinting coins.

The hidden Wish Eaters craned closer. Van could feel their appetite in the air, sharp and stinging.

Mr. Falborg said something to Pebble and gestured at Van again. Pebble threw a panicked look in Van's direction.

"What did he say now?" Van asked the squirrel.

"He said, 'A worthy wish,'" the squirrel repeated. "'Why don't we fix that problem once and for all?'"

Mr. Falborg was already lifting a silver coin out of the pile.

Can't hear. That problem. Once and for all.

Realization seared through Van's brain.

He thought of the horrible, pounding blur of sounds that had plugged his ears all night. Of all the times he had wanted to reach up and yank those sounds right out again, but couldn't.

He didn't want that. Not once and for all.

"No!" Van shouted.

He rushed forward, trying to swipe the coin out of Mr. Falborg's fingers. Mr. Falborg raised his hand out of Van's reach.

"Don't wish that!" Van yelled. "I don't want that!"

Mr. Falborg blinked down at him, looking politely surprised. "Well . . . some . . . better . . . squirrel translator . . ." Then, too quickly for Van to block it, Mr. Falborg tossed a coin toward the fountain.

Van felt his heart echo the coin's path, pounding upward, then falling, falling, falling.

The coin splashed into the fountain.

Pebble dove after it.

But a huge, many-legged creature had already surged out of the shadows and thrown itself into the water. Van saw a spark of light wink once before vanishing into the creature's mouth.

The air filled with fog.

A breeze that came from every direction at once battered against Van, pressing the air out of his lungs and forcing his eyes shut.

When he opened them again, the breeze had stilled. The fountain glittered. The smoky creature hovered beside the fountain, looming even larger than before. And there was something in Van's hand.

He squinted down at his palm.

His hearing aids.

Van took a deep breath. He could feel the air rushing

in and out, but he couldn't hear it. He could see the leaves rustling, and the fountain trickling, but he couldn't hear them either. He was still himself.

He looked up at Mr. Falborg.

The man in the white suit gazed back at him with an expectant expression, as if he was waiting for Van to thank him.

But Van didn't feel thankful.

He felt the opposite of thankful.

Van shoved the hearing aids into place, glowering at Mr. Falborg the whole time.

Mr. Falborg waited until Van was finished. "I was only trying to help," he said mildly.

"You weren't HELPING!" Van exploded. "I didn't *ask* for your help! And you didn't ask *me* what I wanted! *SHEESH!*" He shouted so loudly that the squirrel on his shoulder jumped. "Why does everybody think I want to hear the way *THEY* do?!"

Pebble stared at Mr. Falborg, her arms folded tight. "People always think everybody else wants to be just like them."

"Or they merely want what's best for everyone," said Mr. Falborg. He fanned his fingers, making the coins on his palm glimmer. Hidden in that little gesture was something sharp and steely. Something that looked like a threat.

A new realization jolted through Van, as clear and sharp as shattered glass.

It was Mr. Falborg who'd made the wish.

Mr. Falborg was the one who had taken over Van's hands and feet and made him open the Wish Eaters' cells, who had made Van feel sick and out of control and powerless over his own body. Then he'd drawn the released Wish Eaters here, in spite of the danger this could mean for Van and Pebble and everyone else—just like he kept the other Wish Eaters in tiny boxes, telling himself that he was doing it for their own good. Mr. Falborg didn't help others out of kindness. He just thought he knew best.

"*You* did it." Van took a step forward. "You wished for me to release the Wish Eaters. You made me do things I wouldn't have done."

Mr. Falborg watched him, calmly shaking his head. "I've told you what wishes cannot do." He held up his hand, ticking the list off on his fingers. "They cannot control Wish Eaters themselves. They cannot kill or directly cause harm. They can't bring things back to life. They can't stop or change time. And they can't make a person do anything he fundamentally *would not do.*" He stared straight into Van's eyes. "But you *wanted* to release the Wish Eaters. Deep down, you wanted them to be free. Especially your own little friend. Didn't you?"

"Well . . . yes! Of course!" Van spluttered. "But I wouldn't—I knew it wasn't the right thing!"

"Are you sure?" Mr. Falborg asked.

A gust fluttered across the yard. Van glanced around again at the monstrous beasts shimmering in the shadows. He thought he recognized one saucer-sized pair of eyes.

"You knew I'd want to free Lemmy," said Van slowly. "That's why you gave me the Wish Eater in the first place. You just used me to get inside the Hold, and then . . ." He looked at the coins in Mr. Falborg's hand. "You lured them all here. You don't want them to be free. You just want them for yourself."

Mr. Falborg sighed. He tipped his head to one side, looking disappointed. "Not just for *myself.*"

"Uncle Ivor." Pebble's voice was loud and clear. "You think doing bad things for good reasons makes them all right. But it doesn't." She threw out one hand, and the circle of smoky, watching creatures shifted. Staring. Waiting. "You can't control them."

"Control them?" Mr. Falborg echoed. "Why would I need to?"

Pebble looked like someone had just asked her why they shouldn't take a nap in the middle of the street. "Because they're dangerous!"

"They are *powerful.* There is a difference." Mr. Falborg gave Pebble a pitying smile. "You think you understand what's happening here. But you are very young, and you're one small piece in a great big puzzle. Sometimes, other people—older, wiser people—know how that puzzle should be solved." He gave the coins in his palm a little toss. The creatures shifted like a pack of hungry wolves. "That's why I am taking my collections away from here."

Pebble's voice was suddenly so small and choked that Van barely heard it. "What?" she gasped. "Where are you going?"

"Ah." Mr. Falborg smiled more widely. "I can't tell you *that,* can I? Not when we're being watched."

Van scanned the edges of the yard again. This time, beyond the hidden, hungry Eaters, he could sense the presence of dozens of small, glittering eyes. Bats. Spiders. Birds. Rats. All gathering secrets.

Mr. Falborg's gaze moved to Van, and Van realized

that he—and Barnavelt—were watchers too.

Mr. Falborg's attention moved back to Pebble. "It's time for you to come home," he said. "Back to your real family." He lifted a bright silver coin between forefinger and thumb. "I want you to come with me, Mabel."

"Did he just call her *Mabel*?" Van whispered to Barnavelt.

But for once, Barnavelt was entirely focused on the situation at hand. He craned over Van's shoulder, leaning as close to Pebble as he could without falling off. His whiskers quivered.

"I wish for my child, Mabel Falborg, to leave the Collectors and come with me," said Mr. Falborg. "And I wish for her to help me care for these creatures, keeping them safe from anyone who might take them from us."

Mr. Falborg tossed two coins toward the fountain.

This time, Pebble didn't even try to stop him. She just watched as the coins hit the water one after the other.

And Van watched her. He couldn't read her face. What did Pebble actually want? He didn't know what to believe anymore. She hadn't even told him her real name. Had anything she'd said—even about wanting to be his friend—been true?

Van's chest ached.

Before he could wonder anymore, two creatures surged out of the dark—the one with leathery wings, and another with an ape's features and horse's body. They gobbled at the glittering waves. Immediately both of them grew even larger, the horse thing stomping its huge hooves, the other unfurling its wings and flapping into the air, its foggy body so large that for a moment it blocked half the sky.

The air misted and cleared once more.

Pebble stood still for a moment. She looked like someone standing in front of a door with something very cold on the other side. Then she took a tiny step forward. And then another. And another.

"Pebble?" squeaked Barnavelt.

Pebble didn't stop.

Mr. Falborg held out a hand. Pebble put hers into it.

"I knew it," Mr. Falborg said. "I knew that, deep down, you wanted to be on my side again." He wrapped Pebble in a long hug. It was hard to be sure in the dimness, but Van thought he saw Mr. Falborg crying. Pebble's face was turned away.

At last Mr. Falborg looked up at Van, his eyes shining. "I am so sorry for the trouble we've caused you, Master Markson," he said. "It's a shame it has to affect you this way. But what you've done has changed so many lives for the better. Losses aren't really losses if they contribute to the greater good. Don't you agree?"

Van tried to pull the meaning from Mr. Falborg's words. Had he heard him correctly? What were the losses? Was he apologizing for controlling Van, or was there something more?

"Sometimes we have to make exchanges," Mr. Falborg was saying. "Sacrifices. We give up one precious thing in order to gain another. Or *many* others." He gestured around at the lurking creatures. "And it's really the only solution. You're not one of them. You're not one of us. But you know too much for either side to let you go off on your own." He cast Van a smile. "You understand."

"I . . . ," said Van. "What?"

Van glanced at Barnavelt. The squirrel was still quivering on his shoulder, his focus never moving from Pebble's face. "Pebble?" the squirrel whispered.

"I give you my *deepest* apologies." Mr. Falborg's eyes were crinkly and charming and warm. "Thank you, Van Markson."

A coin arced through the air.

Van felt himself plummeting with it, just like he had fallen from the top of the water tank, knowing more surely with every passing second that there was nothing at all that he could do.

In a foggy daze, he saw Pebble lurch forward, her mouth forming the word *NO*. But the coin had already touched the water. Something slithered out of the shadows—something that looked like an eel the length of two swimming pools. It gulped down the glint of light.

Van didn't have time to move or fight or scream as the eel, swelling even larger now, lashed its head back from the fountain and closed its smoky teeth around him.

Van was whipped up into the air. Barnavelt tumbled from his shoulder, and Van's one remaining slipper flew off his foot, and then he was zooming through the city so fast that streetlights turned to glowing ribbons and buildings were only one long brick blur, and then there was only darkness.

It was dense, tarry darkness—darkness so thick that Van couldn't see his hands when he waved them in front of his face.

The force that had carried him suddenly backed away. Van dropped down onto a solid surface. He tripped forward, catching himself with both hands. When he glanced up, the eely creature was already writhing out of sight, its body as faint as a ghost.

Van crouched for a moment, breathing hard. The air smelled like metal and dust. He couldn't hear anything over the rumble of his own pulse.

Where was he? Was he dead?

No. Mr. Falborg had said that wishes couldn't kill anyone.

Slowly he rose to his feet.

He was somewhere enclosed. Somewhere underground. Somewhere man-made. Could he be somewhere inside the Collection? From far away, he could feel the weak tug of moving air.

Then, gradually, the tug grew stronger.

The surface under his bare feet began to tremble.

Van turned around.

Another monstrous eel was headed straight toward him.

This one was made of metal. Its eyes were headlamps. Its body was split into rocking, rushing cars. It barreled down on him with a roar so loud Van could feel it in his teeth.

The facts hit him with a crash.

He wasn't in the Collection. He was in an underground train tunnel. He was standing on the tracks. He was deep, deep below the earth. There was not a platform in sight, and the nearest one could be miles away. The train was coming fast. There was no safe space to escape to, and no time to run.

Still, Mr. Falborg had told the truth. The wish wouldn't kill him. Not directly.

The train would do the job.

27
The Second Train

VAN closed his eyes.

At least he wouldn't have to watch the blaze of those headlamps zooming closer. He wouldn't see the flash before the darkness, when everything winked out.

His mind flew to his mother. Her smile. Her smooth hands. He wished he could see her one more time, feel her folding him into a last lily-scented hug. But she was far away, in the Greys' house, her leg in a cast, with no idea that Van was anywhere but the guest room upstairs. She wasn't coming for him.

Van hadn't wanted to hurt her, but it had happened. Indirectly. His choices—his wishes—had started it all. A sob ached in his chest. The wishes were too much. Too big, too wild, too full of what-ifs. Too vast to control.

He wasn't sure the Collectors were right about eliminating the Wish Eaters forever. But they were right about the risks of the Wish Eaters' magic—magic that could destroy someone with the toss of a coin, or the snap of a bone. Nobody, no matter how wise or kind he seemed, should possess that kind of power over everyone else.

The train's light flared over him. Its brightness seared through his closed eyelids.

The engine roared. The brakes screamed.

The train hit him with astonishing gentleness. It lifted him straight off his feet. Van felt strangely safe, held up by its speed and size, his body streaking backward through blackness, oily wind rippling through his hair.

Light swelled around him. It squeezed into his closed eyes, growing brighter and brighter, and Van wondered if this was the light that waited at the end of death's long dark tunnel.

He opened his eyes a teeny bit.

But this light was electric. It came with street signs. And graffiti. And advertisements for shampoo and cell phones.

He was soaring past a platform. And the thing that

was carrying him wasn't a train at all.

It was a creature made of fog and dew. It had ruffled ears, and nubby, tender fingers, and round, gigantic, lemur-like eyes.

"Lemmy?" Van breathed.

The Wish Eater made a sudden swerve away from the tracks, flying up over the deserted platform. Just behind it, the *real* train went shrieking onward, its brakes screaming as it charged into the next tunnel and vanished from sight.

Lemmy soared over the turnstiles, up another flight of cement steps, and out into the dawn. It kept Van cradled to its foggy chest. Streets fell away below them. They rose up, up, above the tops of buildings, over the green plumes of rooftop gardens, past rows and rows of windows that glimmered with the coming sunrise. Lemmy held Van tight.

It was like being carried by a thick patch of mist. The Wish Eater's body was cool, almost cold, and as wispy as cotton candy. Van could see straight through it to the ground below. This would have been frightening to someone who hadn't flown through the city in a plastic sleigh. But Van wasn't frightened. In fact, he hadn't felt so safe in a very long time.

Lemmy arced down over a park, swishing past the treetops. Leaves pattered against Van's legs. Then Lemmy pulled upward again, coasting over blocks of dozing row houses and cobbled alleyways, finally descending as lightly as a cottonwood seed on the edge of a familiar roof.

Van looked down. They were perched above the Greys' backyard. Behind him, the window of the red guest room was still open.

Lemmy's misty hands let go.

Van steadied himself on the ledge. He looked up into Lemmy's dinner-plate-sized eyes.

"Who made the wish for you to save me?" Van asked. "Was it Pebble?"

The creature tilted its head to one side. Its ruffly ears perked.

"Did she steal one of Mr. Falborg's coins?" Van pushed on. "Or did somebody else know I was in trouble? Did Barnavelt do it? Can the Creatures even *make* wishes?"

Lemmy blinked.

"Who was it?" Van repeated. "Who wished for you to save me?"

The Wish Eater gazed at him for another moment.

Then it lifted one nubby-fingered hand and patted at its own chest.

"You?" Van whispered.

Lemmy gazed back at him.

"The Collectors said—they said that all of you become dangerous. That if you get too big and powerful . . . you *change*." He reached out to touch Lemmy's fuzzy arm. "But you don't seem dangerous. You're bigger, but . . . you're still you."

Lemmy touched Van's shoulder. Its hand was as light as a breath.

"Thank you," said Van. "Thank you, Lemmy."

The Wish Eater's mouth curled up at the corners.

It lifted gently off the ledge, hovering in front of Van for a moment. Then it whisked upward, its long tail sweeping behind it, and flew out of sight.

Van stood there for a very long time, staring up at the sky.

He climbed through the open window and shut it again behind him. Out of habit, he checked the corners for spiders. He peeped under the bed and into the closet.

Would Jack and the guards still be after him? Had the Collectors learned what had happened with Pebble and Mr. Falborg? Did everyone finally know the truth?

The truth. The words froze Van to the floor.

Did *anyone* actually know the truth?

If Pebble had really wanted to return to Mr. Falborg, had she just been manipulating Van all along? Was she tricking Mr. Falborg by going with him now? Whose side was she really on? Or—maybe—could you understand something deeply enough that you could no longer take either side at all?

Van turned toward the window. The sun had finally crept over the horizon. The sky above the city was turning peachy gold, with wisps of cloud unraveling here and there. It lit up the city, street after street after street, house after house, all of them full of collected secrets. To Van, standing in that quiet bedroom, the world seemed larger than it ever had before. Turning away from the window at last, he climbed up onto the wide, squishy bed. He took out his hearing aids and buried his face in the thick white pillows. He hadn't even pulled up the blankets by the time he fell asleep.

28
The Rock and the Hard Place (and Chuck)

EVERYBODY in the Greys' house slept late that morning.

Van's mother and Mr. Grey, who had stayed up very late talking and laughing, dozed until almost noon, Van's mother on the sofa in the downstairs study, Mr. Grey in his own upstairs room. Peter's door stayed shut until it was past lunchtime. And Van slept like a rock that someone had dropped onto a queen-sized bed.

He woke up to a room filled with sunlight. It took him several seconds to remember where he was, and then to trace back through the twists of the long, long night before. Giant Lemmy. The oncoming train. Pebble and Mr. Falborg. The loosed Wish Eaters. The beasts in the Hold.

It made his head feel like a cup that was full to the very brim.

He rolled out of bed and wriggled into pants and a shirt. He fitted the hearing aids into his ears. Then he hurried down the staircase.

The kitchen held the fading smell of coffee. Emma looked up from a book with a smile as Van came in.

"Good morning," she said. "Or good afternoon, really. Would you like me to make you some brunch?"

"Could I just have a bowl of cereal?" Van asked.

"Of course you can!" The nanny bustled to the cabinets.

"Where is everybody else?" Van asked, over the clunking of doors.

"Mr. Grey . . . off his . . . meetings all day. Peter's still upstairs . . . video games . . . and your mother's resting in the study."

"I'm going to go say hi."

Van tiptoed to the study door.

His mother lay on the striped silk sofa. Her coppery hair was piled into a loose coil on top of her head. Her leg in its thick white cast stuck out beneath a fringed blanket. She was reading a copy of *Opera News*. Van could smell the lilies of her perfume even through the doorway.

Maybe she could smell him too, because she lowered the magazine and craned around.

She smiled.

"Well, hello, sleepyhead." She held out her arms for a hug. "Did you sleep well?"

Van dove across the room and let his mother wrap her arms around him.

"You look tired." His mother cupped his face with one hand. "I don't think you did sleep well."

"Not really," said Van, looking at the sleeve of his mother's ivory silk robe rather than into her eyes.

"I know it's strange, being here." His mother lowered her voice. "But it's temporary." She squeezed Van's hand. "And even if we're staying with the Greys, it's still you and me. A duo. For good."

Van nodded, but there was a lump in his throat that made it hard to speak.

"What's wrong, Giovanni?"

"It's . . ." Van swallowed, and felt the lump go down into his chest, where the aches from last night and the night before still waited. "I'm sorry, Mom. I'm so sorry. I'm sorry you got hurt. And I'm sorry we have to stay here. And I'm sorry that it's my fault."

His mother stroked his hair. "It's all right, *caro mio.*

I'm all right. And you're all right. And that's all that really matters."

Van didn't argue—even though, for the first time in his life, there were a few other things that really mattered to him too.

A little while later, after telling his mother that he was going to visit Mr. Falborg, Van hurried out the Greys' front door and onto the shady sidewalk.

The city was a bit of a mess that morning. In the Greys' neighborhood alone, Van noticed an oak tree full of squawking red parrots, a mountain of mystery novels towering in someone's tiny front yard, and one turreted lawyers' office that had been turned into a bouncy castle. On another corner, he spotted an ice-cream truck that had skidded into a hydrant, scattering boxes of melting treats all over the street. Van skirted the crowds of smiling people helping themselves to spilled ice cream and darted around the corner. He wondered if these odd things were wishes come true, or if they were made by the Wish Eaters' unpredictable magic, and if anyone else in the city would guess the truth either way.

His legs were still rubbery-tired from the night

before. He trotted as fast as he could down the shady streets, to the spot where the tall white house loomed into view.

There he slowed.

Mr. Falborg's house towered behind its hedges, looking as neat and bright as ever. But the closer Van came, the more he sensed that something had changed.

Van tiptoed into the shrubs. From their leafy cover, he checked the windows. Each one was covered with thick white curtains. When he was sure no one inside was peering out, Van darted down the narrow path where Pebble had led him the night before, into the walled backyard.

Yes, something had changed.

The yard had a hushed, disused feeling. The benches and chairs had been put away. The sculptures on their pillars were hidden in knotted burlap. If Van hadn't stood in the same spot only the night before, he would have guessed that no one had visited this place in months.

The fountain had been turned off. And it wasn't only off—it was *empty.* Its scalloped stone bowls were dry, the pond surrounding it drained and cleared. The skulking koi and their lily pads were gone.

Turning away from the silent fountain, Van inched toward the house's back door.

Mr. Falborg had tried to kill him. But Mr. Falborg was obviously gone now—taking Pebble, and the truth about his plans, with him. Van wasn't afraid of Mr. Falborg's empty house . . . was he? Besides, if there was some small, forgotten clue, some hint about where they had gone or what they were going to do next, Van had to find it.

The knob turned easily in his hand.

Van shoved the door open.

He stood on the threshold of an empty kitchen.

It wasn't just empty of people. It was *hollow.* Every piece of furniture, every bit of decoration, every cup and plate and saltshaker had disappeared.

Like someone in a dream, Van trailed through the kitchen and into the hallway. The masks, the vases, the framed antique postcards—gone. He wound his way through the front parlor. Empty. No books on the shelves. No cut-paper silhouettes on the walls. He stepped through the archway and switched on the lights. The cases full of glimmering paperweights had vanished.

Van turned around, moving faster now, and ran back

along the hallway, up the stairs, past the bare walls and hollow corners and nooks where treasures should have been. He burst into the room with the red curtains. Then he nearly jumped back out again.

A man in a long black coat stood between the hidden room's open doors.

At the sound of Van's steps, the man turned around. The faces of two black rats peered out of his coat's front pocket. Above a high collar, Van saw Nail's high, hard cheekbones, sharp nose, and tousled hair.

Like Mr. Falborg last night, Nail didn't look surprised to see him. Unlike Mr. Falborg, Nail didn't look relieved. His face stayed hard and cool and calm, but Van could see a tiny touch of sadness in it.

Nail tilted his head toward the hidden room. "They're gone."

"He took Pebble," Van blurted at the same time. "He *wished* for her to go with him."

Nail nodded. "We were watching."

"Do you know where they went?"

Nail shook his head. "It could be almost anywhere. Ivor Falborg is a man of vast resources, of both ordinary and extraordinary kinds."

"We have to find her." Van took a few steps into the

room. The emptiness around him made the space feel larger and colder than it ever had before. "We have to get her back!"

Nail's craggy face was unreadable. For a long moment, he didn't answer at all. Then he said, "We can try."

"Try?" Van repeated, exasperated. "If you and your Creatures are always watching, if you know so much, then how come you didn't keep this from happening in the first place? Why didn't you *stop* him?"

"You know what he had." Nail's voice was firm. "What he *has*. Imagine the damage that hundreds of those creatures could have done if he'd felt the need to use them against us."

Van moved closer to Nail. Beyond the taller man's silhouette, he could see into the hidden room, the rows of wooden shelves all completely bare. "The Wish Eaters . . ." he said slowly. "Did he take *all* of them? These little ones, and . . ."

"And the ones you released?" Nail's voice grew even firmer. "Some of those we trapped again ourselves. They've been returned to the Hold. A few *did* leave with Ivor Falborg. And a few—we believe—are loose. By now they could be almost anywhere."

Van swallowed. So Lemmy might not be alone out

there, in the huge, open world. He wasn't sure if this thought was comforting or frightening. "Razor said *all* Wish Eaters get dangerous and unpredictable if they grow too big. But . . . what if some of them don't?"

Nail's eyebrows drew together. He tilted his head quizzically to one side.

"I mean . . . ," Van went on, "what if some of them are *good*?"

Nail's mouth moved into a tiny smile, although his eyes didn't smile at all. "It isn't a matter of good or bad. It's not about kindness or evil. It's not even a matter of intention. You can *mean* to do good and still do terrible things."

Van took a little step back. Pebble had said nearly the same thing to Mr. Falborg last night. And now Nail was saying it to him. Van had used wishes with only the best intentions. And where had it led him? His mother had been hit by a car. Her leg was broken; her job was lost. He and she were stuck in the last house in the city where Van would have wished to be.

"If you give someone, *anyone,* too much power," Nail went on, "enough power that they can control everyone around them—then you run a terrible risk."

The next words flew out before Van could weigh

them. "But isn't that exactly what you Collectors do when you trap all those wishes and Wish Eaters? Control everyone around you?"

Nail straightened. His eyebrows rose. His mouth softened. "You are a smart boy, Van Markson."

And that was all.

For a moment, the room was quiet.

Then Nail said, "Come. We should leave before any-one notices us."

They made their way back through the hallway and down the steps, both keeping mum. They'd just turned into the lower corridor when a furry silver streak bounced past them.

"I checked the fourth floor," reported Barnavelt, skidding to a stop in front of Nail's boots. "Maybe I should check the third floor again, just to be sure."

"You've already checked the third floor four times," said Nail.

"Are you sure?" The squirrel blinked. "All of it?"

"All of it. Four times."

"Maybe I should check the *fourth* floor."

"You just checked the fourth floor."

"All of—?"

"All of it. Yes," said Nail. "Four times."

The squirrel flicked its tail. "What about the basement?"

Nail sighed. "Barnavelt. She's gone."

"Gone?" The squirrel repeated the word as though he'd never heard it before. "She's *gone*?"

"Yes." Nail's voice was very gentle. "She's gone."

There was a beat. Barnavelt stared up at both of them, his whole body trembling. "Maybe I should check the third floor."

"You should climb up onto my shoulder and come home with me," said Nail. "We'll try to find her. And we'll bring her back. If we can."

As slowly as Van had ever seen the squirrel do anything, Barnavelt clambered up the fabric of Nail's dark coat. He sat on Nail's shoulder, even his tail keeping still.

They all slipped through the hollow house and out the back door, into the hushed daylight of the garden.

"Will he be all right?" Van asked, nodding at Barnavelt.

"We'll take care of him," Nail promised.

"And if Pebble comes back, will you—will you let me know?"

"We will." Nail gave a small smile. "We'll be nearby. We always are."

He put out one hand. Van shook it.

"Take care, Van Markson."

With a sweep of his coat, Nail turned and strode away.

"Good-bye, SuperVan," Van thought he heard Barnavelt say—but by the time he looked after them, Nail and Barnavelt had vanished.

Van shuffled around the edge of the empty pond. The rocks lining its bottom were gray and dusty. A couple of coins glinted dully on the stones. Van reached down and picked up a nickel. He turned it between his fingers, wondering if it had held one of Mr. Falborg's wishes. Maybe this one had transported Mr. Falborg's stuffed snake collection, or moved the pond full of giant koi. But moved them *where*?

Van let out a long, tired breath.

Slipping the nickel into his pocket, he turned away.

A fluffy gray cat stood just behind him.

"Renata?" Van whispered.

The cat's eyes narrowed. It glanced to either side. Then it said, in a gravelly voice, "Call me Chuck."

Van blinked. "But I thought your name was—"

"*Renata?* Hmph." The cat snorted. "Only to Mr. Fancypants. My mother named me Charlene. I go by Chuck."

"Oh," said Van. "My mother—"

"Your mother named you Giovanni, but you go by Van. I know." The cat squinted her blue-green eyes at him. "I pay attention. You know, most of the time, cats are just *pretending* to be asleep."

"So do you . . ." Van glanced around too, making sure they weren't being overheard. He dropped his voice to a whisper. "Are you one of the Collectors' spies?"

"I'm a free agent." The cat raised her chin. "I go where I like. I talk when I like. *If* I like."

"Is that why Mr. Falborg left you behind?"

"Oh, he didn't mean to leave me. But you can't force a cat to do something she doesn't want to do. Certainly not just by wishing." The cat took a lazy glance around. "Life here was getting stale anyway. I'll have a few weeks of adventure on the streets, maybe go back to my old job, mousing in a downtown diner. And then . . . maybe I'll move in again when he comes back." She flicked one ear. "Mr. Fancypants *does* always spring for the top-shelf tuna."

Van's mind sparked. "So he's coming back?"

"He always does." The cat gave her paw a lazy lick. "He's got places everywhere. The country, the city. Italy. Russia. Japan. But he always comes back here eventually."

"Do you know where he went?"

The cat paused for a moment. Van couldn't tell if it was because she didn't want to tell him, or because she didn't want to admit that she didn't know. "Not this time," she said. "But if I were you, I'd forget about all of this. Falborg is a dangerous man. He always knows exactly what he wants. And he's not going to let anyone get in his way. Then again, I wouldn't want to get on those Collectors' bad side either." The cat paused again, gazing up at Van. "You know that old saying about the rock and the hard place? You're the thing that's stuck between them."

"But I thought, with Mr. Falborg gone—"

"Oh, this isn't over," said the cat. "They all know about you. They know what you can hear, and see, and do. It's *far* from over." The cat turned with a swish of her silvery tail. Over her shoulder, she gave Van a little nod. "So long. Watch your back."

She stalked into the shrubbery. In an instant, she was out of sight.

Watch your back.

Van glanced over his shoulders. For a split second, he thought he caught sight of something shifting and smoky and huge lurking within the leaves of a big maple tree—but then a breeze stirred the leaves, and the thing was gone.

Van headed along the hedge-lined path.

At first he was too occupied by everything that had just happened to pay any attention to the ground beneath his feet. But when he finally looked down and, out of habit, started scanning the gravel for any lost treasures, he noticed something strange.

There, half hidden by the glossy green leaves of the hedge, was a marble. It was made of sparkling blue glass, and it held a spiral of glittering gold. It was the marble he had given to Pebble. And arranged around the marble were other small things: three mossy pennies. A half-burned birthday candle. One branch of a broken wishbone.

It was a sign.

A sign for him.

Pebble knew that Van—maybe *only* Van—would notice.

But he wasn't sure what it meant. The marble had been his gift to Pebble, and she'd kept it in her pocket ever since. The other objects seemed to represent kinds of wishes. Was this a message about collecting? Was it just her way of saying good-bye? Or was it a sign that she knew he'd come looking for her? That she wanted him to keep looking?

Carefully Van collected the marble, the coins, the candle, and the broken bone. He slipped them all into his pocket. They were such tiny things, and the world was so big.

Big enough to hold creatures that ate wishes, big enough to hold an army of underground people in long dark coats, big enough for spiders and ravens and talking cats and distracted silvery squirrels. And somewhere out in that huge world, there was a tall, gray-haired man in a white suit, and a girl with eyes the color of mossy pennies.

But small things could be powerful too. Van knew it. He ran his fingers over the little objects in his pocket once more.

Then he set off toward the Greys', keeping his eyes sharp.

There were treasures everywhere. You just had to know how to look.

Acknowledgments

I'VE got a lot of people to thank for making my writerly wishes come true:

Van and his story wouldn't exist without the help of several deaf and hard-of-hearing students and their teachers: Shanna Swenson in River Falls and students Austyn, Noah, Brian, and Kennedy; Amanda Kline of the Minnesota State Academy for the Deaf and students Dalina, Gifty, Dexter, Amber V., and Amber H.; and Angela Dahlen in Red Wing and Cannon Falls, and students Ella, Cara, Nikki, and Maddie. Thank you all so much for letting me hang out and bombard you with questions. I hope I've reflected a tiny bit of your brilliance in this book.

The magical Martha Mihalick, for her enthusiasm, honesty, and faith in this story, and for pushing me harder whenever I deserved it. And to Laaren Brown, Lois Adams, Virginia Duncan, Paul Zakris, Ann Dye, Meaghan Finnerty, Gina Rizzo, and all at Greenwillow: Thank you for making me and the Collectors so at home.

Danielle Chiotti and everyone at Upstart Crow: I'm so lucky to have you on my side. Danielle, thank you for your (endless!) work, insight, and guidance. Whenever things get dark and twisty, I know you've got the flashlight.

They didn't actually see this one in progress, but my critique group—Anne Greenwood Brown, Li Boyd, Connie Kingrey-Anderson, Lauren Peck, and Heather Anastasiu—has made me a happier human, a smarter reader, and a better writer. Giant hugs and cupcakes to you all.

Adam Gidwitz, for the GI Joe story.

Stephanie Watson, for hosting the Hoverdraft panel where I read the opening chapter of this book aloud to strangers for the very first time.

All the music teachers and opera singers it was my good fortune to study with over the years.

My family. Thanks to Mom and Dad for literally everything (especially the babysitting!), to Dan and Katy and Alex, and to all the grandparents and aunts and uncles and cousins and in-laws who make me feel so supported and who make family get-togethers so loud. Love you all.

And finally, lastly, mostly: Ryan and Beren. I can't wait for more adventures with both of you.

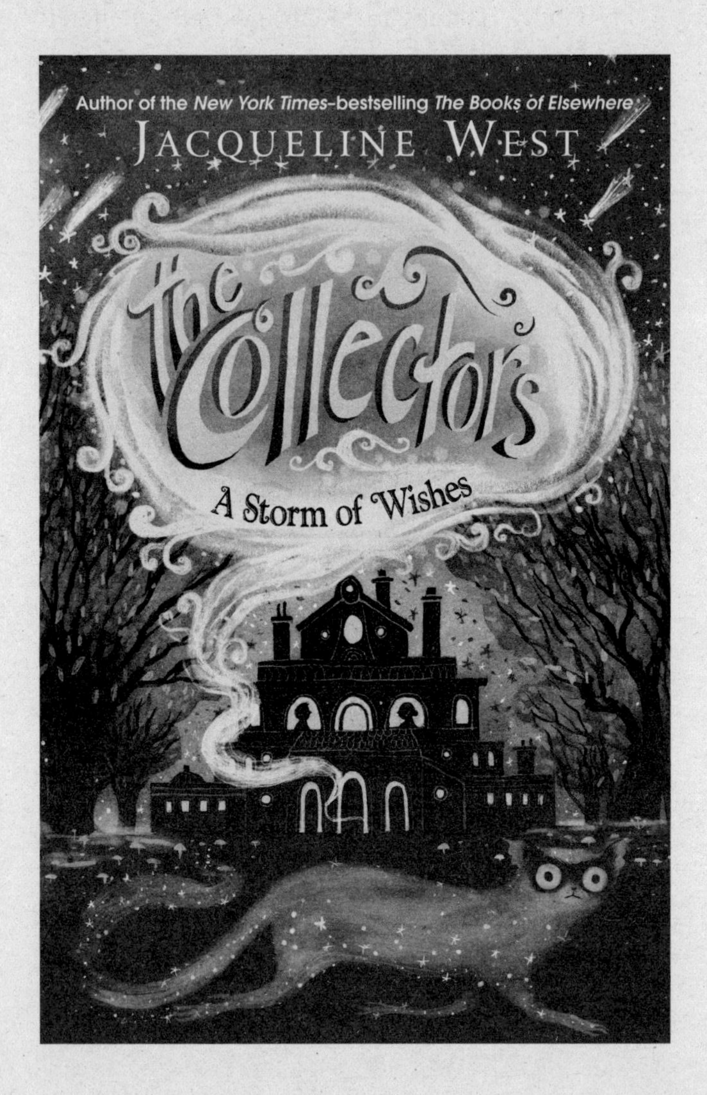
Author of the New York Times-bestselling The Books of Elsewhere
JACQUELINE WEST
the Collectors
A Storm of Wishes

Can Van find Pebble?

And can he help protect the Collection

and the magic it holds?

To find an excerpt from his next adventure,

close your eyes.

Make a wish.

And then turn the page.

1
The Thing at the Bottom of the Well

The thing at the bottom of the well was asleep.

It had been asleep for quite some time. The thing itself didn't know how long, because it no longer measured time at all. Light slipped into darkness, warmth dissolved into cold, and the thing remained where it was, drowsing, occasionally staring out at the soggy shadows through the slit of one gray eye.

The well was ancient, dug and used centuries ago. The thing at its bottom was older still. Its great gray body stretched through the tunnels that branched from the well's shaft, filling the courses where deeper water used to run. Its claws sank in the black dirt.

People brought it offerings now and then, but the thing at the bottom of the well rarely took them. It was so vast and so old that it rarely felt hunger. It rarely felt anything at all.

But once in a great while, between stretches of sleep, something small and new would catch its eye.

Late one summer afternoon, a family came walking through the woods: a mother, a father, and a five-year-old boy. They'd had a picnic in a clearing, and now they were rambling along the overgrown paths. It was the little boy who spotted the well—the crumbling and mossy wooden roof, the circle of stacked gray stones. His mother gave him a coin. The boy tossed it into the well. In half a heartbeat, it had slipped out of reach of daylight and vanished into the deep, deep dark.

The woods rustled. The little boy's parents steered him away.

Far below, at the bottom of the well, the coin landed with a delicate *tink*. It struck a mound of other coins that had piled up above the shallow water, most of them eaten away by rust and mud and time. It lay there, glimmering against the darkness.

The world is full of wishes like this one.

Secret wishes, birthday wishes, wishes scribbled in diaries, wishes mumbled to no one. Most wishes are merely words. *I wish I didn't have school tomorrow. I wish*

I was rich. I wish I could just disappear. But some wishes—the ones made on birthday candles and broken wishbones, the ones hung on falling stars or thrown down certain deep, dark wells—are more than that.

Some wishes, with help, can come true.

The thing at the bottom of the well opened its eyes. With one huge, clawed hand, it reached for the wish glinting on the pile of coins. It scooped the wish into its toothy mouth . . . and swallowed.

Mist, thick and silvery, filled the air, rising up through the well like smoke from a chimney.

And in the forest above, a unicorn leaped from the underbrush.

It galloped past the path where the family was walking, its silver mane and tail gleaming, its hooves so swift and soft that the little boy was the only one to notice it at all.

He raced off the path after it.

His parents turned a moment too late. They shouted for the little boy. They chased after him, screaming now, trampling through the bracken. Before long there were other sounds: motors and sirens, dogs snuffling through the brush, booted feet moving in lines. By the time the little boy was found, cold and scared but safe at the bottom of a ravine, nearly two days had passed. He kept insisting, while his crying parents hugged him and the EMTs checked him over, that he had wished for a unicorn, and his wish had come true.

The thing at the bottom of the well heard all of this.

It listened distantly, indifferently, the way it watched the weak shafts of sunlight that ventured down to its tunnel before being consumed by darkness.

The thing had caused far worse trouble than this.

Digging its claws deeper into the earth, it settled back to sleep.